THE TAF

SARGAS

BY LARRY YOAKUM III

The 1st book of the
Targothian Trilogy

Introduction by James Rosenthal Jr

Well....where to begin....

Larry has been a friend of mine for a time now. We have sat around, drank beer, talked of old military stories, and done some karaoke, as well as attended Octoberfest in Addison, Tx. Needless to say, he has got some stories to tell....but to be able to put thought to words to a book is truly amazing. He has got a knack for describing what everyone feels but cannot say. I have enjoyed his books and continue to look forward to what he has next.

Larry, my friend, my bruder from annuder mudder.....this book tells of the Motherland, Targoth....where we were conceived. I am humbled and proud to know you and be a part of this.

TACTAB....it's not just letters or a fancy saying...it's our life motto.

Dedication to my family

I wanted to take the time to thank my incredible wife Allison who stands by me and can deal with my eccentric brain. Thanks to my parents for raising me and not stifling my creativity when I was young. Thanks to mein bruder James, for being a brother to me, though we share not the same blood, there is more to family than mere blood.

And especially, thanks to all my readers. I may write for myself, but you people are the ones who keep me in business. I feel that a writer must write for his or herself, and if others enjoy the stories told, then that is icing on the cake.

Prologue

It has been an incredibly long time since my little journey began. My life from before everything changed was a regular ordinary life. I was born in 1975 and I grew up in the quaint little town of Valley Center, KS. A lot of weird things occurred in that town.

Over the course of my life, I've encountered sights that most people would assume to be caused by either insanity or instability. I learned rather quickly that the universe as we know it is so much more than what we see in front of us. There are realities in between the shadows. Worlds far out in the depths of space.

I had name given to me by my parents. That is a name I haven't gone by in a long time. Sometimes, I don't even remember it. I suppose it doesn't matter much at this point. My old name I wouldn't even answer to now if someone used it. I am now someone else, different then that young man who was taken and changed all those centuries ago.

I am now Sargas and that won't ever change, and though much, oh so much, time has passed from then to now, rest assured that my memory is accurate.

So now, let's start this.

Chapter 1

I graduated high school in Valley Center in the year 1993. I never really felt like I fit in with all those people. I know that sounds like such a cliché. In all the movies and books, there is the person who becomes some sort of savior or a vampire with a soul or they find out that they are part witch and go on to protect the world from some evil coven. Well, I am not that savior. I was thrust into a situation that I wasn't prepared for and it may have even been truly destiny, but I am no liberator. Some might say that I am, but I've never felt that way. In my opinion, the word "prophesy" is thrown around entirely too much, a plot device used in stories in order to explain away why the hero is the one to perform the particular quest in question.

As I said, I graduated in 1993 and got my first real job, not counting bagging groceries my senior year of high school. I fit in more with my coworkers than I ever did in school. But, I knew I didn't want to be there forever. Since I was a small boy, I had wanted to join the Air Force like my father did. He served for four years and was a military cop. My father and I looked a lot alike. We both shared the same dark hair, though his was much darker whereas mine was a medium brown, much like my mother's hair. My father and I had the same eyes. Sometimes when I shaved I would squint my eyes for a second and think my dad was looking at me.

When I was younger, I used to look forward to following my father's footsteps. I wanted to join the Air Force, be a cop, and get out and be on the Kansas highway patrol. My dad himself was on the Wichita Kansas police department for over twenty years before he retired.

Alas, my time in the military didn't bring that dream to fruition. Instead, I ended up becoming a survival equipment technician. They are the people who inspect and do maintenance work on parachutes, life rafts, and other pilot survival gear. Don't ask me how I got that job, I don't even remember after all this time. But, it was probably for the best, as I think I wouldn't have made a good cop. My temper is quick to flair and at times I have a problem with authority.

I had enlisted in 1995 at the age of nineteen and turned twenty right after basic training ended and I went to tech school at Sheppard Air Force Base in Wichita Falls, Texas.

Not too long after I went to my permanent party base, Eglin in the Florida panhandle, I met a woman named Jennifer, and I fell in love with her way too fast and did the stupidest thing imaginable and married her. If I hadn't though, perhaps my life wouldn't have taken the turn that it did and I wouldn't be transcribing my long life right now. I'd have died of old age centuries ago and not even been a blip on the Universe's radar. Looking back at that possibility, I wonder if the Universe would have been better that way. Who knows? Not like you can change the past. Well....I suppose if that were entirely true, I wouldn't be doing this right now.

I found out after we had married that she had a drug problem, and soon thereafter, I was back to living in the dorms on base. I didn't know what I was going to do.

In my brain, I had a hard time reconciling the situation. I treated her great. She treated me like shit. In my youth, and even later on, I'd see sweet women with men who were bastards, and I would always think that once I found a woman, I'd treat her great and she'd be in love with me. Not always, as it seems. Again, I digress. Forgive me. I am old and I tend to ramble. I might not look my age, but believe me, I am way past the point of what humans consider a senior citizen.

I might not remember every single detail from my life before, but I remember this night. It is burned into my memory like a branding that will forever mark my soul.

In the Earth calendar, it was the second of October of 1998. It was a Friday. I was taking one of my usual walks in the evening. Since I was living in the dorms again, I was distant from everyone off duty. I wasn't unfriendly, but I enjoyed my privacy. Inside I was a wreck. I would take walks at night once the sun went down. It cooled the humid Florida air quite well, making my constitutionals much more comfortable. I didn't walk any place in particular. I'd just go towards the base post office and around and towards the library and then eventually back to my room. I was lucky enough to get a single room. Before I was married I lived in the base dorms and had a couple of different roommates.

This night, I had a weird feeling inside. I didn't quite know what to make of it. All my life, I had been having these dreams on and off. I never remembered much about them when I woke up, but three things always stood out in my mind afterwards. Two of these things were words and the third was a symbol. Since I was seven years old this happened every so often. Until that night, I never knew what to make of it.

That night on the second day of October, in the year of 1998, I, a young man of twenty-three, had his life change in the most unimaginable of ways.

It had just turned 2100 hours and I put on my shoes and headed out the door on my nightly walk, ignoring the feeling of foreboding. I didn't pay much attention to the time on my watch until I reached the post office. Only fifteen minutes had gone by. Sensing something was out of place, I looked to my left and thought I saw something move out of the corner of my eye. Must be my imagination, I assumed. I couldn't shake the feeling that someone was eyeing me from somewhere I couldn't see. I turned to head back to the dorms, but as soon as I turned around, I froze. I couldn't move. I tried to call for help, but my voice wouldn't come out. Something was keeping me from moving or talking.

Something was eerily familiar about all this. Like something from a long-forgotten dream. Inside my own mind I was screaming. I saw a faint glow coming from my flesh. I was shining slightly, but from a source I knew not what. It was a lot like sleep paralysis.

I managed to move my gaze up and saw that above me was a hole in the air. It was about ten feet above where I stood. It was a large black nothingness, barely visible against the night sky, but I saw it clearly enough. The hole was growing bigger.

Wait, no, it wasn't. It was growing closer. How the hell can a hole in the sky like that even exist, let alone move on its own?

My feet were firmly on the ground. The hole was moving down towards me. It was now inches from my face. I heard faint voices coming from the other side. Was this in fact some sort of nightmare? Had I not gone for my walk but instead passed out on my bed?

The hole stopped moving for a brief second, then it overtook me, engulfing me whole. Was this how Jonas felt? The blackness enveloped me, and the sense of vertigo was overwhelming. I felt like I was falling, yet I could still feel my feet on the ground. Whatever was happening, it could not be anything of the normal, everyday world.

The falling feeling eventually stopped and I could tell that I was indeed standing on solid ground, but I was no longer outside in the slightly humid Florida night air. Where in the hell was I?

Chapter 2

It appeared that I was standing in some sort of dark cavern made of stone and steel. I could see the walls, but barely. The room was circular and about twenty feet around. The dark gray walls surrounded me, going high up into the obscurity above. There was a chill in the air, yet I was sweating. Not profusely, but as if I just did a small sprint in the warm and sunny afternoon. I quickly patted myself down to check for injury. I had all my limbs. I didn't feel like I had lost any organs, but as I wasn't a medical professional how could I know for certain?

I was still wearing the same clothes: jeans, black sneakers, and my AC/DC t-shirt. Interesting. Did I somehow end up going down a highway into hell? I looked at my watch, more out of nervous habit than needing to know the time. It was dead. Not like it would matter if I knew if it was noon or midnight.

The silence was intense. I could swear I heard voices mumbling, but maybe that was just my thoughts arguing in my head that this is just a dream or some sort of psychotic episode. Never before in my life had I felt such a deep fear. Looking up and around, all I saw was blackness. But, yes, those were voices. Knowing I might regret it, I called out. "Hey! Who's there? What the hell is going on?" The mumbling noise stopped. Above me, a light came on, illuminating the faces of thirteen people. Some were men, some were women. All looked at me with an intensity I have never experienced.

"Greetings, young one!" I heard one of the people say to me. I spotted the speaker. He looked to be just a few years older than I but with close cropped jet-black hair and clean shaven. Though he looked to be in his late twenties, for some reason he came off as a tired old man. His accent was hard to place. Somewhere between German and British. "Forgive us if we don't speak your language properly. We only recently learned it. I am Arakus P'Tan Arak of Elginia. I am one of the thirteen council members of the High Council of the Elginian Imperium, and on behalf of Emperor Bar Roma the Fifteenth I welcome you to the Citadel of the Bah'Tene."

I didn't know what else to do in the situation. I waved. For such a strange circumstance to be involved in and the powerful fear I felt, I was handling things rather well.

"You must forgive us so abruptly bringing you here, but we can assure you, it is important. But, come, let us speak more face-to-face." With that, the floor beneath me vibrated a bit, and it appeared that I was standing on a platform. It began to rise very slowly, bringing me to face level with my hosts. It wasn't that high up after all. Now I could see their faces more clearly. They all appeared to be my age or just a bit older, but all had an air of superiority to them. They all seemed arrogant and judgmental, viewing me as something of an insect. The only one who didn't give off a bad vibe was Arakus, who spoke as soon as the platform stopped moving.

"First, young man, some introductions are in order. As I said, I am Arakus P'Tan Arak. To my right is Lord Vontorlad, Lord Mil'R Ot Fortuna, Lady Sardonia of Vinspirion Prime, Lady Conratlaton, Lord Tarkuun, Duke Dengos of Elginia, Zonglabesh the King of Moon Imperium

Seven, Baroness Syltron and her brother Master Smoth, Yun'op, Master Bradloy, and finally, Kop Va of the Imperial Clericdom. We are the thirteen council members of the Bah'Tene, as well as the advisory council to the Emperor." None of them had anything that really stood out, except for Syltron. She was pretty hot, for a blonde. I was more into brunettes and occasionally redheads.

So many questions. Where to start? "Why don't you all have titles?" I can't believe that was my first question. But, all things considered, I wasn't freaking out like you'd think I would have in the situation. Was it because I was jaded by being married to a drug user? Did I perhaps think I was still sleeping and having the most vivid nightmare possible? At the time, I just didn't seem that threatened. Scared? Yes. But I didn't feel in danger. It is hard to explain.

The one called Duke Dengos spoke next. "The ones that do were born into them. All of us are pure blood Elginian. Only the nobility and their most trusted servants and military leadership may join the ranks of Bah'Tene." Lady Sardonia mumbled to herself. It was in what must have been her native language. Though I didn't understand the words, from the tone I could tell it was rude.

"Excuse me?" I said. "Why don't you speak so that the alien in the room understands?" Looking back I have to smile at my hostility towards them. Here I was, a twenty-three year old guy from Kansas, being brought before thirteen mysterious strangers, yet I still managed to show my usual sarcasm that I exhibit when annoyed.

"What I said," Sardonia continued, "was that only worthy Elginians may join our ranks, and I don't like how some primate tene..." Arakus cut her off with a wave of his hand.

"Young man," Arakus spoke, "there is much to tell you before we send you into the Grand Test."

Test? Grand Test? Somehow I knew this test wouldn't be something that I had already learned in high school. I asked what sort of test they were talking about.

The one I remembered as Syltron stood, making her seem very tall next to all the seated members. I remembered thinking she was one big bitch.

"The Grand Test is a test of heart and soul to see if you are worthy of being Bah'Tene. You already have the rare genetic sequence that is required. Now, we have only to see if you can pass."

Arakus nodded. "Yes, and if you do, you will have power and ability you would not possess as a mere tene." He must have noticed the puzzled look on my face. "A tene is what you may call a mortal. While we Bah'Tene are not really immortal, we do live a thousand of your human years, without aging, until our life span is expired, and we instantly age to a millennium old, and turn into dust and bones."

One of the other's spoke up. I wasn't sure who it was at the time. "We are much harder to kill, but it isn't impossible."

Arakus nodded and looked right at me. "I will tell you the truth, even if you succeed in the Grand Test, you won't be the same man you are now. We won't force you to take the test, but rest assured, if you don't, you will have to remain here the rest of your days, looked after, of course, but you won't be allowed to return to your own home."

"Why the hell not?" I blurted out.

"Because," Arakus continued. "You are no longer in your own time." My eyes glared at him. "You were in the Earth year of 1998 before. We need you specifically to join our ranks, but you were not born yet. We had to open a tear in reality to bring you here to Elginia. It isn't easy, requiring an intense burst of subatomic energy and to do it again might cause catastrophic danger to the solar system, if not entire galaxy. Right now, on your home world, the year is 1498. Sometime in the month of June. I don't really remember, I am terrible with Earth's calendar."

"Fourteen hundred and ninety-eight!" I yelled. "Ok," I said through clenched teeth. "Let me get this straight. You brought me five centuries into the past because you need me for your club? Aren't there other guys you could have kidnapped in this year? Why did you have to bring me here and screw up my life?" All thirteen council members stood together. Arakus cleared his throat and spoke. (Please bear in mind that this happened a very long time ago and I might be paraphrasing a tad, but my kind have incredible memories.) As he spoke, my mind swirled with images and sounds I had seen only in my deepest state of dreaming.

"Fifty thousand years ago, here on the planet Elginia in what your people call the Andromeda Galaxy, our fifty greatest warriors gathered and met with the Archangel Michael. Michael's brother, Lucifer, had long been stranded on the primitive world of Earth, while his minions of darkness spread throughout the universe, seeking out civilizations that had left Earth in the time before the creation of the second generation human, Adam. Many humans left their world and colonized distant galaxies, many long forgetting their own origins. Lucifer's men went out to seek them, to corrupt them, to use them. Several scientists from Atlantis, the last great Empire in the time before Adam, had come over to Lucifer's side, and they went to another galaxy, the one your people call Triangulum and on a world in the galactic core they engineered several abominations.

The Orions, the Reticulans, the Reptoid Men, and, perhaps worst of all, a corruption of the very core of mortals. A sickness of the spirit that brought the dead back to life, their bodies devoid of their souls which have since gone into the spirit world. A soulless being that craved the very blood of the living. Nosferatus Exmortus, what eventually came to be known on Earth as a vampire.

Michael had gathered our ancestors and bestowed in them a great power, only a fraction of an archangel, but nonetheless impressively powerful. Our kind stopped aging at that point, and the lifespan extended to a thousand years. We became hard to kill. We developed a sense of our surroundings. We alone had a special gene in us that allowed us to carry this power. It is a rare thing to have. In our native tongue, we named ourselves the Bah'Tene, which means Beyond Mortal. We are the Sons of Michael.

Over the millennia, we have fought the Nosferatus and the Grays and many evils of the universe. Eventually, some of us broke off and formed the Fallen, who sided with the Nosferatus and the other demonic hordes of the universe. A great civil war happened that drove the Fallen from our galaxy and they traveled to the furthest reaches of the Three Galaxies."

I interrupted him and asked what the Three Galaxies were. It was the Milky Way, Andromeda, and Triangulum galaxies, all close together and were easy to travel around in with highly advanced light speed engines. There were many smaller satellite galaxies nearby, too, but they were devoid of life. The smaller galaxies had hundreds of thousands of stars instead of the billions in the larger galaxies. There were very few colonies there from times past, but no life had ever originated there, though they did hold thousands of inhabitable worlds.

Arakus continued. "Since that war over thirty thousand years ago, the Fallen have occasionally come back, but we have always driven them away. But now, they have corrupted more of us, and we need to replenish our ranks. That is where you come in, young man. You have the blood of a powerful Targothian leader. Sargas ot the Central Valley. He led many of his people to Earth a thousand years ago and has since blended in with the Terrans of Earth. You are a child of Earth, but also a child of Targoth. You are the descendant of Sargas."

Sargas? Sargas! That was one of the strange words I've had in dreams since I was a child. That and Targoth. I figured that eventually that bizarre symbol would turn up. Dazed from the sudden influx of information, I looked back up at the council. They seemed to be silently pleading with me to join their ranks. But why me? Even if I was descended from some alien warlord, I am not a warrior myself. I'm an Air Force guy who does maintenance work on pilot's survival gear. I'm married to a druggie. I really had no clue as to why I was here or if I'd even pass this test of theirs.

I looked at them. "I'm in."

Chapter 3

Arakus stood and gestured to me. "Thank you so much. We look forward to you joining our ranks. Pending your completion of the Grand Test." I asked what this test was.

Vontorlad answered me. "The Grand Test was developed to harness the power of the gene that all Bah'Tene have in them. It isn't a guarantee that you'll succeed. Pass or fail, you will die. We all die in the Test." I swore under my breath. "Your subconscious will manifest itself and you will fight. After you die, if you are worthy, you will resurrect as Bah'Tene."

I asked what happened as a Bah'Tene. "First, you will be virtually immortal, as we said. It will take much to kill you. But don't get arrogant. There is plenty out there to end one of us. You will heal fast. You will learn fast. You will have much of your brain unlocked to give you a perspective that you've never had before."

A plan was formulating in my head. If I really was the descendant of this Sargas guy, then I was confident I'd pass this test thing. Then I would come back as a Bah'Tene, and I would be able, hopefully, to live long enough and catch up with my life in 1998. Five hundred years was a long way off, though. It felt very overwhelming.

I told them I was ready and wanted to get it over with. If I were to die here, I wanted to be done with it. I was lowered back down into the depths beneath my feet.

I stood there and looked around at the walls. Five centuries in the past on a planet somewhere in the

Andromeda galaxy. According to these guys, I have alien blood in me. Alien from the perspective of Earth, that is. Something called Targothian. Another word from that dream from long ago.

I was curious as to how this ancestor of mine got to Earth and why didn't anyone in my family know about it. Perhaps if I can get out of here, I could meet them, I thought. But that might not be a good idea. I'd seen enough movies to know you don't alter the past, which my presence might.

Wasn't I already altering it by just being here? But what if that past was supposed to be altered by me and if I didn't do it, then I'd be screwing things up. It is enough to make you go mad. I'd just go find that Targoth planet first chance I got, if I survive the testing, that is. I called out to my hosts. "If I make it, can I go to that Targoth place?"

Arakus shook his head. "Sorry, young one, but that world is no longer around. Qal Dea destroyed it. Nothing but debris remains, floating in the void." That was horrible news. It felt like a kick to the crotch.

My thoughts were abruptly interrupted as I heard footsteps behind me. I turned and saw the last thing I really expected, yet somehow knew would happen. I saw myself standing there.

My doppelganger was dressed in a black robe with the hood off. He was grinning at me in a way that made my blood run cold. It reminded me of a nightmare I had years ago in a house I could have sworn was haunted.

When I was about ten, we lived in this house on Park Street in Valley Center, Kansas. It had a basement that even into adulthood gave me the occasional nightmare. In the dream in question, I was walking through the house and I stopped in the living room and turned to my right and looked into the bathroom. The door was open and some guy was standing there looking at the mirror. He slowly turned his head and looked at me and grinned, much like my doppelganger right now. He bolted at me and it scared me awake.

The doppelganger began laughing lightly. "Don't worry. I won't rush you like that. I'm going to gut you nice and slow." He walked leisurely to me, a very annoyingly slow walk that made me want to run up and punch him. Screw it, I thought to myself, and rushed the guy that had my face and clocked him in the jaw. He grinned even wider to where I thought his face would break in two. He reached up and grabbed my throat and choked me hard. I couldn't breathe, and the world was growing dark around me. I kicked my feet at him and he vanished, and I found myself standing there choking myself, both hands around my throat in a death grip. I let go, shocked at that fact. I heard laughing and I turned and saw him there again, this time in some awesome looking all black battle armor. It was form fitting and not bulky at all. A chest piece covered the torso and there were pieces on the arms and legs. Heavy leather boots and thin black gloves completed the look. Where was the helm?

"This is traditional Targothian armor from thousands of years ago," he said to me. "It is stored in your collective unconscious. You must have some sort of DNA remembrance. But what do I know? I'm you, and you're not too bright." Laughing louder and quite manically, he bolted towards me and before I could blink, he impaled me with his heavy battle sword that came out of nowhere. I could feel my life leaving me, and I felt a flash of anger. I wasn't supposed to die, not like this. Not today. I grabbed the sword by the blade and pulled it from my chest, slicing my hand open but I suppose now stitches were a moot point. I turned the blade and thrust it into his gut.

I hoarsely whispered at him, "I go, you're coming with me." My twin winked at me and simply vanished as if he wasn't ever really there, as did the sword, but my wounds still remained. I shut my eyes, preparing myself for whatever awaited me in the next life. Everything went black.

Chapter 4

I opened my eyes, seeing all the council members standing above me. Arakus held out his hand to help me up. I noticed my wounds were gone. My shirt still was torn and had blood all over it. At least I was still breathing.

All the council members nodded their heads at me and in unison spoke, "Welcome, brother Bah'Tene."

Arakus shook my hand, as he told me was custom on my world in my time. I thanked him. I took in my surroundings. Nothing was different than earlier, but I perceived things in a different way. I got a sense of each council member. I could feel that they were like me. They had power and didn't age. I could sense what they were. I looked up and noticed for the first time that the chamber was full of guards with exotic looking rifles. They were tene, as I could sense. I knew they were actively aging and would die in a few short decades.

Short decade? I was even perceiving time differently now. I could feel inside me. My organs were powerful. My small beer gut was gone. I had a stronger physical presence. I knew now that going through this change also made you physically better. The peak of endurance. The blessings of archangel essence.

I was told to go outside and test out my abilities. Arakus led me to the outer door and I for the first time since I arrived here saw the sky. I saw stars that were unfamiliar. I knew a bit about the constellations, but I saw new ones above my head. Three moons were orbiting this world.

Elginia, home of the Bah'Tene. I was now one of them, a Son of Michael.

Now, it was time to see what I could do. I began to run. I ran very fast, faster than would be humanly possible. I leapt in the air and at the same time I shot a fireball from my left hand, destroying a small platform. When I landed, I immediately turned and saw what I had done.

Arakus appeared next to me. "You're a fire master. That is rare. Most Bah'Tene don't have that ability, let alone any secondary powers. Only a fraction of a percent. Some can produce energy from their hands and eyes but that is even rarer. Most of us just have enhanced strength, endurance, healing, mental capabilities, and the rest. It is a rare treasure for one of us to have the ability to create fire. Learn to control it, my friend. Otherwise you may incinerate yourself."

I smiled what was probably a goofy, nerdy smile, and stared at my right hand. I focused my mind and saw a small ball of fire forming in my palm. It didn't burn me like I thought it would. Turning my head towards the sky I spotted a flying insect. I thought of the fireball as a solid rock and I threw it as such, and it flew from my hand, incinerating the bug. I felt slightly drained but the energy quickly returned. It would take practice to create fire like that. The first time as I leapt earlier was just a fluke in all the excitement.

I saw a sword rack near me and I reached out and tried to pull one of the blades to me. Arakus pointed out that telekinesis is another rare talent for our kind, even more unlikely than fire or energy. I went over and took a sword and I began wailing on the practice targets. They were androids that moved lightning fast. I was faster. One of them managed to slice open my arm, but it healed in a matter of seconds. The pain was comparable to a slight papercut.

"Healing is quite easy for us, my brother," Arakus said. "You can regenerate lost limbs and organs, save one. You lose your head, and you're dead, but that is pretty much for all life forms. It is how you kill nosferatus, demonoids, just about anything you will come across. In fact, I can't think of any physical creature that can't be killed that way. Angels and true demonic dark spirits, well, that's a different story. Our bodies can also be damaged quickly beyond our healing. It gets better with age, but even the strongest of our kind can die in a massive fire. We can survive in space with no protection, but eventually must get out of it otherwise we will implode. And as for your fire abilities, it will be weak for now, but in time and with practice, you will be able to create great flames. Eventually it will consume less of your energy and require much less recuperation. Come, there will be time enough to learn everything. For now, we must celebrate."

I was taken inside and escorted to a great banquet hall. Apparently, we still had to eat. It was a large hall, and all the council members were there, along with many others who I could sense were Bah'Tene. There were hundreds of them, along with powerful warriors who were mortal, but nonetheless were not to be trifled with. I even met the acting Emperor, a young kid in his mid-teens. His father had grown ill and he had been sitting on the throne and running the Imperium with the help of the Council's advice. Something about him seemed oily and untrustworthy. He resembled a stereotypical pimply faced kid who had trouble with girls.

I took the seat of honor, as was custom to the newly made. For the remainder of the night, we drank, we laughed, and they listened as I told them my story. Where I came from and how I got there. Some of them were surprised that Earth lasted another five hundred years. Much of the Imperium thought of us as barbarians. Well, I supposed in the fourteen hundreds, we were, and even in my own time, they would regard us as such.

There was one Bah'Tene in particular who stood out to me. I had an instant fear and respect for him. His name was Gostal, and they called him the Phantom Lord, for he had killed thousands in battle in his life before he became Bah'Tene.

His hair was in a short militaristic buzz. He was in his forties when he was changed so he was one of the few that looked like an older being. He was a powerful warlord on this planet and conquered many worlds for the Elginian Imperium. One of his monikers was "Conqueror of A Hundred Worlds in A Hundred Years." He commanded several armies on different planets. I could sense that many of the others feared him, too. He had an air of madness to him, though he was very charismatic. It was during this dinner that I found out that I was assigned to him as a protege. He would show me the culture of our kind. I really had no choice but to graciously accept. Besides, I had to do something to occupy my time for the next five centuries.

After the dinner, we all retired to our chambers, and I prepared myself to go with my new boss. I fell asleep much easier this time. Was it all the mead or was it the fact that I was just wiped? Who cares? I slept a dreamless sleep that was more refreshing than any other night's sleep I could remember.

I had nothing really to pack up. The tailors had mended my AC/DC t-shirt and washed the blood out of it. I was given new clothes but kept the shirt underneath. I was dressed in all gray and white, in an armor that looked almost similar to what my doppelganger wore, but it was certainly different. It bore the seal of Gostal, a winged skull with snakes in its eyes. The armor was made out of what they called flexiton, an artificial alloy made from iron and several other ores that existed only on Elginia and nowhere else in the known universe. It was strong enough to take a point-blank blast from several assault rifles and not even dent or give you a bruise underneath, but it was flexible enough to not have your movements encumbered. I figured it would be strong armor, but I was sure that in this place there were weapons that could still damage it.

I announced that I was now going by the name Sargas. I wanted to take the name of my ancestor. My own birth name seemed weak now. Since my ancestor was dead for the last thousand years or so and the people of Targoth were no more, wiped out by some psycho named Qal Dea, I wanted to honor their memory. I traveled with Gostal for several years. I was now in his army, and the Council seemed a bit worried about me going off with him, but they were the ones who sent me, so what the hell was up with that?

I now wore his emblem upon my chest. I was taught how to speak Elginian. I learned it almost instantly upon my lesson. I picked up every language I heard just as fast. Soon I was speaking over two hundred languages fluently. Elginian was the primary one spoken, so that is what I used most of the time. I even taught Gostal a bit more of English. More than he already knew, anyway.

That was one of the biggest benefits of being Bah'Tene. Our brains could pick up a language after hearing it spoken for around five to ten minutes.

I also learned a lot more about nosferatus. In Earth folklore, vampires were believed to burst into flames in the sun. That is not true, although they do seem weaker in sunlight. It is speculated that a star's light in a planetary atmosphere caused their cells to become heated and weakened. They can still exhibit superhuman strength, however, when threatened and snap out of their lethargic state caused by a sun. Beheading works best. That works on most things in the universe. That could on occasion work on demons as well, but not always in a permanent fashion. They were more spirit-like, as nosferatus were physical creatures empowered by supernatural means. In a nosferatus, the mortal soul was gone, transitioned to the spirit world. The body and its memories were powered by pure darkness and fed on the life force of the living: blood.

I learned that a vampire's bite didn't turn you as it often did in Earth's fiction. The only way to become one of them was to ingest their tainted blood. It would force the body to shut down and die in a day, give or take several hours, only to resurrect as one of their horrid kind.

Another benefit to being Bah'Tene was if you were ever somehow forced to drink the blood of a vampire, it wouldn't turn you. It just made you feel ill like a stomach flu. You'd likely puke yourself into near dehydration, but you'd heal from that soon enough. Perhaps not soon enough for a vampire to take you out of commission, though. Other supernatural creations, such as werewolves, that would change a tene into a monster with a mere bite, also had their bites neutralized by the active Bah'Tene gene.

I learned more about my new culture, such as the Challenge. When two Bah'Tene had issue with one another, one would initiate the Challenge. This was basically a duel. The one who issued it picked when the fight would be. The one who was challenged picked the place. There was one main rule: no powers nor enhanced abilities of any kind. It would be a straight up fight, usually to the death, but if one of them surrendered, there was no shame in it. It merely meant that you honor your opponent and agree to stop the fighting. That was rare. In the history of the Bah'Tene, it usually ended in the death of one or the other. You were not considered a murderer, be you the challenger or the challenged. You won a duel.

The no powers rule was important, as not every Son of Michael was blessed with an extra gift. If one of them used a special power, they'd be honor bound to cease the attack until the other Bah'Tene struck next and could use an ability if he possessed one. This was implemented because, as Arakus had told me earlier, since not everyone developed a special ability then the duel had to be fair. My fire was rare. Rarer still was the ability of creating energy blasts. After a power was used and the other fighter struck, then all bets were off, and powers could be used. That was dangerous as it could level a city if the fight went on too long.

The Bah'Tene culture was interesting, and now I suppose it was my culture as well, along with my old one from Earth.

I learned about other races in the universe. We didn't go beyond the three galaxies of Milky Way, Andromeda, and Triangulum, for the closest galaxy out there would take several hundred of our longer life spans and our tech level only allowed for travel between the Three.

Two races of note were Arturians and Alturians. There are many who get those two beings mixed up. Arturia is in the core section of the Andromeda. The Arturians look pretty human, except they have no nostrils on their nose. They require no air to breath, even though their world has an atmosphere almost identical to Earth's. They get drunk on carbonated beverages and alcohol has no effect. A lot of times they get fake nostrils in order to pass as a humanoid race that can be affected by booze. They have drinking contests with alcohol and always win as they can't get drunk. Many have been arrested for this scam.

Alturians are different altogether. Their jungle plant was on an outer spiral arm of Triangulum. Their males are around five feet tall and are covered in thick, dense hair. You literally cannot see flesh. The women are on average seven feet tall and utterly devoid of hair. Interesting how a race could evolve with such a difference in their genders. Another thing to note, Arturians and Alturians hate each other. To call one the other will result in violence. Often in killing.

The world of Pax Draxia was seventeen solar systems away from Earth. The Pax Draxians looked more or less human, as well. They are generally very tall and have a darkish tan or red hue to their flesh. They heal beings by touching them, but would have to reserve this for the very ill or wounded, as a healthy person would often die painfully as their system overloaded. The females usually found employment as a dominatrix. They'd beat a man to near death and then have sex with him, healing his wounds in the process.

One of the most unusual creatures I came across were Mullet Men from Hyaline. Just imaging a human covered in fish scales and a head of long blue hair. Their world wasn't even a water planet. There was only about ten percent water on the surface, yet it managed to evolve a species that lived ninety-five percent of the time under the surface of the one ocean.

There were the Aryans, tall humanoids with mostly blonde hair. They would eventually arrive on Earth in the late 1920's to help a young man named Adolf rise to power. Upon his defeat, they leave the Earth alone, going back to Arya, located on the opposite end of the Milky Way galaxy. They use a wormhole near their planet that takes them into the asteroid belt between Mars and Jupiter, a dangerous route indeed. They haven't the technology to fly light speed, though, so that is the only way for them to reach Earth. I thought about stopping them now in this time before they had a chance to help with the Second World War, but deep down I knew that was an event not to be toyed with. Not only would it possibly prevent me from returning to the same world in which I left, but it would cause catastrophic mayhem with the immediate galaxy. As a Bah'Tene, I could sense things like that. Time travel was something so rare that it hadn't been attempted in the lifetimes of any living Bah'Tene, but it still let my mind open enough to tell me what events can be changed and what couldn't.

Of all the beings I learned of, the worst of the bunch were the Orions, the Reticulans, and the Reptoids, which the Council told me of as well back when I first met them.

The Reticulans, or Grays as Earth people call them, resided on an Earthlike world in the Zeta Reticuli star system, thirty-nine light years from Earth. They were half the size of a human, only around three to four feet tall. Highly intelligent and scientific, they were designed to perpetually study the genetics of life, and would often abduct Terrans off the Earth for scientific experiments. They never tried it with the other humanoid races around the Three Galaxies as the people of Earth were kept in the dark about the truth of alien life and were thus easier to scare and manipulate.

Orions, identical in facial appearance to Reticulans, only differed in their height, being around six feet tall, and their mental capacity only allowed them to be servants for the Reticulans.

The Reptoids, tall and horned and green scaled, were the warrior race that defended the Reticulans. Two castes had evolved from the genetic manipulation done long ago by Atlantean scientists. The leadership caste, slender of build and small tails that served no more than an extra appendage. The soldier caste were a few feet taller and more muscular, and they had large tails capable of lashing and acting as an extra arm in combat.

In addition to these and other mortal races (yes, the Orions, Reticulans and Reptoids were mortal as they are born, mate, grow old, and die), there were supernatural demonic races as well, such as the Nosferatus.

While most demons were spirit beings that could take physical form at will or if they preferred, possess a living being, there were demonic races that came from demons intermingling with mortals. These were often referred to as demonoids. For the most part, demonoids appeared in a wide variety of forms. Sometimes they looked like classic demons from folklore with horns and tails. Other times, they looked more human of face but with an inhuman body. But, since they weren't pure demonic spirits, beheading was always a good option when dealing with them.

The first time I encountered a demonoid was on my first mission with Gostal.

Chapter 5

Several days after we left Elginia, we fought a band of demons called Nefarium that were pillaging a small moon base that was orbiting a world called Nordia.

The Nefarium were brutal bastards, among the worst you'd ever come across. They looked more or less human but with bald heads and eyes that were blood red. Their mouth was full of shark-like teeth. A set of small horns came up from their temples.

They weren't proper demons, I should indicate. They were what we call half-breeds. The Bible refers to them as Nephilim. This particular breed came about when the demon Belial mated with several homeless prostitutes somewhere in the slums of the capital of Elginia thousands of years ago. The results were beastly infants that grew into the abominations that are the Nefarium.

They were very tribal, a leader had to prove himself strong at all times, lest a power-hungry subordinate tried to take his place. Many a time, a Nefarium would kill his own son to keep from being cast down from their leadership position. I could only assume they had females, though I never personally saw one. No one quite knew how they reproduced, but many speculated it was either an asexual being that could self-impregnate or they raped tene females to create their young.

Gostal and I had been flying around in his personal craft, the Skull Hunter. He wanted to teach me to fly it in case I ever needed to take it out for a solo mission, or until I acquired one of my own. It was a small shuttle, no bigger than a bus. It was a nice craft, but it lacked the awe of his flag ship, the Reaper Blade.

A large capitol ship, it was about two miles long and looked like a very large oval UFO. This must be one of the types of ships that caused people of Earth to see flying saucers back in the old days. Gostal had an entire fleet of these.

He was indeed a powerful warlord on Elginia. All his troops seemed to fear him and served out of that fear and a sense of wonder. I felt that awe at times myself. Gostal had a presence that wasn't to be messed with. But, I think it was safe to say at the time, that I was the closest thing he had to a friend. But, let me get back on topic about my first actual encounter with the Nefarium.

While flying around the upper atmosphere of a nearby gas planet, we got a distress call and headed to Nordia to investigate. I asked if we needed to summon some troops from the ship. Gostal laughed and said that he needed no help against a common band of half-breed demonoids. I shrugged my shoulders and went with it. I activated the LSD, which is what we called the light speed drive, and within moments, we were on the other side of the solar system and docking on the moon base.

As soon as we landed, we were greeted with bullets and arrows flying at our shuttle. Looking at each other, we both smirked and ran out of the ship, my sword held high and his two axes in his hands. He liked to fight with two weapons as he got to kill faster that way. He didn't like the sword. Gostal felt that the sword was too common of a weapon. He preferred his axes. Both were identical. They were as long as a sword, but the blade had an intricate design on it, something almost dragon-like.

Rushing down the boarding ramp, I threw my sword at the head of the nearest demon, slicing the top of his skullcap off. I jumped into the air and landed right behind the demon's corpse, my hand immediately grabbing my blade and I swung it around and gutted two Nefarium that were coming up behind me.

I felt so alive in battle. Me, who up until recently was an Air Force survival equipment tech who spent his days inspecting and repacking parachutes. Now I was five centuries in the past and battling intergalactic demons. I loved it. It was my new thought process that was unlocked from the Grand Test. It did change me. I still had my sense of humor and would say Earth things that confused my space brethren, but I also was a viscous animal in combat. I loved the kill. Taking the head of a demon or throwing a nosferatus into a burning pit was as exciting to me as anything else I had ever experienced.

Gostal was off about fifty feet away having his own fun. He was like a whirlwind of death, hacking and slashing and dropping demon bodies all over the place. I held up my hand and let out a fireball that engulfed an oncoming trio of Nefarium and turned them into a smoldering pile of bones. It took a lot out of me and I hadn't yet mastered the ability to create fire effectively. That was just a lucky shot.

Gostal looked over at me and smiled almost fatherly. I had a father in the twentieth century, but at that moment,

I felt like Gostal was a good substitute, given the insane circumstances.

I could sense something else in Gostal. There was a madness right below the surface. I felt an abrupt fear for him and almost got my sword hand taken off by a demon swinging a pair of bloody daggers. I snapped out of it just in time and took the demon's hands instead. He fell to his knees in pain and I lopped off his head and walked off as he plopped over lifeless. I often pondered where these creatures went after death. Was it Hell? Was it reincarnation for them? Or were they simply gone from existence, like a light-switch that is turned off and can never be turned on again?

The battle only lasted moments, but the rush was intense, nevertheless. After we dispatched the attacking Nefarium, we watched as many more fled in personal crafts. Gostal got out his communicator and called the Reaper Blade and ordered them to send out their superiority fighters to wipe out the fleeing demons.

We received much gratitude from the people of the base. Gostal took a liking to the wife of a technician and seemed as if he was going to just take her with us.

"Lord Gostal? What are you doing?" I asked. He looked at me like he wanted to kill me for bothering him, but the look of anger swiftly passed, and he smiled and said he was just admiring a beautiful woman. I nodded and we went back to the Reaper Blade, but the entire time I was wondering if maybe Gostal wasn't really who I thought he was.

Later that night I sat in my chambers and meditated. It helped to clear my hectic thoughts at times. I knew Gostal for only a short while, but he was still my mentor and friend.

But, there was always that nervousness from other Bah'Tene, especially from the Council. They seemed to be genuinely afraid of Gostal. I wonder, then, why did they invite him to join the ranks of Bah'Tene? Did he serve some purpose, or perhaps, it wasn't until after he turned that they realized he changed more so than they thought?

An image came into my mind as I meditated. It was Gostal standing on a hill overlooking the valley below. Thousands of his soldiers were slaughtering an army of primitive natives. An image of Arakus came into my vision and he had a look of sorrow. The vision in my head had no sound. The bloody battle was silent, but no less violent. Gostal laughed at the carnage below. Arakus looked directly at me and said "Stop him"

I snapped out of my meditation at that. "Stop him." Was that a vision of something that actually happened or did my brain misinterpret something? I knew Gostal was a bit mad. You'd have to be to be called Phantom Lord.

But, he was still Bah'Tene. He was still one of the good guys. My concerns were unfounded and ridiculous.

Chapter 6

Gostal and I continued to travel around the Three Galaxies, seeking out Fallen Bah'Tene and whatever evils we could smite.

On several occasions we encountered Nosferatus Exmortus. I would usually refer to them as space vampires, and that annoyed Gostal, but he took it in good humor. Using their technical name was a bit of a mouthful.

I remember the first time I went head to head with a vampire. It was several weeks after fighting Nefarium.

Vampires had an air of cold about them. You could almost smell the grave emanating from their pores. I never gave much thought to vampires in the past, but to know that they originated from space and that the devil basically made them with corrupted Atlantean scientists was something you'd never expect to know about in a million years. If only Bram Stoker could have known that when he wrote his book. It would have taken on a science fiction vibe as opposed to gothic horror.

A vampire looks completely human, or tene, I should say, save for that aura of death. The vampire's curse could affect not only humans from the various worlds, but any mortal tene being. Gostal told me he once encountered a Mullet Man vampire. No matter its tene body, it was always the same form of vile evil.

A creature with no soul. I knew that their soul moved onto the afterlife upon becoming undead, so that person at least got to rest in peace. It was unfortunate for their families that the vampire had their memories. The vampire didn't even really realize that they were not the whole person they once were. They don't register that their soul is gone, and if they do, they don't care.

It isn't like in the movies where a vampire bites you on the neck and you become one of them. They have to choose to make you like them by feeding their blood to you. Blood is life, full of the energies that make a mortal the person they are. In a way, when a vampire feeds off of a person, they are not just eating their blood. They are consuming their hopes and dreams and desires. A poet is a poet because of their soul and their blood. A vampire will take that poetry from the poor bastard and feed on them until they die.

Vampires are extraordinarily cruel and vile. They take pure joy in slaughtering infants and young girls and gentle old men. The screams of the innocent arouse them in an almost sexual manner. When Lucifer had his minions create these fiends, he got his money's worth.

Undeath isn't a purely vampire issue. The undead have been around for as long as there were mortal beings. Vampires, children of Lucifer, are merely the kings of their kindred.

This vampire I encountered for my first time, it was young. It was freshly made. Its maker must have left it alone after turning the poor tene into an abomination. I found the beast while I was patrolling a small outpost in the middle of a heavily forested planet on the edge of Elginian space on orders from Gostal.

I had been given the basics on how to kill one of them. It isn't as easy as it sounds. The creature was confused as to its situation. I thought I'd be able to give it a quick death and take my leave. I was wrong.

As I moved my blade to its throat to claim its head, it leapt impossibly high into the air and took shelter in a tall tree. It swore obscenities at me in Elginian. It jumped out of the tree and fell towards me. I stepped back and swung my blade and took its head off. Sensing that there was more going on, I turned around and instinctively swung my sword again and took the head of another vampire that had been circling the area. He thought he could sucker punch me. How wrong he was.

Several more vampires came from the trees. Some of them were former human, but there were several other tene races in the mix, including one Arturian vampire. My blade swung fast, my left hand held up and I managed to conjure up a few balls of flame. I hit a few of them with the fire, but the rest made it through. One had gotten behind me and clamped its teeth on my neck. I healed as soon as it took its fangs out. It spit out my blood. For some reason it didn't like the taste.

"Awe, what's wrong? Don't like my herbs and spices?" I took the head of the one that bit me. I now had five more to contend with. Wanting to try something I had been hoping I would be able to conjure up, I held my hand up in the air and focused my attention, and within seconds, a dozen fireballs rained from the sky. My energy was draining at the excessive use of my unique gift, but it was worth it. The remaining vampires all screamed in the most inhuman way as their clothes burst into flame. Their bodies followed suit, and in a matter of moments, they all lay on the ground in a pile of dust and bones.

Vampires were strange creatures in death. Sometimes they crumpled to dust and bones, much like a Bah'Tene one day would. Other times they just fell over dead, their body still maintaining the features of their undead nature. I think it had something to do with their age and just how violent their death was. Of course, a rain of fire would dust them, no matter their oldness.

Patting myself on the back I slowly and painfully made my way back to the rendezvous point and met up with Gostal, reporting on what happened. He was very impressed with my story. It took me a few days to recover from the fire rain I created. I wasn't ready yet for that amount of fire. One day, I would hopefully be able to do it at will. Gostal had even speculated that maybe I could give up the sword and fight with only the flame.

Over the next few years, Gostal and I traveled around the Three Galaxies in the Reaper Blade and killed vampires where we found them, and killed a few Fallen that were helping them find victims. It just floored me how a Bah'Tene could fall so far from his duty and help out one of those pale corpse abominations.

While the two of us traveled, his armies battled the forces of the Fallen, who also had tene soldiers that were either forced into service or they chose to follow the Sons of Lucifer. Either way, they all faced the same fate. The Universe could be a brutal place. Many times, we joined them on their engagements, but not always. Much of my time was spent in battling the vampires and demonoids out there in the vastness of space.

I encountered a particularly nasty vampire out on the edge of Earth's solar system. We picked up a distress call from a merchant ship flying around the Milky Way, its destination was planet V'arl orbiting Kronis, or what Earth people call Alpha Centari.

The ship for some reason just stopped dead in space, probably an engine breakdown, and then the beacon went out. Gostal and I found it and he sent me onboard. No life forms were read on our scanners, but I went over nonetheless to be certain.

I found the problem very fast once I docked with the merchant vessel. The crew was all dead, their bodies drained of blood.

I sensed it before I saw it. A very old, very powerful nosferatus. He looked like a middle aged man, dressed in some sort of law enforcement garb from a world I didn't recognize. I could only assume he killed a space cop and took his clothes. He laughed when he saw me. "Pitiful Bah'Tene. No wonder so many of your kind fall and help my brethren. Is this the best that the Council can send out here? You have the stench of a Terran on you." Earth people were called Terrans due to Earth being called Terra on old star maps. It sounded better than Earthling or Earther.

I held out my blade. "You have a problem with Terrans?"

He grinned. "Yes. You taste too gamey. Too primitive. How did they manage to grab you off of a primitive rock like Terra and put you through the Grand Test?" His accent was that of the lower class of Elginia. I knew he must have hated the elitist royal family.

But how did he know about the test? Damn Fallen giving information that they ought not be giving. No matter. Powerful vampire or not, I was going to send him to whatever passes for the afterlife for their kind. Since his soul was long gone, I had inkling that he would be facing nothingness.

I hurled my blade at the vamp's chest and leapt at the same time, launching a small fireball from my right hand. The vampire moved out of the way, faster than anything had a right to move. I grabbed my sword that had stuck in the wall and took the vampire's left hand as it reached for me. It howled deeply and punched me in the jaw with an uppercut from his remaining hand. It grabbed onto me and bit into my arm, drinking some of my blood. It hurt like fire, and I saw that the thing's left hand had now grown back. "Oh. Terran blood is normally gamey but yours is different. What is wrong with your blood, Bah'Tene? Did taking your test taint your flavor even more so? Make it dirty?" Its eyes turned black and it ran off in the other direction.

I took off after it as fast as I could run. My enhanced Bah'Tene abilities allowed me to keep up with it. The halls were blurred from the speed. Finally, it came to the end of the corridor and halted, turning to face me. Lifting my blade, I impaled the undead bastard through the heart. I knew that wouldn't kill him. He couldn't flee, however. My blade had pinned him to the wall of the ship.

As the vampire tried in vain to pull himself from the sword which pinned him to the wall, I stepped back. I focused on my sword and the blade burst into flame. The vampire cried out for mercy as his body burned from the inside. A moment later, he returned to the dust from which his mortal body came.

I reported back to Gostal, and we hauled the merchant ship back to Elginia. On Gostal's request, each member of the crew was buried with honors and their families were to be paid handsomely as to never have to work the rest of their days.

Gostal may have been borderline nuts at times, but he did have his moments.

Chapter 7

On Earth, the year would have been 1501. I had been traveling and apprenticed to Gostal for four years at this point. I had continued to perform solo missions on my own, reporting back to Gostal, always onboard the Reaper Blade. He was never actually on Elginia much anymore. He only ever would go if there was a new Bah'Tene that had survived the Grand Test, but that was rare. Just because you had the gene in you didn't mean you'd come back. He would only go if someone survived and returned as one of our brethren. Even then, that was only twice in four years. The second time, I got to go with him and I met the new Bah'Tene, the son of a nobleman. His name was Stave or Steve or something like that. I don't really remember. He died not long after while being ripped apart by some strange unknown creature.

It wouldn't be unknown for long, as Gostal sent me out to find it.

The newly made Bah'Tene was looking for Fallen on a very distant rock that didn't even have a real name, just a number. The world was called Trentia Seven Seven Five. It was a single planet orbiting a lone star out in the void between galaxies.

How a star wound up in interstellar space was actually a common thing. As the universe expands, galaxies can collide. Sometimes, a star gets pulled from its orbit around the galactic central core and goes off into the depths. Occasionally it takes one of its planets with it. This was most likely the case. Top Elginian scientists had speculation on where the world originally sat, but they were always bickering on who was right. I didn't care.

One of my kind died there by some unknown beastie. He was found literally torn into dozens of pieces, though some of the pieces were gone.

There were a few primitive villagers on the planet. How did they get there? One could only wonder. If a planet gets dragged off into space, wouldn't that kill all life? I suppose the atmosphere could stay on the planet. That is for the scientists to finally figure out.

Needless to say, there was life on the world. Humanoid, as was many lifeforms in the universe. Not all looked human, but pretty close. There were differences of course.

These people in particular were tall and slim, clad in leathers. Since there was no other animal life known on this rock, I shuddered to think that they made their dead into clothes. It was hard to tell the men from the women, as their women lacked the bodies you'd expect on a female.

They were all scared of whatever was out there. An old man, possibly one of the elders of the tribe, kept saying the word durmivol, over and over. I asked what that meant.

One of the younger tribesmen told me that durmivol was an ancient demon in their old language, from before they were dragged out into the void. Most of the tribesmen said they never saw one, but the old man claimed to be a witness to the stranger from beyond who was torn apart.

The durmivol was twice as tall as a man. It had an animal's face that had a longish muzzle and its flesh was dark gray, like the sky before a harsh storm. Large leathery wings sprung from its back. It usually wore a loincloth made from the skin of its victims.

In my travels, I had heard of descriptions of mythological beings such as this. They never had a name to it, though. They were always called the Horse Bat or the Demon Steed. I knew that if these people here had ever seen a horse, they old man would have referred to the creature's face as such. I assured them that the creature would die that day and not kill any of them. They were happy and praising me.

I set out into the wilderness beyond the village. As I walked along, I noticed how the atmosphere of this planet was just like Earth and a lot of other worlds. I couldn't help but wonder again how the air had stayed in place as the planet went out into space with its host star. My thoughts were soon interrupted as I felt eyes watching me.

I caught a whiff of a strange scent I've never encountered. My Bah'Tene senses could detect it, almost like an animal picking up on a minuscule odor. Whatever was near, it was big and hungry and considered me to be a late lunch. I could feel the beat of its wings before I even heard them. A dark shadow fell over me from up on high. I looked up and saw a great winged beast swooping down on me. I jumped to the left and rolled, popping up and throwing a fireball at it. I hit its wing and it fell to the ground.

With a loud thud, the beast swore in English. How did it know English? I drew my blade from my side and held it up. The creature crawled up onto its feet and glared at me. I could feel that it had pheromones spraying from its pores and that I was supposed to be frozen in fear. If I were a tene, I would no doubt be, and the thing could take its time eating me. The beast looked puzzled when I moved slowly towards it, my eyes never leaving it.

"How do you move? What sort of man are you?" The thing did speak English pretty well. This is the first time I'd heard the language since I left Elginia after taking the Grand Test.

"I'm Bah'Tene," I responded. "Not exactly something you can just freeze with fear." It snorted at me. "You're the durmivol, I presume."

Growling, it answered me. "How do you know that word?" I told him the locals referred to you by that. "Yes, that is my kind, but not my name. My name is not pronounceable by the mortal tongue. This was once our home world, so long ago, when even the ancients of Elginia and Atlantis wore loin clothes and died of old age at twenty-five"

"Interesting," I said, still keeping my eyes on the monster. "How do you know English?" It asked me for my name first. "Sargas."

It shook its head. "That is not the name I sense in your brain, yet I know that is how you are addressed. Your name from before you became powerful and tough. The name I sense is..."

I cut him off. "Never mind that name. Sargas is how you'll address me now, durmivol."

The creature sniffed. "You are so like the other off-worlder I found a few days ago. He had a power like yours. Maybe that is why he was so hard to rip up, but the taste was divine!"

That set me off. In my rage, I launched another fireball at the beast, feeling weak immediately after from the sudden surge of power, and it jumped in the air and took flight, being missed by mere inches.

It hovered in the air above me again and smiled. "I suppose you'll taste just as well, Earth man." How did it know? "I can sense things from your brain, even if just a small detail or two. You have a powerful block in your psyche." It flew straight at me and I leapt right over its head as it came close. I landed on its back and with my sword I sliced off its right wing. The beastie fell down hard on the ground and I was almost crushed under its weight but managed to roll out of the way.

The beast stood, growling and screaming profanities in English that would make a drunken sailor blush with shame and embarrassment. I rushed at the durmivol, sword held high and ready to strike. The beast swiped a powerful arm and hit me, knocking me thirty feet into the air and landing hard on my back. A few vertebrae did break, but healed seconds later. My anger flaring, I summoned up another fireball and hit it square in the chest. As it flailed about trying to put out the flame, I flung my sword at it, hitting the mark and slicing off its head.

It was as I had learned upon becoming Bah'Tene. Taking a head kills pretty much anything. The corpse of the monster lay there, its head at its side. I picked up the head and tossed it on the flaming corpse. Going back to the village, I told them the beast was dead, and they tried to offer me the chief's daughter as a reward. I politely declined, telling them that I was already married, which was more or less true.

My wife won't be born for several centuries but in my own time I was married to her. But, I wasn't above having sex with beautiful women while I fought my way back to the twentieth century. I just didn't want to sample one of their women. Not to be rude, but she looked rather mannish.

I told them that though I killed that beast, there might be more out there. I told them I couldn't guarantee their continued safety out here this far from civilization, so I convinced them to come back with me to be relocated. They were the only lifeform on this rock, so I only had to arrange transport for three hundred and fifty natives. When I reported back to Gostal, he rolled his eyes and called me a soft-hearted fool, but he smiled as he said it. We relocated the tribesmen to a settlement on the far side of Elginia. Even unto this day, they live the same way and their population never gets bigger than several hundred.

But that was the end of that, and I never bothered checking on them again. I had other things to do.

Chapter 8

Over the next several years, Gostal and I traveled around, putting our hunting of demons and undead on hold and instead doing battle with Fallen. The Fallen were raising armies of tene and forcing many of them to take a Grand Test in an unknown location. For a very long time, the only way to become Bah'Tene was to take the Grand Test at the Council Chambers.

The Fallen had somehow found a way to duplicate the process. It was creating incomplete Bah'Tene. They had some strength, but none of the skills and mental abilities and other things that a true Bah'Tene could do. They were, more or less, just very durable tene. They died a lot easier than a real Bah'Tene. Whatever the process was, it lacked that piece of Archangel primordial energy that permeated the chamber walls during the Grand Test, the very power of Michael himself.

Together, Gostal and I fought many of them. Though the two of us could easily decimate a regiment of these half-ass Bah'Tene, we had Gostal's personal army of tene soldiers with us. He and I would be in the front, hacking and slashing at the enemy, and I'd throw some fireballs for good measure when my strength allowed for it.

At a battle on Moonan, several solar systems away from Elginia, I first caused an enemy Fallen to burst into flames from within. During the fighting, I saw a young soldier of Gostal's lose his skull cap, and my anger grew in a flash. The Fallen that killed the young man screamed in pain, and it took a few seconds to notice why. I had set his innards on fire, without even launching a fireball. The flames engulfed him in mere seconds. I could feel some blood trickle from my nose as I fell to my knees, weakened.

I looked over at Gostal and he smiled like a proud father at me. As he looked on, several enemy tene troopers had surrounded him. He held up his hand and plasma-like bullets shot forth from his fingertips. Even after all these years together, I had no idea he could do that. The bullets went through them like they were made of paper. His face showed that he was greatly weakened by that move, but it also showed satisfaction.

That battle lasted for hours, and in the end, we lost over a hundred men, but we completely wiped out the Fallen present and took several thousand of their troops prisoner. The council didn't waste any time in getting rid of them. As punishment for siding with the Fallen, they were loaded into several transport ships and launched into the sun of Elginia. I felt no remorse, no regret. They were the enemy. They made their choice, and they got a much swifter death than many of our soldiers out on that field.

I had gone back into my chambers on board the Reaper Blade. Since the battle where I witnessed Gostal zapping people with laser fingers, I had a feeling deep inside of my soul that something was amiss in the universe.

Gostal was a powerful Bah'Tene, that much has always been certain. But the way he fired his laser fingers really had me floored. That was just strange. I didn't even know that was a thing for us. I knew, though, it wasn't his ability that unsettled me. It was that he never told me about it and the feeling I got from him when he used it. I knew that couldn't have been his first time doing that power. I never sensed such sadistic delight from anyone before

Don't get me wrong. I have taken joy in killing of an enemy. Slicing off a vamp's head or running a blade through a Fallen. It was something that gave me a sense of accomplishment, and, more often than not, satisfaction. But, as far as I knew, I was sane. I was starting to doubt the same thing of my mentor. Or maybe I was just being hypocritical.

Gostal was a mighty warrior even when he was a tene. Having power like we do, that does change you. Maybe it had been slowly driving Gostal mad and the time of his sanity was running out. I just didn't want to accept that possibility.

I was brought from my thoughts as Gostal summoned me to the dining hall. I went straight there and was greeted by the Council, guests of his for dinner. I waved at Arakus, the first being in this time and place that showed me any care, as I was just a barbarian half-breed to the others on the Council, and no doubt to a lot of my brethren. Gostal didn't seem to regard me as such, but he was a bit of a barbarian himself.

I sat down in my seat at the main dining table and broke bread with our leadership. Gostal was in great spirits that night. We all laughed and drank and told stories of our latest adventures. Gostal told of our recent battle and I told them of my encounter with the durmivol. Arakus spoke of the Emperor finally dying and his son taking the throne full time. Political issues never bothered our kind much. The Council may not have been the rulers of the Elginian

Imperium, but they held great sway with the royal family and their advice was always sought out.

As the meal ended, Arakus told us of the main reason that they came for a visit to the Reaper Blade. There was a small world, Korbironna, that wanted to secede from the Imperium and be their own sovereign world. The Council was tasked with negotiating with them to get them to stay. The new Emperor had no desire to have a member world leave so soon after he took the throne full time from his dead father. They decided that Gostal would be the perfect candidate to talk to King Dortna, ruler of Korbironna. Gostal's reputation as "Conqueror of One Hundred Worlds in One Hundred Years" would hopefully sway the good king from leaving the Elginian Imperium. Gostal took the mission with a smile and a nod.

During the conversation, I noticed that Arakus, as well as the other councilmembers, kept darting their eyes over to me nervously. Did they think that I'd say something against the mission? That wasn't my place to do so. I figured a diplomatic undertaking would be a nice change of pace after spending the last decade traveling the stars and killing monsters and enemy soldiers.

The Council soon boarded their transport to go back to Elginia. Strange that they came all this way and not just send us a transmission. Maybe they just wanted some free food. Before boarding the shuttle, Arakus looked back at me, and the look on his face reminded me of something. A vision I had several years ago about him telling me to stop Gostal. Our eyes locked and he nodded grimly at me. He sensed that I was remembering that vision. As the shuttle took off out of the hanger, I glanced over at Gostal, who was busy giving instructions to his ship's captain. For a moment, I saw a dark shadow cast over him, but it was soon gone like the sun coming out from behind a cloud and taking away the darkness.

Within the hour, we were changing our course to Korbironna, right on the edge of Elginian space and what we called the Wild Zone, an area of the galaxy that was uninhabitable by even our kind. Lightning storms the size of Jupiter continuously went on since the galaxy first formed back in the birth pangs of the universe. Why the hell would anyone want to live on Korbironna?

We came out of light speed and I saw the planet on the monitor. It was a beautiful green and purple world. The purple was the water of the oceans, colored that way because of the unique atmosphere of the planet.

Far beyond that world, you could see the lightning of the Wild Zone. There was an energy field blocking the planet from the storms. The view was frighteningly beautiful. Soon after arriving, we, along with several dozen of our troops, boarded the Skull Hunter and flew to the surface of the planet to the capitol citadel. The sky had an unusual purplish tinge to it. You could barely see the lightning storms off in the vast distance.

We requested permission to land and were soon setting down on the docking platform of the capitol. We were greeted by several members of the royal guard and they led us to King Dortna and his wife Queen Millor. The king was a pleasant looking old man, almost grandfatherly and his wife reminded me of Barbara Bush. You would half expect her to bring out an apple pie and some chocolate chip cookies. Those would be nice as I hadn't eaten that kind of food in a long time.

Gostal and I bowed before the king and greeted him. He smiled and told us to speak our peace. "Your grace, I am Gostal of the Bah'Tene serving the Elginian Imperium. We have come to negotiate your world's continued membership in the Imperium."

The king nodded his head. "I was sure they'd send some immortals to try and keep us from freeing ourselves."

Gostal shrugged his shoulders. "We are not immortal. Only compared to your kind, your grace." The queen mumbled under her breath. "Excuse me, my good queen. What was that?"

She looked directly at Gostal, her pleasant grandmotherly demeanor turning fiery. "I said, we've been on our own as a world for centuries with no help from the Imperium, so why should you even care if we leave or stay?"

Nodding in agreement, the king spoke. "Yes, is the young Emperor that hungry for subjects that he has to keep even a small world such as ours just to collect our taxes and take our sons off to war?"

Gostal was getting impatient, I could sense it. We were very tuned to each other as we fought side by side for a long time now. I could feel his anger starting to perk up.

"Your grace," Gostal's speech disturbingly calm. "It isn't that the Emperor wants your taxes so badly. The member worlds of the Elginian Imperium have a responsibility..."

The king held up his hand to silence us, and he ordered us to leave. I sensed it before it happened, and to this day

I wish I had acted on it. Gostal held his finger up ever so lightly and our troops piled into the room and opened fire on the king and queen, cutting their bodies in half. I could have probably done something, but it was too late. He could be violent and hardcore in combat, but he had never acted in this fashion before, gunning down a civilian. I didn't want to believe Gostal had it in him.

After a decade together, I now saw his insanity, fully bared in the open for the universe to witness. He was a true madman. Psychotic. He may have fought the Fallen on behalf of the Council, but was himself was more or less a Fallen as well, in action, at least.

Screw my duty to him and the Council, I thought. I brought out my sword and went for the kill. I was going to take his head. If I didn't, he'd most likely kill everyone on the planet. He sensed my actions before I could carry them out. He unhooked his axe from his belt and swung it at my neck. I quickly caught the blade before it touched my skin and held it there with all my strength. He reached with his other hand and began choking me. It wasn't going to kill me, but I could still black out and then he could decapitate me at his leisure.

I could sense that my time was almost up. I was going to die here, in 1507 on Korbironna in a far-off galaxy. I would never see the twentieth century again.

Not like this, I thought. There was one way to save myself right now, or at least postpone my demise. I tried to speak. Gostal released his grip enough to let me continue. "Challenge," I managed to cough out. He let go and put his axe away.

"You? You challenge me? That is laughable!"

Recovering from my attack, I smirked, "You afraid to accept, Gostal?"

His eyes narrowed. "That is Lord Gostal to you! I accept! We do it on Mount Korn outside of the Elginian council chambers! When would you like to die, Sargas?"

"Tomorrow morning at the rise of the sun. That is when I should like to kill you, Gostal." He laughed and walked out the door, his men following him.

Chapter 9

I got on my communicator and called into the Council. They told me they already knew as Gostal informed them seconds before I did. Wow, that was fast. Arakus noted to me his disappointment that I would do something so foolish, but he was glad that I didn't bow down to the Phantom Lord like everyone else did.

I acquired a small shuttle and flew back to Elginia. I wanted to get there in time for the fight. I eventually arrived back on Elginia and went directly to the Council. Gostal was there already, and he smirked at me as I entered the chambers. "Greetings, challenger."

Ignoring him, I spoke directly to the Council. "The time of the Challenge is going to be soon, as you know. I have one request." They all listened. "If I die, take my body back to Earth. I don't care that it is way before my own time. Take my body back, cremate it, and scatter the ashes at these coordinates." I pulled out my communicator which also had maps of thousands of worlds stored in it. I brought up a holographic image of the Earth and showed them where Valley Center would be in the future. "My ashes go here."

Gostal rolled his eyes and left the room, calling out before he left, "Sargas, I'll take your cold corpse there myself, old friend."

I went back to the ship I commandeered and tried to rest, but sleep was elusive. Sooner than I would have liked, it was time to face the Challenge. I lifted off and headed towards Mount Korn.

All of the council members were gathered there, along with probably every Bah'Tene in the tri-galaxy area. Everyone wanted to see Gostal fight the barbarian from Earth. Snooty bastards. Gostal was standing out in the middle of the mountaintop, his axe in hand, his men all in hovercrafts around the mountain. They wanted to watch their master fight, too.

"Ah, Sargas," Gostal shouted. "Good of you to be on time for your death. It isn't too late to back out, cowardice might be preferable to oblivion." Many of the Bah'Tene laughed at that. His men all stood silently watching.

I got out of the craft and walked towards Gostal. As the challenged one, he had his weapon out already, prepared to strike first. He had a rather wicked looking two-handed axe that he held easily in one hand. Not his usual weapon, but I knew he'd be skilled using it. I stood three feet from him, a former friend and mentor to me, and prepared for him to strike. I sensed it a split second before it happened. The axe came towards my neck, and I deftly blocked it in a move he taught me.

He looked impressed. We continued to trade strikes with our weapons, the sound of metal on metal permeated throughout the mountains as two pseudo-immortals fought to the death.

Under the cloudy sky he thrust his axe at my neck and I'd block and swing at his. He was holding back his power. I knew that if he lost control and struck with his lightning fingers (not sure of the proper name, but that is what I called it), he would decimate me. He felt no need to, however. He was clearly enjoying this, fighting with me, man to man, the way the gods intended.

After long minutes of trading blows, I could sense something I hadn't expected. He was growing a bit fearful. He hadn't really fought sans powers since becoming Bah'Tene. No advanced reflexes or strength or agility were used. This tene fighting was making him start to wonder if he could take anyone in a fair fight. I had a renewed sense of strength and I sped up my strikes, as I could tell he was wearing down, ever so much.

To the untrained eye, there would be no sign of weakness. Only a Bah'Tene could sense it. I saw my chance, and I took it. I ran my sword through his stomach, slicing many organs in the process. I knew he'd heal, but it still felt good to do that to him. The madman butcher of Korbironna. So much for friendship, I guess. I withdrew my sword and Gostal fell to his knees, pained and not healing quick enough. I decided to end it. I would love to punish him further, but I didn't see the need.

I raised up my blade and brought it down on his neck, forever severing head from torso. His body immediately fell forward, and in a lightning fast move, I kicked his severed head off the mountain. No one cheered for me. Everyone was shocked. I was too. I really didn't think I'd pull it off, but I won. I killed the Phantom Lord.

All of Gostal's soldiers landed their ships and marched up to me. I knew no one would help, so I prepared to slaughter all those men. I didn't relish the thought, but the challenge was over. I was allowed to use my powers to protect myself. The men all stopped about ten feet short of me. All of the Bah'Tene in attendance watched silently. The main soldier, who I knew was named General Mukaoy, knelt down, placing his rifle at my feet. His men followed suit. They were surrendering to me. It suddenly dawned on me. These soldiers had seen me kill their cruel master, and they were pledging their loyalty and service to me. I had just inherited the Phantom Lord's army.

All his soldiers, from all of the worlds he controlled, would now follow me. I told the general to rise. He told me that on behalf of the soldiers under the rulership of Gostal, they pledged their lives and service to me. Long had they wanted to leave his rule, but Gostal was too powerful to just walk away from. He held them though their loyalty to his being their master, but many of them were also forced into service on pain of torture. He had their families held captive in their own homes. I knew Gostal was crazy, but I didn't realize just how far he had gone. I was too close to him. I didn't want to see his madness, but there it was before me. Better late than never.

General Mukaoy put his fist in the air. "Sargas! Sargas!" Soon, the soldiers joined in, chanting my name.

I thought it was amazing. The Phantom Lord's army, loyal to me. The Reaper Blade was mine as well. I nodded at General Mukaoy. "Thank you, General. It is an honor to have you at my side."

The Council of Bah'Tene approached me, and I noticed a change in their demeanor. They were happy and thankful, two emotions that I've never felt from them before.

"Sargas," spoke Arakus. "We are extremely grateful for what you've done for us. The Council wishes to extend our eternal thanks to you."

"Well, you're welcome," I replied. I turned to the General. "Get all the men back on the Reaper Blade. Leave the Skull Hunter. I'll be flying it back up to the Blade shortly." The General bowed and left to follow my orders. "Arakus, there is no reason to thank me. I did it to save my own ass. Gostal almost killed me, after he killed the king and queen of Korbironna." I explained the story to him.

"Yes, Gostal told us pretty much that."

I was shocked. "What? You knew, and you didn't punish him? And don't give me any crap about you didn't want to interfere with the Challenge. Did you send him there to kill the king and queen?"

"No," Arakus assured me. "But, we needed you to be there with him for that assignment. I know about your vision from so long ago. You knew that Gostal was capable of so much death and destruction. We needed you to stop him." I asked what he meant. "We couldn't stand against him. He had an army, which now belongs to you, one of our faithful. He needed to be stopped, and we knew it had to be by you. We had a vision, as well. You and your Targothian blood, barbaric as it is, It's the only thing powerful enough to stand against the Phantom Lord. That is why we reached into your time to bring you here. You weren't born yet. We tried to get you sooner, at birth, to raise you as one of ours, but we could only get you at the specific time that we did. Opening a portal in time is not an exact science."

I was truly angry. "You ripped me from my life because you were too pussified to take on Gostal? You figured that I was just an expendable Terran, eh?" I was tempted to bring a fireball on Arakus but controlled myself. "Is Targoth even gone or did you lie to me to keep me from going there?"

"Yes, it's true," Arakus answered me. "We altered our archives so you'd never know. We didn't want you leaving us. We needed you to fulfill our vision and kill the Phantom Lord. It happened as it was meant to. The universe has its ways and its own reasons for things that be."

It hit me. Targoth was still around. It wasn't gone like they had told me. The place my ancestors came from. I wondered if my dad knew he was descended from aliens. He never let on if he did. Maybe he didn't know. I'd have to wait several hundred years to ask him. But, Targoth was still out there. "Where is Targoth? Tell me!"

Arakus sighed and told me the coordinates. It was located in the outer region of the Andromeda galaxy, not unlike Earth being in an outer spiral arm of the Milky Way. Very far away and in an area of space that according to maps and archives is empty, showing it as several stars with no world orbiting. I never would have known it was there.

"I know I can't stop you now, Sargas, but if you're truly going to Targoth, be warned. There was a reason your namesake left the world. A Fallen Bah'Tene rules over it." I couldn't believe what I was hearing. A Fallen ruling over Targoth. "One who has somehow managed to live far beyond his one-thousand-year span. We know not how he does it, but he is still there, but so long as we don't interfere, he stays in Targothian space. Our predecessors on the

Council told us of him when we were appointed as successors."

"You mean to tell me, you know of a Fallen out there doing evil shit and you don't stop him? Why? Afraid that he is powered more than you? Because he's lived beyond the thousand? You, Arakus, are revealing the Council as cowards." He glared at me. "We never run from a fight with a Fallen."

Vontorlad stepped in. "Sargas, watch how you speak to Lord Arakus."

I smirked. "Oh? Fuck off." I said in English as I walked away. Then, returning to speak Elginian again, "Consider this my resignation from the forces of the Imperium. I am going to my homeland to deal with this Qal Dea myself."

"But he's a tyrant and insane!" Vontorlad burst out. "You haven't a chance!"

Arakus called out to me using my birth name. I turned to look at him and he flinched. I turned back around and continued to walk off. "Sargas! If you do this, you'll be cut off from the Elginian Imperium. No more will you be considered a Son of Michael! Your fate in Targothian space is your own."

I didn't bother turning around this time as I answered. "You've not been any help to the Targothians so far anyway, so what does it matter? Goodbye, council of cowards."

I didn't need their help, I decided. I had my own army of badass troops. I had a small fleet of warships. It was time to go to Targoth and kill another insane Bah'Tene. Just another day at the office.

Tyrant and madman. He didn't sound that much different than Gostal, except Gostal was my friend, at least in the past. Dea is a complete stranger, and a fulltime Fallen. Killing him would be much different than taking out Gostal.

Chapter 10

I flew away from Elginia in Gostal's flagship. It was mine now. All of his soldiers, no, my soldiers, saluted me as I walked past. General Mukaoy escorted me through the ship. It was a ship built for war and siege. I now had over twenty of these under my command, each one had three thousand men onboard, and dozens of squadrons of space fighter jets. They looked a bit like an F-15 but with a more streamlined look, and seated three men. One was the pilot, one was the navigator and the third was the gunner.

I was taken to the bridge where there was bustling activity. The men scurried about carrying out their daily functions. It was awesome. They saw me standing there and they all stopped and saluted until I dismissed them. I had been on this ship before but following behind Gostal. He had his own private chamber behind the bridge that only he was allowed in. It was mine now. It was a place to meditate and have quiet time. I invited the general and he was surprised at the gesture, but followed me in.

I asked him to tell me about his people. He was Elginian, but not from the main world. He was from a colony seven thousand light-years from the main planet. His was a caste raised as soldiers for the Emperor of the Elginian Imperium. Emperors. Who needs them? I was done with those chuckleheads.

I told the general that I'd need a good advisor for the military leadership of the fleet. I appointed him High General, a new position I had just created, and told him

I'd defer to his good judgment on the day to day defense operations. I still wanted to be kept apprised of everything. He heartily agreed and told me he was unworthy of such an honor but would serve me until his death. Taken from his parents at age five, he was raised to be a warrior and a leader. He never knew his family. They all died in a joint Fallen/ nosferatus attack when he was ten. He knew he'd never see them again, so he never thought about them. His men were his family. I could honor and respect that. But, if luck was on my side, I'd see my own family again, though I'd be a lot different than the young man they knew.

I was still trying to understand how the Fallen and nosferatus could team up, even after all these years it was hard to fathom the two forces uniting. A Fallen is still a Bah'Tene at heart and yet they could tolerate being around the vamps. Just being around those undead bastards pisses me off. It is in our very essence to hate them. Yet, they did manage to collaborate to spread havoc and death. Evil befriends evil.

I told the general to order the ship to stop and put me on an open channel. I called out to all my new soldiers. I ordered the fleet to my location. We were done with Elginia. We were heading to Targoth. Within an hour, I had all twenty battleships there, along with several civilian transports. These were the families of many of the soldiers. That was fine. They all deserved a better life than the fascists of Elginia could provide. Only after a decade of serving the Council of Bah'Tene I grew tired of their crap.

If my ancestral home was under control of someone like Gostal, I had to free them. I would liberate the people of

Targoth that stayed behind after my ancestor led the rest to Earth. They had spent enough time in servitude to a fallen Bah'Tene.

It took a matter of hours, but the fleet arrived in Targothian space. The solar system itself was average in size. There were ten planets, most had moons except for the first two and outer three. The bridge crew scanned the entire system. I was told each planet except for the first two had colonies on them and had been terraformed to be just like Targoth. There were also other outposts in the surrounding systems.

As soon as we hit the system, I was notified we were being scanned. No doubt they hadn't had visitors in their lifetimes. Qal Dea had the system to himself as the Council didn't care to come here. They considered him a big fish in a small pond and wanted to keep him left alone so he'd be content with that. Things were about to change.

I sent out a message to all of the colonies at once, and to the main world of Targoth itself, fourth planet from the sun. The message was in Elginian, but it got translated into Targothian. They only had one language, one dialect. On the trip over I had read what little information I could find on Targoth. While its location was gone from the archives, much of the mythology and history was easy to dig up. Legends spoke of other races that inhabited Targoth a very long time ago, before the visitors from Elginia discovered the planet. Creatures found only in one other place that I had heard of...Earth mythology. Elves, goblins, and other fairy creatures. Perhaps they originated on Targoth and went to

Earth. It was possible they were still out there somewhere in the universe.

The message I sent was simple. "Sargas has returned."

Needless to say, that message didn't go over very well. Within seconds I had over a dozen Targothian battle cruisers surrounding my flagship, and their weapons were primed. I know they couldn't possibly think I was the first Sargas, or could they? That was all centuries ago. I was in the past, but not that far back. For the Targothians, my ancestor had been gone for centuries. Maybe Qal Dea sensed that a fellow Bah'Tene was here. The response back was a simple one, too.

"You are not welcome." Well, now. That was rude.

"This is Sargas, formerly of the Elginian Imperium. I wish to speak to Qal Dea about a possible merging of our forces in the name of Targoth." It felt like a long time, but it was merely a matter of minutes. A face appeared on the monitor. He was about my age, physically, at least. He had a long mane of fire red hair and a beard to match. His eyes were a dark hue of crimson as well. This fallen one had been soaking in his own corruption for a very long time. "Hello. I presume you are Qal Dea, leader of Targoth?"

He glared at me. His voice was deep and heavy. "That face. So familiar, yet not. You are not the same man who took my subjects away all those centuries ago. I sense your power and have taken notice of your fleet. It looks like you got the best of the Phantom Lord. I knew him by reputation only, as I do keep abreast of the events of the Imperium when I grow bored." I nodded. "Well, that is a tale I should want to hear. You have permission to land in a small personal craft.

72

You may have three comrades with you. But your fleet must stay where they are." I agreed to the terms.

Something about this guy was very off. I knew he was basically a Fallen, but even so, he should have crumpled to dust already. He conquered the planet over a millennium ago. That is beyond the lifespan of one of our kind. I had already seen a few of my kind turn to dust after reaching their maximum life limit. Not many ever get there, except for council members, as they no longer do anything useful other than debate and hide in their over glorified office building.

I made my preparations to land. I put on a fresh set of armor, along with a cape. It had the seal of Gostal on the back. I'd have to find another symbol soon. I wouldn't want to continue to wear Gostal's seal, nor would I want my soldiers to have to either. I had Mukaoy stay behind to command the fleet in the event of an attack. I took his second in command, Colonel Barsid, and two soldiers with me. Getting into Gostal's personal shuttle, I flew us down to the surface of the planet. Targoth, my ancestral home.

After breaking through the outer atmosphere, we soon were close enough to see the planet. It was beautiful and somehow extremely familiar. DNA remembrance, perhaps.

The hemisphere I was in right now had one large land mass, about twice the size of Europe. To its east, I saw another large land mass, about a third of its size. Many islands were strewn about the vast sea. One island in particular caught my attention. It was shaped almost like a head with horns. Scans indicated there was another large land mass on the opposite side of the planet, about the size of Asia and India combined, though it was covered in ice and snow with extremely low temperatures. Life forms currently read to be approximately 500 million humanoids. Much smaller than the population of the Earth of my time. Perhaps many were off world right now. After all, they entire solar system was inhabited by colonies. I came in closer to the coordinates given to me. I could see almost in the center of the main land mass was a large valley.

I took notice of a large castle right at the northern tip at the edge of the valley. The valley looked very deep, several hundred feet at least, and there were various paths leading down to it. Doubtful they were used much anymore. More likely transports took them to the bottom and back up again.

Another thing of note at the north part of the valley was a small forest. There were a couple of ponds and many small villages. Motor vehicles, not too different from our cars on Earth were driving around, but there was no exhaust. The atmosphere read to be almost identical to Earth. Slightly more oxygen and less nitrogen, and zero pollution. Whatever they were doing, they were doing it right.

The castle on top of the valley had several landing platforms. I was directed to land on one. It was time to meet the natives.

Chapter 11

I was greeted by a platoon of Targothian troops. The uniforms were almost like the military BDU of the late twentieth century, but a dark solid gray. The leader approached me and did what must have been their salute, a fist over the chest. He greeted me in Targothian before realizing that I didn't speak it.

"Tolm. Atla toik Jama Tymber ot Gen Gantad". When he was finished, he spoke in Elginian. "Forgive me. I have not spoken Elginian in a long time. Dea has it taught to our children in school. What I said was, 'Hello. I am Commander Tymber of the Imperial Guard. I must say it is an honor to meet another like the Master."

I sized up Tymber. He was taller than me and looked to be in his late twenties. He must have hit six foot four. He wore his dark hair in a buzz. On his armor was what must have been his rank and the symbol of Targoth. It was a red square with some sort of bird of prey colored green. "I would like to ask you to follow us please to Master Dea."

I followed behind. I got a good sense of this guy. He had a lot of power and strength but was only tene. He'd make a formidable Bah'Tene if he survived the Grand Test.

Whenever he said the word 'master' I could sense that his temper flared, but due to the soldier's control, it never showed to the untrained eye. He only served his master because there was nothing else. Hopefully, when I did what I needed to do, Tymber was one of the ones still standing. Seems a shame to put down a potential ally.

I was led up the steps. I insisted on the walk up for him to speak in his native tongue. We conversed about the beauty of the planet and he mentioned that his family was currently living in Ansaka, the nation in which the Central Valley resided. The Central Valley had a unique position on the planet. Due to the axis of the planet and the position from the sun, it created a specific weather pattern in the valley below. It never went below forty degrees and never above fifty-five. Those are in Earth's Fahrenheit, of course. His family preferred the temperature in Ansaka. Right now, it was springtime. Beautiful weather in which his children could play.

I was listening very intently for a dual purpose. Being a Bah'Tene unlocked parts of your brain that most mortals never get a chance to experience. One of the benefits was that if were to listen to a language being spoken for more than ten minutes or so, you could learn it fluently. There were bound to be words and phrases you'd need help on, but more or less, you could converse. By the time I was led into Qal Dea's throne room, I bowed and greeted him in Targothian. Needless to say, he was impressed.

"Ah, Sargas of the Elginian Imperium. No, wait, sorry, formerly of the Imperium. I must admit, I wasn't sure I'd ever see one of my Bah'Tene brethren again."

I put up my hand. "Excuse me for being so blunt, but I must ask. How have you lived this long? By my calculations, you should have dusted long ago." He smiled while his men looked visibly nervous. They weren't offended by my words, but rather in fear of his potential response.

"Well, Sargas. Let me explain. Long ago, after I became Master of All, I discovered a meteorite in the caverns beneath this castle. I could feel power from it. It came from a galaxy that was no longer alive, far on the other side of the universe. It had been on Targoth since before the times of the Faery folk. I could just feel it. I knew it deep inside. This was ancient. And being near it had seemed to prolong my life. I couldn't just leave my precious Targoth behind. Not since I claimed it from its former ruler, Lord Lorancano, the father of Sargas, that is, your ancestor." My ancestor was the crown prince to this world.

Qal Dea yelled out something in a demonic sounding way and his men all drew their rifles and aimed at me and my three companions. "I cannot allow you to remain here, Sargas. I would not mind you leaving, but as I have probably rightfully guessed, you have come to claim your old home." Growling again, the men all opened fire, but I immediately pushed my companions down and rushed the troops with my sword in hand. All the soldiers ran for cover. I pointed my sword and demanded Dea surrender. He laughed at that. It was an insane, maniacal laugh that you might hear in a cheesy mad scientist movie from the fifties. He commanded his troops to stand down and took out his own weapon.

Upon seeing the sword, I knew that it belonged to the former ruler of the planet. It looked like a katana but with a straight blade. On the hilt, it had an emblem. It was a gray circle with a gold triangle, that itself had an upside down black triangle in the middle. Two red bars with three black dots each came from its sides, one in the upper left and the other in the lower right. I could feel it in my gut. I had seen this symbol before, in a dream I had as a kid at the age of seven. I have seen it several times since in dreams. This was the Seal of Targoth. The symbol of the world before Qal Dea conquered it. He took notice of my expression.

"Oh, I see you like this sword. You should. It belonged to Lord Lorancano. It is Sargotha, the Sword of Targoth. Possessed by the rightful ruler. After I took Lorancano's head and chased his son away, I claimed it for my own. Targoth refused to join the Imperium. I don't blame them," he continued. "That was when I knew that I wanted to more to do with the Imperium either. This world was mine for the taking. I forced the other Bah'Tene to leave. I felt a power here, beneath his castle, and it has made me more powerful. How could they not leave me here? They couldn't face my new supremacy. Cowards." I did agree with him on that point. As he continued to drone on and ramble about the cowardice of the Council, I couldn't take my eyes off that sword.

Sargotha. I knew that if I were to take it from him, the people of Targoth would follow me. They must have already known that this guy was not the rightful ruler, though he has ruled since before their great grandparents were in diapers.

I could sense it from the soldiers. They wanted to cast him down, but he was too strong. They wanted me to take the sword. They needed me to. I needed to take the head of the Bah'Tene that took the head of my great, great ancestor.

I readied my weapon and charged. He was a fire lord, too, and caused flames to erupt all around me. I dove right through it and brought my blade to his throat, but he blocked it one-handed. "A proper fight it is, Sargas."

Our swords clashed back and forth. I managed to give him a quick knee to the crotch, causing him to double over. No Challenge was issued, but we both wanted to fight blade on blade now. Qal Dea sliced me across the stomach with his sword. It hurt like a son-of-a-bitch, but it healed almost as quickly as it opened. I ran my sword through his throat, piercing it and my blade coming out the back of his neck. I sliced it out and to the right, which normally would have removed his head. It didn't.

His head stayed on the shoulders. I knew then that the meteor which seemed to give him a prolonged life had also made him stronger than the average Bah'Tene. Where the hell did that meteorite come from? There were millions of galaxies across the universe, though they were too far to reach with the current level of technology of the Imperium. It could have come from anywhere. Some great force in the universe must have hurled it across the void to land it right on Targoth in ages past.

This was possibly a fight I wouldn't win. I might die before I had a chance to catch up with my own time. Once again, I found myself facing the possibility of dying before the 20th Century. Dea walked towards me in a cocky stride, grunting and laughing at the same time.

"You foolish child!" He shouted. "Did you really think that you had a chance against me? I am Qal Dea, the Master of Targoth!" He held up the sword. "I have Sargotha! He who holds the sword holds the world!"

He began hurling fireballs at me, which I dodged as I fled the chamber. I barely made it out of there. I grabbed my companions and we all fled back to the shuttle, but not before the Colonel took a shot to his back from the Targothian troops firing on us.

As I flew us back to the Reaper Blade, the Colonel continued to bleed out. Several Targothian fighters left their hangers from the citadel and pursued us. Flying as fast as the shuttle would take us, we docked back in the Reaper Blade and I ordered the ship to take off at light speed and leave Targothian space. We quickly left the system. The fighters eventually broke off their pursuit and went back to Targoth.

If I was going to take the planet from that madman, I was going to have to come up with a better idea than just trying to kick his ass in a straight fight.

Chapter 12

Several parsecs outside of Targothian space, I called for a meeting with General Mukaoy and his command staff. Colonel Barsid had died upon arriving back at the Reaper Blade, and his replacement, Colonel Trave, was with us now.

Trave was a good man. He hailed from the capitol of Elginia, growing up on the streets of the city, with no family or home. He joined the Elginian military at the age of consent and was a loyal soldier to the Imperium up until several years ago when he was placed in the service of Gostal. He was forced to occupy worlds that held no threat and imprison people that did no wrong. Disenchanted, he contemplated desertion, but couldn't bring himself to do it. He felt trapped by the Phantom Lord. Now freed of that psycho, he was happy to be a soldier again.

"My lord, I don't know how we can take the capitol of Targoth without a fight. They have much more superior ships than we do. And they outnumber us as well."

It was true. The Targothian fleet had almost forty ships, all with more firepower. They had three times as many fighters as our fleet, as well.

Dea seemed like the type to kill anyone who found their way into his domain. He was simply a predator guarding his den and eating all the smaller animals that scurried by.

"I am forced to agree with you, Colonel," I answered back to his words of concern. "In a straight fight, the fleet would likely be decimated. On top of that, we'd have to kill many Targothian people. I don't want that. They are good people, they have been under the thumb of that Fallen bastard all of their lives, as their parents and grandparents before them. I am going to have to go in alone." They all gasped and started arguing about how dangerous it would be for me. "Please. I'm not the one in danger down there. Ever since I came to this time, I've thought about my ancestors that I was told were wiped out centuries before I got here, and that on Earth, they had intermingled and most likely forgot their origins. Now that I know they're alive, and down there and under oppression, I have to free them."

"But, my lord," General Mukaoy interrupted. "They are too far gone. There is no way to reach them. We should cut our losses and find a new home out there in the stars, far from the Elginian Imperium. Would be hard to do in any of these three galaxies, but we can go further out there. Try for a galaxy out in the other side of the universe."

I shook my head. "General, could you turn your back on your people? I can't go back to Earth just yet, as I don't want to accidently screw up the timeline and possibly wipe myself out. Getting to another galaxy would take centuries, even with our advanced craft. Most of you would never see it. This is where we stay. This is my home. I'll relieve you all of service to me and let you go on your way if you like, though I'd rather you stay at my side."

The general nodded, "Lord Sargas, we want to stay. We have no desire to set out into the universe without you."

I smiled and continued talking. "In my studies of this planet, I read something interesting. The Council tried to bury the history, but I dug some of it up. My ancestor, Sargas of Targoth, after his father was murdered and he led tens of thousands of Targothians to Earth, he gained a title. It means "liberator" in the Targothian language. Yo-akum. I want to be worthy of the title Yo-akum to my people on Targoth, as my ancestor was."

I hadn't learned yet how he led the people to Earth, as Targoth had no interstellar ships at that point in time. Dea had brought that technology to the planet upon his taking over. I wanted to learn how they made it to Earth. I wanted to know all of Targoth's history from the people themselves.

"Gentlemen, this is what I want you to do. Stay here, outside of Targothian space. Don't go into the system unless I call for you. I am going to the planet incognito. I'll not be able to remain in contact with you, but stay out here. Understand? I don't want them arming up against the fleet. I'll stop Dea somehow and then the rest of you can come on down planetside. Trust me. I know that the Targothians are ready to get rid of that asshole."

"What if we don't hear from you?" Mukaoy inquired. I simply told him that if I didn't contact them in a two weeks' time, then to leave and seek their destiny elsewhere. If it was my fate to die on Targoth, then I didn't want the entire fleet to face the same. I told them I was going to my chambers to rest before going back to Targoth. I'd be leaving in an unusual way. We had several meteor samples on board the ship for scientific study. I'd hollow one out and hide inside and be launched at one of the planets in the system, where I could commandeer a Targothian craft and fly to the planet. But for now, time to rest.

As I lay there, I reached out with my mind, my senses, and meditated, focusing on Targoth. It was a beautiful world, indeed.

My mind opened itself up and I looked into the distant past, seeing it before my eyes like a movie. I wasn't actually there, I was merely an observer.

I saw my ancestor, Sargas. He looked a lot like me. He and his father, Lorancano, stood in the throne room and were confronted by Qal Dea, the ginger madman.

I couldn't hear any words, only could witness the action. Sargas and Dea were having a heated argument, and Dea took his blade and rushed at lightning fast speed towards Lorancano, taking his head in an instant. He grabbed Sargas and threw him across the room, knocking him into a nearby statue. Dea bent down and took something from inside of Lorancano's robes. It was Sargotha, the sword of Targoth. Everything went black then, and I was alone in the dark. Footsteps came from behind me. I turned to strike, realizing I was unarmed. Instantly I felt no fear. Sargas, my forefather, was standing before me.

"Hail and well met, my descendant," he spoke to me. He looked enough like me that I had a flashback to the Grand Test. "Don't fear. I'm not your subconscious. I'm your ancestor."

"You're the Yo-akum," I whispered.

He smiled. "Yes, it is as you say. But, that was over a thousand years ago. I have moved on to the realm of spirits, but I had learned that you were brought from the distant future to this time because of who you are. A Targothian." That was true, I explained to him. I told him of how the

Council told me Targoth was gone and how my blood was strong enough to kill a madman like Gostal. Though I was from five centuries ahead, my particular DNA and blood made me the one they chose instead of a long line of my ancestors they could have picked. "He and Dea are very much alike," ancestor Sargas said.

"With one exception," I responded. "Dea still has a head."

"Well, my great descendant Sargas. That is where you can help, by taking his head as I should have done a long time ago. We had never encountered a Bah'Tene. Such strength. I may have led many of my people to Earth, but not all of them came. Many stayed behind to fight and make us able to escape. My father wanted me and as many survivors as possible to flee. A great wizard had opened a portal to Earth using old magics, where we settled in what would later become Germany and the Slavic regions." For a second, a dark thought passed through me. "No, my friend, Hitler was not one of us. He was one hundred percent Terran, though he did have some help from advanced aliens." I knew all about the Aryans from the far side of the Milky Way.

I felt relief at that. I'd hate to think one of the biggest genocidal maniacs in Earth's history was one of my people. I asked how he knew of someone from my world's past, which was still the future from his perspective. In the spirit world, time is fluid and can flow in either direction.

"Sargas, my descendant, you need to make your way to Targoth. You must defeat Qal Dea. You must issue the Challenge to him, in person, as over the video monitor would be a grave insult. Issue the Challenge and defeat him.

He'll be no match as long as he doesn't break the no power rule. Kill him and claim Sargotha for yourself. Take care of our people." With that, my ancestor, the original Sargas, faded away, back to the spirit realm.

I snapped out of it and realized it was morning. That meant it was time to go. I said goodbye to my troops and had them launch me towards a small outpost on the edge of the Targothian solar system. I could have launched to Targoth directly, but that proved to be difficult to get a straight trajectory.

From there, it was easy enough to steal a small shuttle transport.

The trip to Targoth would be long and boring as this ship I swiped wouldn't fly past light speed. It moved fast, however, and within a day I was closing in on Targoth. Things in the universe always have a way of sneaking up on you and throwing a wrench into your gears.

As I got closer, a small meteor happened by and hit my shuttle, knocking out the navigation. I spun around and around, falling towards the planet below. There was no way of steering this busted up shuttle accurately now. I was going nowhere near the citadel that held Dea. I found myself on a course towards the island that looked like a head with horns.

Chapter 13

Fortunately, I managed to steer the ship just enough so that I came in, rather abruptly, into a fairly level landing. Most of the ship had broken off in the process, but soon enough, I was on the ground, somewhere on the big horned island.

I thought about setting my distress beacon and getting picked up by someone, but thought better of it. Who's to say that they wouldn't try and kill me? For all I knew, Dea had posted my image and ordered his men to vaporize me. Well, try to, at any rate. But I had no desire to kill any Targothians. They were only following the person they were conditioned to. They were all raised in this world to obey Qal Dea. Maybe they regarded Sargas as a myth.

Well, Targoth was a world that once had creatures of myth living on its very surface so if Sargas was a myth, he would soon be fact again. I had read that great lizard beasts with wings used to travel the skies. Dragons. But, they were all gone, faded into legend.

I wandered the island for almost an entire day before I found a fishing ship docked. It was a large vessel, not unlike the sailing ships of Earth. It even had sails to steer by the winds. A world like this that had such great flying machines and they still preferred old school sailing. I couldn't help but appreciate that. A simpler way of living. That was very appealing, especially to someone who had spent the last decade killing demonic beings in the stars.

I quickly removed my armor and discarded it. I hoped that jeans and a black shirt with a rock band on it wouldn't be too conspicuous. Nearby was a small house. Perhaps it belonged to one of the sailors. Hiding my sword behind some bushes, I knocked on the door. No answer. Listening carefully, I heard no one inside. Turning the knob, I opened the door which was apparently unlocked. The inside was one large room. It was very sparse. A bed, several cloaks hanging from the wall, and a cooking pot. I took a cloak and went back outside, retrieving my blade and hiding it under the cloak.

Walking towards the sailing ship, I began to hear voices. The crew was busy preparing the ship for departure. "Hail!" I called out in Targothian to the men on the deck. One of them waved back. "My ship crashed back there. I seek passage to the mainland." My Targothian was surprisingly good. Even I could tell I had the accent of a native.

The tall and burly sailor, who identified himself as the first officer, lowered the ramp and let me on board. "I don't have any money," I told him.

He laughed a deep, jolly laugh. "Tis no problem, good sir. We'd be happy to take you back to the mainland. We're just fishermen. If you help out cleaning on deck, well, that is payment enough."

I thanked him for the ride and he took me to the Captain, a shorter man named Davron. Most Targothian men seemed to be at least 6'4, so Davron was a bit below average height. I too must have seemed like a short guy to them at only 6'1.

I introduced myself as Jack. Figured it was as good an alias as any. They took me to the mess hall and fed me. The meal was fish, of course. A very delicious fish. It was fried in butter and served with what must have been a potato on this planet.

After the meal, I spent the next several hours mopping the deck. I didn't want to risk them finding out who I really was. If anyone found out, it could endanger them as much as myself. Soon enough, night was falling, and I was relieved of duty for the evening and invited to partake of their supper with them. Again, a fish dish, but cooked differently. It had a garlic flavor to it. Before going to my bunk, I asked how long the trip to the mainland would be.

"Should be no more than five or six days," the Captain answered. "We're done with our haul and heading straight for the processing plant." I thanked him and retired for the night.

I was sleeping on a bunk in a small room with seven other bunks. All of the sailors were passed out in deep slumber. Thankfully none of them snored. I lay there on my back and shut my eyes, letting sleep find me and soon I too drifted off to the dreams of my subconscious mind.

Over the next few days of the trip, I discovered a small library on board. The men liked to read in their spare time. I found several books, one called Tales of Targoth, which held many stories of Targoth in the time of mythology. I found a book on the planets of the solar system, too. I had no doubt that this was basic knowledge for most Targothians. I read it on an evening that I wasn't required to mop the deck.

I learned the names of the other planets in the system. The first three worlds in the system were desert worlds, devoid of life, and hardly an atmosphere to speak of. The first was Iolat, named for the creator of dragons, beasts that long ago flew the world freely, but have since vanished into myth. It earned its name by being so close to the sun. It was believed to be the place that bore the ancient flying lizards.

The second world was Lilith, named for the goddess of lies and corruption. Strange enough, I remember that name as being the first wife of Adam, supposedly before Eve was created, at least according to apocrypha literature from Earth.

The third was Dar, named for the god of storms and weather and the father of the goddess Zabra, who herself was the matron of lightning and thunder. Dar had a moon that was named Zabra after the god's daughter. Dar also had an underground colony of Targothians. Long ago they had dug a vast cavern and set up atmosphere processers to make the air breathable. Much of the ore used for building ships and weapons came from the miners of Dar.

The fourth was, of course, Targoth. The origin of the name of Targoth was lost to the mists of time, but many believed it was what the ancients had called the Great Power, the creator of the cosmos, god of the gods. Targoth itself had two moons, named Shal and Bal. They were ancient generals of a long ago war, fought when the very gods themselves walked upon the land. Legend says the fight was so terrible that two mountains broke off from the surface and launched into the air, forever to orbit the planet, and they were named after the generals. Others say the generals were named after long forgotten gods that resided on those moons.

The fifth world was called Hanch, after the god of the forest and creator of the mythic elven kind. Legends told of how long ago the elves settled the kingdoms of Silverstone and Kumbernestia as well as the Goldmoon Kingdom of Elves on the border of the Grey Sea and the Rarl Ocean. This world had only one lifeform when they settled on it. A large bat-like creature, but it fed on decaying plants. They dubbed it a boglmin. It had six moons, all uncreatively named Hanch Two, Three, Four, Five, Six, and Seven. I suppose colonists have better things to worry about than naming moons.

The sixth world was named after the god of the balance between good and evil, Jilion, and its two moons were Heli and Heni, named for the goddesses of night and dark magic and of day and white magic. This world needed no terraforming as its atmosphere was completely identical to Targoth's. It is the only planet to have indigenous life other than Targoth and Hanch. It had over two hundred documented animal lifeforms and five hundred plant types. The list of animals and plants is too great to name here, but I will make note of a few that stood out to me. There is a plant that actually uproots itself and moves across the landscape in herds. They feed on minerals in the soil and on their own dead. Horrible to think, but circle of life and all. They were called cannibal weeds. There is also a form of whale that can come up on land and crawl. The creature's fins have flexible fingers on them, aiding in their movement. The colonists called them finger fish. A large reptile creature resembling a snake but with miniature legs lived in the trees and fed on the cannibal weeds. Simply enough, they were dubbed weed snakes. Other than those I named, there are others, but I don't feel like describing them all. You can probably go to the library and get the Intergalactic Flora and Fauna Guide.

The seventh world was named Kao, the goddess and creator of insects. The world itself was host to thousands of insect and arachnid lifeforms, brought long ago by travelers. None of them were sentient, but there was one race called the Kaonitetas, which meant "Children of Mother Kao" in an ancient dialect of Targothian. These beings were as tall as a man and practiced cannibalism with their wounded. Apparently, wounded meant weak and weakness was not allowed to thrive. They were similar in appearance to the common grasshopper found on Earth. A few Targothian explorers in the past had met their end in the bellies of some Kaonitetas. There were three moons around this world, which worked out in its orbit that one side of the planet got to see one moon and the other side got to see the other two. They had been long dubbed Kaoplan 1, 2, and 3. Kaoplan was "Guardian of Kao" in that same ancient dialect.

The last three worlds in the Targothian solar system were totally devoid of life except for Targothian colonies and they also held no moon with the exception of an artificial moon space station located around the eighth planet Athena. Athena was named after the Targothian goddess of war, which is interesting as on Earth the goddess holds the same title. Perhaps Targothian refuges took their faith there with them. Or perhaps Athena was a being of immense power and had traveled to both worlds. The artificial moon base was named Athena 2, and had been there since Dea took over the world so long ago. It had a primary function of going to the planet below and mining fuel used for the space fleet.

The last two planets are Ba'al (after the god of Death and Rebirth) and Temash (god of undeath). Even before the nosferatus came into this system, legends spoke of the dead coming back and feeding on the blood of the living. Both of these worlds were dead rock. Not so much as a microbe had ever existed on those worlds until they were colonized. Each world held over a dozen domed cities, each one populated with over thirty thousand beings. They were all there for a two-fold purpose. To defend the outer perimeter of the solar system and to observe the stars and deep space via telescopes. I could only assume that they also monitored communications of the Imperium and this was how Dea kept appraised of the goings on of Bah'Tene business.

You go beyond the outer planets, and you reach the edge of the Targothian solar system. The next solar system was about seven light years from the Targothian system. Halfway in between was a single planet called Kale, named after the Targothian god of justice. This world stayed in place due to the gravity pull of Targoth's star and the next closest star, called Shelanor, keeping the planetoid locked in its location, never revolving around either star. It didn't even rotate. How the atmosphere stayed in place was unknown.

There was one facility there, and it was used as a prison for only the worst possible offenders. It held no guards nor offered parole or reprieve. Once you were in the House of Kale, you were there for life. It even held prisoners from beyond Targoth. No doubt they were left in there to keep them from causing trouble with the citizens of Targoth and exposing the people to events from the Imperium.

The Captain called me into his chambers and told me that tomorrow by midday we'd be on shore. I thanked him for the ride and went back to my bunk to prepare for my journey the next day. Studying a map of Targoth, I tried to ascertain the best way to the Central Valley.

Chapter 14

We docked at a small port town where the crew began to unload their haul of fish. I thanked them all and bid them farewell as I set about my trip.

We were in the small nation of Southern Abnu, which long ago had been one nation with their neighbor, Northern Abnu, until Dea arrived. They used to be separate in the ancient times as well but united as Abnu about a century before the arrival of the psychotic Bah'Tene Dea. He used the military prowess of the northerners and turned them against their southern brothers, who were fishermen and miners. They split apart and continued to force the southerners to mine their ore for the weapons of the northern army and to feed them with their fish, leaving little for their southern kinsmen.

If I headed up the western coast, I'd end up in Kashm, which was once a mighty empire, now they served as the army of Dea, along with their Northern Abnu compatriots. I decided against that. No doubt I'd run into trouble with them and had no desire to kill any of my Targothian brethren.

I ultimately decided to head up the eastern coast into Kendaria, a small nation that was made up mostly of farmland. They grew many crops to feed the planet. The land was fertile enough that they yielded enough crops to feed the entire system. If I made my way north through that land, I'd end up in Ansaka, where the Central Valley resided.

The Central Valley was in a very unique location on the planet. It was in the dead center of the continent. It was in a unique place in terms of weather. It was like it was perpetually late autumn or early winter. There were many other areas I wanted to visit as well, but this was not a social call. I'd have plenty of time to see my new home world. For now I had to focus on getting to the Central Valley.

I didn't want to fly as air traffic was closely watched here. Transportation by ground was my only safe option. I went to a local inn and procured a small vehicle, basically meaning I stole it, but it was for the greater good.

The technology level of the vehicles was reminiscent of late 20th century Earth. Most of the vehicles were two or four person in size. Many of them had wheels, though the vehicle I took didn't. Hover car is a pretty accurate description. These cars had one great advantage over the cars of Earth. They didn't require gasoline. I don't want to call them hippie cars, but they did run on solar and electromagnetic power.

I drove due east and came to the coastline and followed it. I was making great time as I drove. It handled pretty much like a car on Earth.

Studying that map helped greatly. There would be a small resort town on the way. It held one of the biggest resort hotels on Targoth and overlooked the Gray Sea to the east.

It seems that all the nations on Targoth held the same names as they did back in the days of legend. The only real difference was all of the leaders answered to Dea. They were more or less able to run things on their own, but throughout the land you'd see garrisons of Targothian troops being forced to watch the actions of their fellow citizens.

You could feel the oppression in this world. It was palpable. It was all they had known for the last millennia. From my studies on the boat, I knew that Targothians were more or less like the Terrans of Earth, but their lifespan was twice that of an Earth tene. Being that I am apparently only part Targothian, I couldn't help but wonder how long my lifespan would be if I had remained a tene. I also knew that Targothians were taller than Terrans. On this planet, I might be considered slightly short at 6'1. Most of the men here were six and a half foot tall on average, and the women were around my height or slightly shorter than I. The females all had beautifully long legs which were accentuated by their form fitting clothes.

I didn't want to just rule these people. That was what Dea had done to them. I only wanted to take my birthright as leader of the planet, but I wanted to have the people want me in charge. I wanted them to respect and honor my lineage. I had to prove myself worthy in their eyes. I had to take what was stolen from my ancestors.

I had to claim Sargotha. That in itself should be more or less doable, with the problem being that Dea was no regular Bah'Tene.

That meteor fragment prolonged his life, and no doubt made him more powerful than one of our kind had a right to be. I debated contacting the Council, but forget that. I was done with their sorry asses. Just the fact that they allowed Dea to gain this much power and let him oppress a world, any world, was sickening. They could have stopped him and freed the Targothian people. They could have gone to Earth and brought Sargas back, or even prevented his departure with all those Targothian refugees. Then again, had that happened, would I even be here?

My mother was of Earth, but would my father still have been born? Would someone else had been born in his place? Possibly the individual sperm that created him wouldn't have done the task. It could have been the sperm to the left, or fifty back to the right. Someone else entirely could have been conceived, and that would have affected my own birth.

Would I have been the same man? My soul, would it have gone into another child somewhere else in the universe? And if so, would that person be exactly the same as me, and I'd be there on whatever world and in whatever time I ended up in, my soul making me the same person in a different circumstance. Even to a Bah'Tene, the nature of souls and birth and chance and time was a confusing thing to ponder.

I had plenty of time driving to think about what I'd do when I encountered Qal Dea. I would initiate the Challenge and then the fight would be a bit more level.

Yes, that was my best bet. Who knows what kind of power he might have developed in his time exposed to some intergalactic meteor? Our kind wasn't meant to live beyond their one thousand year life span. First thing after killing Dea, I'd have to take that meteor and dispose of it. I'd launch it into a black hole if I had to. I couldn't afford that power corrupting me. I didn't know what Dea was like before coming to Targoth, but that space rock must have enhanced the darkness that was already there. I knew my mind and soul. I would be afraid to enhance the darker parts of myself. Targoth may truly be reduced to rubble then.

I was starting to get hungry, so I decided to stop for a while and get some food. Seeing a settlement up ahead, I noticed something different about it. I got close enough to see that it was a military garrison. The flag of Gostal swayed in the breeze. I was about to turn and go the opposite direction when I found myself surrounded by dozens of troops, all of them pointing their weapons at me. I prepared to fight, but didn't relish the idea of killing any of my kinsmen.

"Halt," I was ordered. "You're the terrorist from Elginia that the Master warned us of. The one that dares to call himself Yo-akum Sargas."

I jumped out of the vehicle, my hands held up. "Look," I said in Targothian. "I have no desire to fight any of you. I have every right to call myself Sargas. He was my ancestor." They continued to aim at me. "I know none of you can have any love for Dea. Help me to cast him down. With him gone, you can all be free men again." Their weapons lowered ever so lightly, then raised up again.

"If you don't surrender, we'll have no choice but to kill you, Sargas."

"It isn't in my nature to surrender, but if I did, where would you take me? To the Central Valley?"

"Yes, off-worlder. We'd take you to the Master and he'd take your head for his trophy case."

This might work well to my advantage, I thought to myself. This will save time and effort if I just let myself be taken to them. Smiling, I tossed my sword on the ground. "Very well, my friends. I surrender."

The soldiers were apprehensive at first. No doubt they thought I'd at least fight. As they looked on in confusion, a large truck-like vehicle came driving up. When the truck stopped and the driver got out, it was the last person I had expected to run into out here in the middle of Kendaria.

It was Tymber.

"Sargas of Elginia, we meet again," Tymber spoke to me, his hand resting on his side arm.

"Tymber. You're the last person I expected to run into out here. What brings you to our party?"

Tymber explained that my arrival had caused some sparks in the planetary community, and it had started to spread to the other planets in the system. As soon as I and my companions had fled earlier, Tymber had gone to his men and told them who I was. They knew that I was there to take Dea out of this life and liberate the Targothian people. He had come out here to attempt to recruit this garrison, as he had done with several of them in Ansaka. His men had gone to garrisons in Kashm, Wheel, and Steel.

The men at this garrison had shown Tymber the greatest of respect and listened to him. It made sense. I had almost forgotten that he was a commander in the Imperial Guard. If anyone warranted respect, it was this man.

The Imperial Guard had been around since Lord Lorancano had ruled the world a millennia ago. It was around the time when his own ancestor Lord Bradlon had first been appointed as Lord of Targoth when the world united as one after the chaos of the time of legend and myth.

The Guard was an honor to serve in. They recruited the finest warriors from the lands. They served for periods of a decade at a time and could continue to do so, retaking their sacred oath each time, or they could leave and start a life as a civilian. Many left the Guard and became leaders in the community or commanders in the Targothian army or navy.

Tymber was instrumental at getting the soldiers on my side. They all wanted Dea dead. Everyone on Targoth did. Everyone in the solar system did. He was just too powerful to dispose of. A Bah'Tene could claim his head as his brethren should have done to him a thousand years ago.

All of the troops gathered around me, Tymber at my right. They all seemed eager to hear my words of encouragement.

"My Targothian brethren. I know what you're all thinking and yes, I am here to kill Qal Dea and take his place, as my birthright demands. But, I don't want to rule over this world without the consent of the people. Call out to your fellow soldiers. Have them all converge tomorrow at dawn at the Citadel overlooking the Central Valley. We will surround that place and I will challenge Dea to a deathmatch. Only one of us walks away, and if the gods are good, it will be me. I would be honored to be Lord of Targoth as my ancestor Lorancano was, but I swear to you, I will only take that position if the people wish it. I am not an oppressor. I am not Qal Dea. I am Sargas."

For a few seconds, there was silence as the men all looked at me. Before I could open my mouth again, all of the soldiers at the garrison raised their right hand, fist clenched, and chanted my name.

"Sargas! Sargas! Sargas!"

I looked over at Tymber. He nodded his approval to me. He joined the men in the chanting. I knew now that I had the loyalty of these soldiers. I somehow knew, too, that the rest of the Targothian military, as well as the civilians, would all have my back in this. That made me feel a swelling of pride and love that I had never felt before in my entire existence. It felt almost the same as when Gostal's armies swore their allegiance to me. Except this time it was better. This time, it was my kinsmen.

I no longer felt like an outsider, out of his own time and place, trapped in a universe where I didn't fit in, surrounded by arrogant immortals and inept political leaders. I was home.

I felt like a Targothian.

Chapter 15

The troops all loaded up into personnel carriers. Dozens of artillery tanks pulled up beside them. Tymber gave the order and the entire regiment of Targothian warriors saluted me in the Targothian fashion: Right hand balled into a fist and placed over the chest. I could have sworn that I had seen that in dozens of science fiction movies, but maybe this is where it originated from. Maybe some of those Hollywood writers were descended from the Targothian refugees from so long ago. I had thought about that on occasion. I couldn't be the only one with Targothian blood on Earth. Maybe I am the one with the least thinned out bloodline. Things to look into in the future.

Tymber whispered into the ear of another soldier, who in turn ran off, returning a minute later with a surprise. It was a motorcycle.

Not one like on Earth in my time, but it looked pretty similar. It was all black, the handle bars were cruiser style. No windshield. The tires were sleek and deadly looking. It looked much like a Harley, but had an air of futuristic design. I asked what this was for.

"My lord," Tymber answered, "This is a classic military transport bike. Many in our military use these for scouting missions and many of our men ride them in their spare time for relaxation and fun. I want to present this to you as a gift, a token of our loyalty to you and your birthright to rule the world."

I was touched. Such a beautiful gift. "It will be an honor to accept this and ride it into battle with you, my brethren."

I mounted the bike and with a powerful kick, I brought the engine to life. The noise of the engine was divine. All my life I had wanted a motorcycle, but always had a reason to not get one. Money. Dangerous. Never learned to ride. Now, almost five hundred years before I am going to be born, I am on an alien world in a neighboring galaxy and about to head into battle on one.

The vehicles carrying the troops and the tanks all lined up behind me. Tymber came riding up on his own bike, his had ape-hanger handle bars. Not my style, but to each his own.

"Give the word, my lord," Tymber said with a glint of fire in his eye.

Looking back at the caravan of Targothian warriors behind me, I smiled and turned to face the road ahead. "Rock and roll!"

I revved the engine one more time before taking off towards the north, one thing on my mind now. Taking off Dea's head and mounting it on my bedroom wall.

As I rode, Tymber was at my side on my right. My sword hung at my side as the dust kicked up behind me. I could sense the determination and excitement of the army at my back.

The further we went, the more people joined our road fleet. The word had spread to the surrounding areas, and many wanted to join us on our quest, both military and civilians alike. I had a surge of power run through my veins. I would not let these people down.

As the miles passed under our wheels, I couldn't help but think back to the long road that got me here.

Me, a young man of twenty-three years, married to a drug addict. A small town Kansas boy joining the military to leave home and see the world. I had seen some of the world. I had been to Alaska's Elmendorf Air Base twice, and spent four months in Bahrain. Now, I had seen much more than just the world.

We stopped on the edge of Ansaka. I pulled Tymber to the side and asked him if he knew of the meteor. "Yes, my lord." That was good news indeed. He told me that it lay in a secret chamber directly below the throne that Dea sat on. The throne that once belonged to Lorancano and his son and heir Sargas.

"My friend," I said to Tymber, "We need to find out how to get to that rock." He told me there was a switch on the right arm of the throne that opened the chamber. "Good. Here's what I want. When we arrive, I'll challenge that bastard. He won't be able to resist. Then, I want you and your men to sneak in and destroy that rock. I don't know how, but I know you're going to find a way. As the challenged, he will decide the place and I decide the time, as the challenger. He will hopefully pick a place outside and away from the citadel, but if not, if he picks the throne room for some stupid reason, you'll have to get the rock while I'm fighting him. Think you can handle that, my brother?"

Tymber looked at me for a moment. The word 'brother' was something he had not heard himself called before. I nodded at him to reiterate that I felt him my brother. A resolve filled his face and he put his hand on my shoulder

105

and swore upon his life and the souls of his ancestors, he'd find a way to destroy that rock. We saluted each other in the Targothian fashion and got back on our bikes. I gave the order and the caravan was off, heading north into Ansaka.

Ansaka itself is a pretty easy to traverse land. We first headed straight north and came to Port Teel, a port town on the edge of Lake Teel. This lake had been here since the days of myth and legend, and once was the site of a battle of dragons in a time long before humanoids walked the world.

From the lake, we went around counter-clockwise and then headed due west and after several hour's travel, we came upon the small village of Remet, home to many tailors and blacksmiths and leather workers that made uniforms for the royal guard and the Continental Rangers, an elite group of outdoor warriors that were adept at archery and singlehanded combat. They wore leather armor and preferred to live in the serenity of nature, only venturing into the cities when it was required for their duty. Otherwise they patrolled the outskirts of towns and aided travelers who were accosted by bands of rogues and thieves. A Continental Ranger was a formidable advisory. A single ranger could hold his own against even multiple members of the Royal Guard. They had been known to put up resistance with garrisons, and Dea only allowed it as he never considered them a real threat against him.

In Remet, we stopped for the night to rest and prepare for the ordeal we'd soon face. I was anxious to go now and initiate the Challenge to Dea, but the men needed to rest. Tomorrow some of them may die. I sat at an outdoor table drinking a local ale, which was a nice and frothy drink, comparable to German beer. It was remarkable that Dea wasn't down here. I wasn't sure if he'd sense my existence or not.

I heard footsteps coming up behind me, and I sensed a new presence. It wasn't one of the men. I turned and saw a tall man with a crossbow slung across his shoulder and a pistol at his side. Dark brown leather pants, boots and a jacket were his clothes, his hair hanging down to his shoulders. So, this was a Continental Ranger.

"You are the one called Sargas, I take it, stranger," He spoke with an unusual accent I hadn't heard yet. It almost sounded Australian but with less twang and a hint of monotone on the second syllable of my name. "I'm Sergeant Rasmussen Von Hendro of the Ansaka Division of the Rangers. I wanted to see if I'd be welcome to join in your fight." I asked him why.

He explained that he was ready to see Dea go. Dea had tolerated the Rangers for the last several centuries as they offered pockets of petty resistance which kept the dictator entertained slightly, but would eventually grow tired of it. He wanted to help cast down the fiend before he turned his attention to wiping out his brethren in the Rangers. I could appreciate that. They didn't want to join in as they didn't entirely trust me, since I was from the Elginian Imperium, even though I claimed to have left their service. He said there was something about me he trusted and wanted to help and was sure the other Rangers would soon follow suit. I welcomed it.

I called over Tymber and the three of us ordered drinks and Rasmussen told us of his ancestor, Nole Von Hendro, who was a great bounty hunter in the time when elves and dwarves lived side by side with Targothians and goblins and trolls roamed the countryside in hordes that looted and murdered whoever they came across. Nole had served in the Kashm Imperial Army in his youth. After he left soldiering behind, he had gone on to be rather infamous, even killing a great wizard named Dragmu. I remembered reading about that in that Tales of Targoth back on the boat.

As we drank, we exchanged more tales. Tymber told of a legend of a half-ogre named Flog who stopped an evil being from another world. I read that story, too. It came to be my turn.

I told them the story of how I ended up in this time and place. Time travel was something no one had ever considered to be a possibility without magic. But then again, some of what our ancestors called magic is just advanced science, though no one denied the existence of mystical energies in the universe that also acted as magic. That is all magic really is when you boil it all down: the forces of the universe harnessed.

Hours had passed and I called it a night. We all went to our sleeping areas, which were simply blankets on the ground with many of us using jackets or coats for pillows. Sleep came rather easily for me, and before I knew it, it was time to get up and go to work.

Chapter 16

A sunrise on Targoth was a thing of beauty that I had never seen before. It is hard to describe. A brilliant crimson and orange orb rising from the horizon, clouds circled at the top like an angel's halo. It was as if an agent of God was watching over us as we prepared for the battle ahead. Thanking our hosts, we rode west from Remet towards the path that lead towards the Citadel. The Citadel was at the very most northern point of the valley, overlooking the land below.

We reached the upper edge of the Central Valley and continued on northwards toward the soon-to-be ex-home of Qal Dea, the madman. As we rode, I looked down into the valley below. I could see some rivers and a great forest at the northern point, and Tymber told me those were the Goblin Woods, once home to a small tribe of goblins that would venture out and hunt people in the nearby towns of Tragidore and Hanuman. His family lived in Hanuman in the house that belonged to his wife's grandfather. After we killed that bastard Dea, I wanted to go down there and explore. Forests and the like had always been a place of interest for me, even as a kid.

I used to love fantasy movies about trolls and dragons and monsters. Perhaps it was my Targothian blood calling out to me, even at that young age. Collective unconscious or DNA remembrance or whatever else you wished to call it. Somehow, deep down, my interests in things like that had prepared me for this life.

We got closer to the Citadel. As it grew closer, I let my mind reach out and flow. I could in my mind's eye see dragons flying in the clouds and elven archers fighting off goblin marauders. I could hear cries of battle and blood oaths of vengeance. Targoth was a place of beauty and history.

I would always consider Kansas on Earth to be my birthplace, especially Valley Center. Smalltown USA had its charms, and as a kid I often thought there was something unusual about that little city. The house I lived in on Park street with the haunted basement, Theorosa's Bridge out by 109th Street, the alley behind my grandparent's house that I walked down once when I was nine and I ended up inexplicably on the other side of town over ten miles away. When I was young I even heard of something called a demon cloak, but no one ever knew what it actually was. There was also something called Dumonkey Dawhans. I had dreamt about them when I was five. My parents thought it was silly children's nightmares, but who's to say they weren't real?

I was pulled from my nostalgic thoughts by Tymber. "My lord! We're almost there!" He had to shout over the bikes, but luckily a Targothian has quite a set of lungs.

I looked up and saw that we were indeed about ten minutes away. A small smile formed on my lips and I couldn't wait to move into my new house. It would be my home for a very long time. What to do with Dea's head after I severed it. Put it on a pike? No, too cliché. I'd probably just incinerate his corpse and launch the ashes into the sun. That's the best way to make sure he was truly gone from the mortal coil, or the pseudo-immortal coil at any rate.

The night before, I had managed to send a subwave transmission to my fleet and let them know that I was right on schedule. I wanted them standing ready to come here, but not to do it until called for. I wanted to take the planet myself. I knew it would win the hearts and minds of my brethren and earn their loyalty. Of course, it was a big system, and my fleet would reside here. Maybe not all on Targoth, but there were plenty of colonies on the nearby planets. Some of the civilian ships could be converted into a ground base for people to live in. I wasn't going to cast away my comrades just because I was going to settle on my ancestor's home world. They swore their loyalty to me after I killed Gostal, and I would never turn them away. As far as I was concerned, they were Targothian citizens, too.

I also ordered them to retrieve any information about Dea. There was none. The damn Council had wiped a lot from the records. If there was anything before I abandoned my Bah'Tene bosses, they wiped it out after I left. No matter. Most of them were old and would turn to dust, for I doubted any of them would ever leave their comfort to fight the Fallen or hunt nosferatus. Too bad I killed that durmivol. Maybe I could have set it loose on those cowards. Just a fleeting thought of violence, nothing more. I'd never do anything that psychotic. Maybe.

We were almost there. As we got to the edge of the courtyard, hundreds of royal guards came pouring out, their rifles drawn. I ordered a halt and the caravan stopped, and my own troops came out, weapons at the ready. I could sense Dea watching. Sure enough, he was at the top of the citadel, looking down at us with sadistic glee. Both his people and mine stood on guard, aiming their guns at each other, both sides unwilling to open fire. No Targothian soldier wanted to kill a countryman.

I could sense things were about to turn violent and ugly, brother killing brother. Qal Dea had a horrid darkness in his soul, and I could feel it all the way down at the bottom. Before he gave the word for his men to attack, I spoke first.

"Challenge!"

That darkness I was sensing became red. He was angry. "What did you say to me, boy?"

Who was he calling boy? Don't let my youthful good looks fool you. "I said, challenge! I issue the Challenge to you, Qal Dea, usurper to the throne of Targoth!"

I could see his eyes flash red, even from the great distance. I never saw a Bah'Tene's eyes flash like fire before. I had forgotten he was a fire master as well. Did my eyes do that when I became angry and launched a fireball? I'd have to stand in front of a mirror sometime and see. Dea slung his feet over the railing and jumped down. The mad fool had just leapt off of a two hundred foot balcony. As agile as a cat. The bastard landed on his feet with no effort. It was as if he just jumped off of a stepping stool.

"Sargas, Sargas, Sargas," he scolded me. "You have barely been Bah'Tene for a decade or so. I have been one with great power for over a millennia. I am protected. I cannot be killed. You really wish to challenge? Laughable, indeed."

I smirked at him, which I've been told is infuriating when I do it. "You going to turn down the Challenge? I suppose you've forgotten how to fight after a thousand years of easy living."

His eyes did the flashing thing again. "You dare call me coward?" He launched a fireball at my feet. I knew it wouldn't hit me. He was just trying to see who had the bigger dick.

"Your avoiding the Challenge is saying that, old man," was my retort.

His anger faded and he looked full of merriment. How psychotic was this guy? "Very well, child. We'll do it right here in the open. When would you like to start?"

Glad to be away from the throne room, I glanced at Tymber and gave him the slightest of nods as I pulled out my sword. "Now is just right, Qal. You ready for this?"

He laughed and pulled Sargotha from his cloak. Sargotha. The very blade seemed to call out to me. "Yes, let's get you killed off so I can go back to ruling my planet." Our blades clashed. Sargotha was a thing of beauty. I've always loved the look of swords and I loved the swords knights used in the legends, but ninja swords always held a certain appeal, and perhaps this was why, as Sargotha looked a lot like a straight blade katana.

Dea swung the sword at my throat, which I blocked with my own weapon. We traded strikes for several minutes, each one seemed to put another scratch on my blade but didn't seem to even scuff up Sargotha.

Our moves were very fast, but I have to admit, he was faster. I was giving it my all to block the shots and keep my head on my shoulders. I was beginning to think that Tymber never made it to the throne room. I had a flash of him lying dead at the feet of a dozen guards. I felt that it was probably my time to meet my Maker on the other side. Dea's fast moves, though, seemed to slow down ever so slightly. He had a look of confusion on his face. Then he was a lot slower. He was having trouble blocking my strikes. He must have seen the look of satisfaction on my face.

"What have you done?" I kicked him in the stomach, forcing him back and he hunched over, holding his gut. Tymber appeared at my side holding a handful of black and gray dust. "Tymber, you traitor!"

Tymber spit on the ground. "That's not what I'd call it. The true Lord of Targoth has come home." Tymber put his fist in the air and chanted "Sargas! Sargas!" The caravan of soldiers and rangers that accompanied us joined in the chant, and within seconds, the men that were protecting Dea joined in as well.

Letting loose a primal scream akin to a demonic roar, Dea jumped forward and drove Sargotha into my stomach, impaling me. The chants stopped. He stepped back, leaving the blade sticking through me. "Sargas, eh! Lord of Fails! Lord of Fails! Come on, chant with me like you did for him!" Every soldier and ranger trained their rifles at Dea and he still mocked them. "You think that will kill me? You think without that meteor bauble I am weak? I am Qal Dea! I am your master! I am..." he stopped abruptly as my hand drove Sargotha into his chest.

I had put my hand on the handle of Sargotha, and something happened. The sword felt warm and alive. I pulled it from me and healed quickly. My touch, which must have activated something in the blade and made it come to life, was all I needed to make the weapon mine. I could hear my ancestor Sargas speaking in my mind. "It is yours now. Your DNA has bonded it to you, as it has all of your ancestors who sat on the throne. Only the bloodline can use the sword to its fullest potential. Use it well." A righteous rage filled my soul, and I ran it though Dea's chest, shutting him up.

He looked at me with almost comical confusion. "But, it's my sword!"

I pulled it from his chest and held it to his throat. "On your knees. Kneel before me, Dea." He did as told.

"You can't kill me! I am Qal Dea! I am the master of this world! I am..." his words ceased when I swung the blade and took off his head. In the heat of the moment, as his head fell, I roundhouse kicked it and it went flying down into Central Valley below. I could see that it landed in front of a pack of wolves, who quickly set about devouring the flesh.

No one moved or spoke or made any sound of any kind for a full minute. I stood there, holding Sargotha and feeling complete. Tymber was at my side talking and I didn't hear him at first. I finally snapped out of my daze and he was saying, "You did it, my lord! You did it!"

I walked slowly up to the Citadel. I climbed the steps to the main door, stopped, and turned around to face the people. Now, granted, this was a long time ago, a very long time. I still remember the words I spoke then. I remember the feeling I had inside as I spoke them. I faced every Targothian on site.

"My good people. My brothers and sisters. Let this go out to every living soul on all worlds and colonies that are in the Targothian system. I am Sargas, and Qal Dea is no more. The time of living under the whims of a madman are over for you. I don't expect you to trade one world leader for another, and if you wish for me to go, I will do so, but, if you'll have me, I would be honored to sit on the throne of Targoth as my ancestor Lorancano did, and as his son Sargas would have."

I half expected them to shoot at me or banish me. After ten centuries of a psycho Bah'Tene, they wouldn't want another one to take over.

Tymber jumped up with me and spoke to the crowds, "What say you, brethren? What say you for the man who claimed the head of that foul bastard who used us as his playthings for centuries?"

Almost at once, everyone began the chant that I had heard many times in the last several days.

"Sargas! Sargas! Sargas!" That never got old.

Tymber saluted me and I saluted back. I looked over the crowd at my people. I was home.

Chapter 17

Home. It is something we all look for. After spending about a decade in a distant past, I found mine. Targoth.

Over the next few months, I initiated some changes. I spoke with all of the leaders from the system. Governors, mayors, and the like. I found one man that was above all others in honesty and desire for change for the people. Dan Catel of the Republic of Free Wills. It was an island nation due east of the main continent. Long ago the southern half of the island was home to the Kumbernestis Elf Empire, but has since been incorporated into the Republic. The Republic of Free Wills was the first democracy on Targoth, but since Dea took over, was the Republic in name only. Catel was head of the senate there, but now, I had appointed him Chancellor of Targoth.

He'd be responsible for running the day to day business of the government. As Lord of Targoth, I'd be supreme ruler, but I wanted Targothians to have freedom, even if I was still the ultimate authority, they had a right to make decisions and run their governments according to Targothian law and traditions. Besides, I knew my time here was limited and I wanted to get these people used to freedom before I left. I'd eventually go back to Earth to resume my life. Or would I decide to stay here? That held an appeal to it.

I brought my fleet down, and eventually everyone was moved to a home of their own. Some had to live in one of the many colonies in the system, but all were Targothians officially now. General Mukaoy was now High General of the Targothian System Army.

I had merged the Royal Guard and the Continental Rangers into one unit, creating the Knights of Targoth. The Knights would travel the system as peace keepers and law enforcement. They'd protect citizens, as even though Targothians were all brothers at heart, there was still the criminal element.

People still robbed each other and assaulted one another. The Knights of Targoth would be there to help. The Knights wore their uniform proudly. Most of them wore black pants and shirts, but the uniform was a simple black leather vest. The Seal of Targoth on the back, and in Targothian script, Knights of Targoth in an arch over it. A second, smaller version of the symbol was on the front of the vest, on the left breast.

Tymber, who was my most trusted friend on the planet, deserved a position in the K.O.T., as he had nothing but honor in his blood. I appointed him First Knight, second only to me in the K.O.T.

I appointed Rasmussen the Ranger as Sergeant-At-Arms, which put him second to Tymber. He would be responsible to organizing the training of recruits and keeping the Knights in fighting form. Both Tymber and Rasmussen had their title of First Knight and Sergeant-At-Arms on their right front breast. I too had a vest as founder of the K.O.T. My rank patch said Lord Knight. I was going to leave it blank, but those two insisted on the title for me.

In terms of planetary and system patrol, I had half the fleet patrolling the perimeter of the system, rotating them with the other half every few months. I didn't want to keep people away from their new homes for long. Many had families waiting for them.

I had some engineers look at Sargotha. They studied it and discovered something very interesting. There was a microchip inside the handle. It was made from a material they couldn't identify but they determined that it was several dozens of thousands of years old. From the time the first Lord of Targoth in my bloodline held it, it belonged to one of us. Only the current reigning Lord of Targoth with our bloodline's DNA could unlock its greatest secret. Teleportation.

I would never have to carry the sword with me. I would leave it in my chambers in the Citadel. No matter how far away I was in the Three Galaxies, I could hold out my hand and mentally summon the sword. Sargotha would materialize in my grip, ready for battle. At will, I could have it materialize back in my chambers. I could leave it on my flagship and go to a planet below, and I could have it materialize to my hand again. With practice and concentration, I could teleport the sword wherever I could see in my mind's eye, recalling it back at will.

In those months, I had had every symbol of Dea removed and burned. I reinstated the Seal of Targoth, a symbol that the world had used to unify as one, even back in the days of legend. Each nation had their own symbol, but the Seal of Targoth came from even older times, and had been my family's seal since becoming lords of the planet.

The symbol was revered by all. The meaning was something I've always considered spiritual. I also had a special love for it as I did dream of it first when I was seven. Thus, that symbol brought to a close the mystery of the three things I dreamt about often in my youth.

One triangle divided into four to represent the division within oneself, yet unified to a single destiny. Three gold and one black, as we have mainly good within but there is a darkness in the center of us all that must be controlled. The triangle is within a circle, as a circle is infinite, as is the energy that gives us all life, as our energy life force goes on forever even as our physical bodies decay. Two red bars, one protruding from the upper left of the circle and one protruding from the lower right, are the blood shed by our ancestors, both from them and of them. The three black hashmarks within the red bars are to remind all that bear the Seal that as is the nature of the universe, many things happen in threes.

I had traveled to every nation on Targoth. Steel, once home to dwarves of legend. Now it was a nation that made great machines of flight and ground travel. Wheel, former home of the gnomes, now held the greatest scientific minds on Targoth. The old Silverstone Elf Kingdom, which was now divided up between Katu and Talford. It was a large wooded area that supplied a lot of lumber, as Targothian trees grew very fast. Kashm, the desert land. Abnu, which upon my taking over saw the north and south nations united into one again. In the Grey Sea I visited Babby Isle and the islands of the Goldmoon Elves, now full of fishing villages. There were many other smaller islands to see, but they were uninhabited, so they became a great place to build many cities for the Elginian civilians who came with me.

On the other side of the planet was a large continent, covered with sheets of ice and home to great beasts that lived in the cold. No need to even go there, but there were some scientific outposts. Scientists enjoyed the solitude.

I traveled to every other planet in the system. I wanted to visit them all to let them know I was here for them. The Chancellor came with me to get his face out there and show the people that he could be counted on in the day to day running of the government. Tymber came with me to talk about the K.O.T. and recruit new probies, which is what we called probationary members until they were ready to become full fledge knights.

During the day I'd be in the throne room meeting with the citizens who wanted to thank me for liberating the planet and living up to the title of my ancestor, the Yo-akum.

On Earth, the year was about to turn to 1518. I had been in the past for twenty years now. Since taking the throne of Targoth, things had been running smooth. I had a great political leader for the daily operations and two trusted Knights to help run the K.O.T. Targoth was my home now, but everyone who knows a Bah'Tene understood one thing about them. The need to hunt Nosferatus and other demonic creatures.

It becomes part of our nature, very difficult to fight that feeling. It is almost like a bloodlust, but only for the minions of darkness and evil.

I made the announcement that though I was still Lord of Targoth, from time to time, I'd have to leave the system to venture out and hunt foul beings. I still had a duty as a Bah'Tene, though I didn't serve the Council or anything to do with Elginia.

The people continued to swear their allegiance and loyalty to Sargas and the Throne. I knew that the planet would be able to handle itself for some time.

I hopped into my personal craft, procured from Gostal a long time ago. I renamed it the Hunter. It was time to go back to Earth and visit for a while and maybe get into some trouble with some Fallen or other demonic bastards.

I was restless and anxious to get out there and see what I could get into. Sargotha at my side, I lifted off and set course for the Milky Way Galaxy, to a non-descript little green and blue sphere in one of the many spiral arms.

I was going to my other home planet.

Chapter 18

I was missing Targoth already as I flew off. True, I had spent the last decade there, leading my people and watching as the K.O.T. grew into a formidable fighting group. My knights, clad in their black leather vest adorned with the Seal of Targoth on the back, traveled the system righting wrongs and protecting citizens. I had every confidence that Tymber and Rasmussen could handle things while I was away, and the Chancellor was one of the wisest men I had known in my life, so I had no doubts about his running the daily affairs of state.

The last decade was great. I had traveled all over the planet. Targoth was a wonder to behold. All of the old ruins from the days of the legends. In what was once the Kumbernestia Elf Empire, I had done some exploring in my free time and found several artifacts that I kept in my private chambers. I had found an elven dagger which was dated at around seventy thousand years. It had traces of blood on it from an unknown source. It could have been goblin blood, or even dwarven blood. The races of legend didn't always get along.

I had gone to the Isle of the Minotaur, which was where I first crash landed back when I was trying to quietly infiltrate the planet. I met with my old fisherman friends, who were very surprised that I was the descendant of the Sargas of history. I ate a meal with them and shared some drinks and then moved on to see more. I had traveled to the Republic of Free Wills just north of the old Kumbernestia ruins and toured their factories and breweries. Targothian ale was very close to German beer. Of course, I had traveled to the other planets of the system, but I was usually on Targoth, either spending time with my brother Knights or seeing the sights of the world.

I had enjoyed attending music festivals and even had some held at my citadel. The music of Targoth varied in style, much like the difference between rock and country and folk music. My favorite was called Working Class Rhythm, which sounded a lot like my favorite band AC/DC. One of the most popular bands in Ansaka was Goldmoon Dragon Revival. I had them play every year at the annual Festival of Legend, which was when all the people of Targoth agreed to set aside their differences and get together and feast and listen to music and sing with family and honor our ancestors and the beings that walked the world back in the days of legend, such as elves and dwarves and gnomes and especially dragons.

Not all of that time was festive adventure and learning. I had also lost a friend. General Mukaoy had passed in his sleep. Already an old man when we met, he had gotten on in years, and not being Targothian but Elginian, he didn't live as long, so finally his old body just gave out on him. He was buried out behind the Citadel in the Memorial Graveyard. When I arrived, it was just an empty field. I commissioned a crew to beautify it so that it would become a resting place for our military. Mukaoy was the first to be buried in it.

I spent a lot of time watching the Knights train. I'd see transport ships with new probies coming. Probies, the new probationary recruits of the Knights, trained here at the

Citadel. Our army and navy were trained at the eastern coast of Anaska's neighbor, Talfurd. General Mukaoy's successor, General Katarn, oversaw the training of the officers and enlisted alike. He was a young general and he was Targothian, though not born on the planet but on Jilion, the sixth planet in the system, in a colony. He would have made an excellent Knight, but I needed him to run the Targothian Army. Mukaoy's nephew Ronato was appointed as Admiral over the Targothian Space Fleet by me when his predecessor had gotten ill and was forced to retire. All three fighting forces of Targoth were highly trained, well led, and not to be trifled with. I had made sure that everything was taken care of, for I knew I'd be gone soon.

I wasn't going to leave permanently, at least not yet. I might change my mind and stay here instead of going to Earth later on to catch up with my life. Only time would tell, and I had several hundred years to think about it.

I had called a meeting before I left to notify them, though they were not surprised, they were not ready to see me leave. But, as I told them, Targoth would one day not need a Lord of the planet. I didn't want them to have to be under a king anymore. Even if I stayed, I wouldn't have to be Lord. I could step down and live out in the country side. Oh well. Things to worry about later, I would tell them.

Chapter 19

I just have to say; the Hunter was and still is a fantastic ship. Gostal had great taste in personal craft. The size of a bus, it was sleek, it was black, and it was deadly. I left all the weapon systems intact, as they didn't need improvements, though I did have a newer LSD put in for smoother transition to light speed and modified my sleep area to be comfortable. Gostal only had a cot with no pillow. I had to have a pillow, and I had plenty of reading material if I ever needed it. My own copy of Tales of Targoth, along with other literature of the planet. My favorite addition to the Hunter, though, was the beer tap. I wasn't much of a beer drinker back on Earth. My drink of choice was Jack and Coke. But, being on Targoth for the last decade I had developed a taste for Targothian ale.

Off I flew, getting closer to the edge of the system. I eventually left Targothian space and went on my journey towards Earth.

Soon I passed by the House of Kale and saw that a new prisoner transport had arrived to deposit some more inmates. I stopped in to chat with the pilot of the ship. The pilot immediately recognized me and the K.O.T. vest I wore. I always wore it when I went out and about. A Knight is always on duty, especially the Lord of Targoth.

The pilot actually knelt before me. That felt weird. After I told him to get up, I inquired as to his mission. He told me that there were a dozen new Pax Draxians being dropped off for attempting to kidnap a governor's daughter from a nearby independent star system. The house of Kale held many inmates from all over, not just Targothian space. In the past with Qal Dea in charge of the system, any outsider who wandered into Targothian space had been put in there. But, I changed that soon after claiming my place as Lord.

Upon my taking over, I visited the prison (though everyone said I should stay away as the inmates would be hostile, but after landing my ship and walking among them, I found that after a few attacked, a couple of fireballs to their craniums prevented others from trying anything) I had found out there were twenty beings that were there only because they had wandered into the system by mistake.

Most of the off-world prisoners, however, were there by necessity. Dea had an agreement with the surrounding systems, and apparently with the Elginian Imperium, I discovered. They could drop off their hardcore inmates there and leave them. That was the beauty of the House of Kale. No guards. No way for the prisoners to leave. The prisoners were placed into pods and dropped onto the planet below. No one gets off. The pods end up being broken up and used as weapons.

There was still the matter of innocents being in there. Beings that had just accidently crossed into Targothian space, or people who had said things to anger Dea. They were tossed in with the animalistic criminals that dwelled the surface.

I had returned to Targoth after that first trip to the prison, and I had brought back Tymber, Rasmussen, and a dozen other Knights.

We had all arrived in a large capital ship to help with the intimidating of the inmates. I didn't think I'd need that ship there, as the prisoners all knew now who and what I was. But, there are always troublemakers in the bunch. With the large ship hovering within visual range of the prisoners, we landed in our shuttle and looked at the prison before us.

The jailhouse itself takes up around half of the planet. It has no roof, just walls and doors. The floor is the dirt of the ground.

As we made our way towards the main doors of the prison, my Knights and I were greeted with over a hundred crazy inmates, all armed with makeshift blades, no doubt from some of the pods and from the looks of it, from the bones of the dead. They rushed at us with an animal ferocity that might have scared most tene. It didn't scare my Knights. They might all be mortal, but they fight on par with most Bah'Tene that I had dealt with.

A Knight of Targoth does carry a gun on occasion. A small pistol for quick defense. The main weapon, though, is a sword. The type doesn't matter, as it depends on the individual taste of the Knight. And, needless to say, a Knight is trained to use that blade as if it were a part of him, an extension of his will.

I and fourteen Knights of Targoth, all armed with just our blades, stood our ground as the oncoming wall of shanks and bone daggers came closer. I called out to attack and all of us rushed towards the madmen of the prison. Our blades met their crude weapons and though a few knights were injured, it wasn't severe. I didn't lose anyone that day, and we slaughtered all of the attackers. The other inmates who at first stood ready to aid their fellow prisoners quickly changed their minds and stood back as we advanced into the walls of the prison.

Several inmates would attack every so often but we made short work of them. Our way was soon blocked by a large crowd who were refusing to move. Tymber started toward them, but I put my hand up to stop him. I focused my mind and brought down a rain of white hot fire onto them, falling from several dozen feet above their heads. They all ran, though a few of them fell from the pain and were soon burned into oblivion.

I hadn't summoned that much heat before. I felt weak for a moment, but it passed. Benefits of a Bah'Tene metabolism.

After only a few hours of searching, we soon found fifteen inmates who were not the vile murderous bastards that most of the inhabitants of this rock were. Most of them were Targothian dissidents from Ansaka and Talfurd, and one of our newly liberated men was the bastard son of an Elginian nobleman, left there by his father in order to keep his wife from finding out about his infidelity.

Another was a young male from Arturia, separated from his cousins during a piloting class and had wandered into Targothian space. There had been five more of the poor innocent sons-of-bitches, but a few days before, they were killed and eaten by a large Mullet Man prisoner.

I led the way from the prison, flanked by my Knights who were also protecting the fifteen liberated men. These poor souls had been lucky to have survived so long surrounded by cannibals and murderers and rapists and other scum that have done things even more vile. Dropped in here as a matter of easy solutions to political problems or just plain getting lost on a trip. Better to just have killed them, but Qal Dea was a sadistic son-of-a-whore.

We had taken the men back to Targoth where they were all placed in jobs and homes. Five of them had joined the Knights of Targoth, including the young Arturian.

I soon arranged to have a capital ship be stationed out there for four months at a time, where it would be replaced by another and it would rotate its shift with another. I wanted to keep a force out there to prevent any other worlds from trying to drop off innocent prisoners.

They could still drop them down there if they were violent criminals, but if they were political dissidents or just say, a poor man who stole to feed his children, they'd be brought back to Targoth to be looked after. I would never again allow the House of Kale to be a place of suffering for good people.

After reminiscing about the harrowing into Kale, I thanked the transport pilot for doing his duty well and continued on my way. I was Earth bound.

I had only been to the Earth system a handful of times since I came to the past. I didn't want to go onto the planet itself, fearing that my presence could alter the future somehow. Fortunately for me, as a Bah'Tene, I could get a good sense for what events I could mess with and what I had to leave alone. I don't know how to really explain it. I can just tell when I come across an event.

Example being that if I were to kill Hitler, true, I'd be saving six million innocent lives. But, I know I can't do that as the future would be altered catastrophically. Someone else could rise to power and bring nuclear war. One of those survivors might eventually have a descendant that may create a plague or become an insane politician who rapes a family of six. I would only get that sense of what is changeable as I came to the event. After all, I wasn't a psychic.

I was Bah'Tene. Virtually indestructible, long lived and not aging, and I was a helluva swordsman.

Chapter 20

Swords, always one of my favorite weapons. I often wanted to take up fencing as a child. I am not sure why I didn't. Back in my private quarters on Targoth in the Citadel overlooking the Central Valley, I had a wall that was adorned with many weapons. In the center of all that was my first sword, the one I carried for years as I served the Imperium before killing Qal Dea and claiming Sargotha. I hung it on my wall, scratches and dings intact. I didn't want it fixed. Those were battle scars and they were beautiful and honorable.

I even had several of Gostal's axes hanging there, prominently displayed was the large two-handed weapon he had tried to kill me with during our Challenge.

There was one sword, though, that I had a special place for on my wall, but it didn't matter as that sword would often be at my side. Above my first sword was a special plaque to hold Sargotha, the Sword of Targoth.

Handed down from generation to generation since my bloodline first became lords of the planet, the sword was out of the family's hands for a thousand years after my ancestor, Lorancano, was murdered by the insane fallen Bah'Tene, Qal Dea. Sargas, my ancestor and Lorancano's son, didn't have time to take the blade, as he was fulfilling his father's wishes and leading tens of thousands of Targothians through a portal to Earth. Perhaps if Sargas disobeyed his father and stayed to claim the sword, I wouldn't be here right now.

Sargotha was a thing of beauty and grace. I found no records of how or when it was made. Similar to a straight blade katana, it held the Seal of Targoth on the hilt and had the microchip tagged with my DNA, and the DNA of my family line. I could summon the weapon, even on the other side of the Three Galaxies, and it would instantly materialize in my hand. It was an ancient technology, but even after the countless generations that the sword has been in existence, it still worked. If I wanted, I could also cause the sword to materialize back in my chambers in its place on the wall.

Maybe one day I'd discover how it was made. If I could do that, arming the entire Knights of Targoth with similar weapons would prove beneficial.

The trip back to Earth was slow, but only because I was taking my time. I wasn't flying at top speed in the Hunter. Sometimes when I flew the ship, I got to thinking about my old mentor Gostal. He had become a Fallen, and no one really comes back from that. I sometimes regretted having to kill him, but as he was a blood-thirsty bastard, it had to be done. I did miss our time together at times, though. He was really the closest thing I had to a friend for a long time after I was brought into the past.

It is hard for a Bah'Tene to keep friends. We're just too, I don't know, full of ourselves. I admit that even I can be. But, I don't need friends. I have brothers. Tymber, Rasmussen, and everyone who wears the emblem of the Seal of Targoth on their backs in the Knights of Targoth.

A beeping noise alerted me that I was closing in on my destination, the edge of the next galaxy, the Milky Way. Only four day's travel through interstellar space from Andromeda to the Milky Way. Not bad. I wasn't at top speed, but I was still going pretty damn fast and taking the necessary LS tunnels, wormholes in space that allowed for travel between the galaxies. They didn't lead straight through, however. You'd fly through one, then travel for a few hours to another. If not for the onboard computer, you'd never know they were there.

As I flew into the galaxy, I felt a presence that was all too familiar. The undead were nearby. Looks like I was to have a little side trip before hitting Earth.

I followed my senses and soon found an uncharted planet in a very small solar system. I was several systems away from Earth, but I still had to check it out. Any chance to kill a vampire.

I scanned for lifeforms. I knew that vampires wouldn't really show up, but if there was life, most likely the vamps would be near it to feed. My scans didn't detect any tene lifeforms, but it did pick up something that I hadn't seen in years. At first I wasn't sure what it was. But, after thinking about it for a few seconds, it came back to me.

Nefarium. I could sense the vampires nearby, and I detected Nefarium, so I knew I'd have an extra special time. I got to kill two demon types with one stone. I kicked up the Hunter's speed and flew into the atmosphere, heading towards the highest concentration of demonic lifeforms.

I saw that it was daylight on this planet. I knew that the vamps would be weakened it. Poor little undead couldn't handle having solar energy in their cells. After a few moments, a large crowd of vampire and Nefarium came into view. With a smile, I opened fire with the front cannons, raining plasma energy onto the demons and vampires, shredding many of them into charred pieces of husks.

Bringing the Hunter into a rather abrupt landing, I quickly opened the door and ran out into the fray without my sword.

I saw a lone Nefarium, clad in brown leather boots and a gray tunic and pants, standing there looking dazed. Calling my blade to my hand, I hurled Sargotha towards the creature, piercing its forehead. For a second, I was afraid that the fun was over already. It appeared that I killed most of the Nefarium with my cannons, and this guy was just a straggler. A cold shadow passed over my soul, and I knew that it wasn't over yet.

I turned to see over fifty vampires, all wearing what appeared to be a uniform of some sort of planetary guard. No doubt they were all former members of a military unit and were turned by a powerful vampire. They all saw what I had done and they appeared very angry, but I didn't really have any concern for their feelings. It looked to me as if this was some sort of waystation for vampires where they could bring tene for food and conversion into their undead brethren. I don't know what they were doing there with Nefarium, but it seems that I had interrupted something.

I suppose it wasn't all that out of place. Both groups were children of Hell. If the Fallen and the vampires could alley with one another, sure, why not Nefarium?

I'd soon be interrupting their very existence. They didn't appear to know what I was. They all growled in unison, sounding like a den of hungry beasts, and charged at me. I just stood there in place, waiting for them to get closer. Soon they were a hundred feet away. Fifty feet. Fifteen feet. Five feet. As soon as they were right up to me, I summoned

Sargotha to my right hand from that Nefarium's skull, and in an instant, I had swung my blade and severed the heads of seven of them before I leapt into the air and landed behind them as they continued to run before realizing where I had gone. They stopped brusquely and turned back towards me.

I laughed at them. That only seemed to anger them further. That was what I wanted. I held Sargotha high into the air and yelled at them to attack, calling their kind a few choice words in Elginian. They understood what I had said about them. I could tell by the look in their eyes. They rushed towards me again, this time only a little over forty of them left. I stood in one place and waited for them to come up to me. Sargotha slashed left and right, hacking and cutting, removing arms and skulls. This fight might have been more difficult had it been night on this world.

My blade, my trusted Sargotha, dismembered many vampires. Before I knew it, it was done. I had killed every single one of the beasts.

I felt a bit of pity for the people they once were. I knew a vampire wasn't the person whose body they inhabited. That person's soul was gone, and what was left was a monster. It was the not the victim anymore, but rather it was the thing that killed the tene it once was.

Feeling a great sense of accomplishment, I walked around the battle site, using my abilities as a fire master to burn the corpses of the vampires, but leaving the Nefarium. Screw them. Demonic half-breed freaks of nature. They could rot in the elements.

Making my way back to the ship, I took a mug from the storage unit and poured myself a cold Targothian beer.

Celebrating with a brew was the Targothian way after a battle. Many legends tell of armies of Targothian soldiers having great feasts with free flowing beer after the day's warfare was done. Finishing my beer, I finally was able to head out to Earth like I originally planned.

Within minutes of taking off, I was out of the atmosphere and before I could plot the course to Earth, my distress alarm went off. I just wanted to get to Earth and it was as if the universe was screwing with me.

Someone wanted help. It was a general distress call, sent out in over two hundred known languages and dialects, and at first I figured that a planetary patrol would receive it and go save the day.

Slamming my hand on the console, I opened the distress call.

Chapter 21

I had not had any dealings with the Imperium since I left them. I had sensed a few of my fellow Bah'Tene flying near the edge of the Targothian system, but that was the extent of it. When I left the service of the Council all those years ago, I would have been happy to have never seen any of them again. But, the universe has a way of making your past kick you in the gullet.

I flew towards the origin of the distress beacon, and I found the last thing I'd expect, but really, I should have realized it was just a matter of time before running into those chuckleheads again.

I saw a medium sized interplanetary cruiser, a model UPU-667 troop transport unit, used by the Elginian military for troop movement and exercises. Roughly the size of C-5 Galaxy that the U.S. Air Force of my home era used for transport of cargo and personnel, this ship was stranded in the middle of nowhere and barely defending itself against several much smaller, but better armed, space superiority fighters. I watched for a split second before I sensed the pilots of the fighters and what they were.

One of them was a full Bah'Tene, and from all of the negative energy that this one exerted, I knew he was a Fallen. The other four fighters were what Gostal and I called the Pseudo-Fallen. They were tene who were given a half-ass Grand Test which produced partial Bah'Tene. They had some superhuman strength and enhanced senses, but only a fraction of what a real Bah'Tene could do. Those knockoffs could die just as easily as any other tene being.

The soldiers on the transport were all tene. Whoever was manning the gun turrets was a very good shot, and had managed to destroy one of the fighters attacking them. However, this batch of young blood soldiers wouldn't last much longer.

Letting out a slight sigh, I accelerated towards the fighters, my forward guns blasting away, shredding one of the ships into a molten mass of metal, flexiton, and body parts. His friends noticed this and stopped attacking the transport and all of them headed in my direction. That was the plan.

I wanted to try something that I hadn't done before, and I sat in one place for a few seconds as they drew closer. I focused all of my energy and thoughts toward the ship that I believed to be the lead. The real Bah'Tene among the group of enemies. I created a small rain of fire in the path of the oncoming force. The flames dissipated in the vacuum of space. Oh well, it was worth a try, even though it sapped some of my energy. I had hoped with time I would have been better with my fire abilities.

Mere seconds before the Fallen had reached me, I fired my guns towards him, destroying his cockpit and causing him to get sucked into space. I knew he wouldn't die right away, but I decided to let him suffocate. The bastard was wearing the uniform of an Elginian fleet commander. His ship continued to come in my direction, so I pulled what they called a Jack-In-The-Box among the Targothian battle fleet. I made the Hunter go straight up vertically, missing the wayward fighter by mere inches. It was close, but it was a success.

Without their Fallen leader, the remaining Bah'Tene wannabes panicked and turned around, fleeing from the scene. Not about to let them off easy, I burst forward, the Hunter giving chase to the fleeing enemy ships. I fired at them, not really aiming, just wanting to scare them further. They activated their LSD and were gone in a flash. Smiling, I turned back around and flew to the transport ship to see if they needed anything.

Coming to a stop near the ship, I hailed them, and they responded. My Elginian was a little rusty, but I never forget a language. They informed me that they were on their way back to Elginia after their training mission, but after being ambushed by the Fallen and his buddies, their engines were out of commission, their LSD non-functional, as well. Their long range communications had been disabled, too. Son-of-a-bitch, I thought. I swore in English, which I hadn't done often before, and caused confusion to the person I spoke to. He no doubt had ever heard my native language spoken in his life. I offered to make the call for them. I regretted it almost immediately when I got a response back.

"Unidentified vessel, this is Elginian Fleet Command." The speaker sounded young. "Thank you for coming to the aide of our troops. Unable to send help at the present." Great. "Request if you can tow the ship back if you would do so."

What? They expected me to haul this transport back? I could do it. The Hunter had the capability to haul back much larger ships. I just didn't want to. I had places to do and things to go to, or something to that effect.

I was about to inform them that I couldn't, or wouldn't, do it. Unfortunately for me, I picked up some anguish from the transport ship. Those boys, young like many soldiers were, were fearing they'd never make it home. Swearing again, this time in Targothian, I agreed to haul that bucket back to Elginia. We Bah'Tene aren't necessarily psychic, but we would on occasion pick up the feelings of others, often at inopportune times.

I calculated that at my top speed, I'd be able to get the ship there in a matter of hours. Just a quick in and out. Just to get the soldiers home in time for dinner. Punching in the coordinates, I locked onto the transport with my tractor beam and I initiated light speed and was quickly on my way back to one place in the Three Galaxies I never had any desire to go back to.

Putting in a disc of music, I sat back and tried to relax as the ship traveled through light speed towards the blasted Elginian home world. I had hoped the soothing sounds of the Grey Sea Orchestra would lighten my mood and help me get my mind off of going to Elginia.

Unfortunately, my second favorite band from Babby Isle that sat in the Grey Sea couldn't do that. But, it was better than sitting in silence while going back to Imperium Central.

Chapter 22

The trip was uneventful. I was almost hoping that I'd be attacked by demons or Fallen or even by Reticulans. Hadn't really dealt with Reticulans much before. But, aside from several mugs of ale and jamming to Targoth's greatest bands, we finally arrived in Elginian space. As expected, I met with a welcoming party.

Fifteen Elginian battle cruisers, looking like giant UFO saucers in all their glory, blocked my path. I received a message to immediately unhook the tractor beam, which I obliged. I was wanting to drop them off and get the hell out of there before anyone recognized me. I doubted any of these guys would. I hadn't been a presence in the Imperium in a long time. I didn't think they'd remember me. Then again, I was the man who killed Gostal and verbally slapped the faces the Council of Bah'Tene. After the transport was released, one of the cruisers launched a relief vessel to come out and fix their engines and get the troops back to their base. I set about to turning around and heading to Earth.

The ship wouldn't move.

I looked at my display and found that now I had a tractor beam on me. They just weren't going to let me go. Figures. I was guessing they wanted to thank me and bake me a cake. Or they thought they could lock me up and interrogate me, wondering how I managed to fight off a group of fighters with my shuttle. They must have noticed the Seal of Targoth on my ship, but would they even know what it was?

"Unidentified craft," the loud voice boomed over my speakers. "You have been requested to let us escort you to the Council of Bah'Tene."

"Crap on a tap," I muttered under my breath. That was a popular saying on Targoth when something annoying happened to you. "May I inquire as to why?"

For a brief second, no response came. I felt the presence on the other side of the communications console before I heard the voice. A voice I hadn't heard since...

"Because, young man, I wish to see you again."

Dammit. "Is that you, Arakus?" I asked, though I already knew the answer.

"Yes, yes it is, and I am most anxious to speak to you again. It has been a long time, old friend."

Friend? Lying sack of fakakta telling me that Targoth was long since destroyed and even altering archives to make it seem so. Still, curiosity got the better of me, and besides, I wasn't getting any older. But, did I really want to speak to those inept morons again? No, but something told me I should hear them out. And I didn't have much choice at this point that didn't involve a fight of some sort.

"Very well, Arakus. I'll head over, but please, lose the escort. I don't need these guys to show me the way. I still remember how to get there."

With that being said, all fifteen of the ships that blocked my way dispersed back to whatever section of the system they were supposed to be guarding.

I wondered if the Council sensed me the moment I got there. No doubt they did. It was strange that I hadn't picked up on their presence, though. Maybe in the years that I have been gone from here, I had inadvertently learned how to ignore them. That was a nice thought. Didn't think I'd ever have to talk to them again.

Maneuvering through the skyline of Elginia, I did recall how beautiful this planet looked in the nighttime. Not enough to make me want to live here, or even visit, but still. It was a sight to behold. The planet was practically one large city. There was probably only about one-seventh of the planet that wasn't covered in buildings, instead being dedicated to nature preserves, farming, and natural bodies of water, and of course those refugees from that durmivol planetoid in the void of space.

Yes, it was a nice planet, but it paled in comparison to Targoth.

Targoth, with its vast farmlands and the fields of Ansaka. The dark majesty of the Goblin Woods. The hardpan desert of Kashm and its several dozen water bearing oasis locations. Even down in the southernmost part of the Kyko Sea with the large land mass referred to as the Dead Zone, which at one time was said to be roaming with the undead, mindless and rotting away. They regarded that as legend, but I've seen plenty of undead, though I've never seen a mindless corpse like that just wandering around other than in a zombie movie. Not to say it isn't out there somewhere. The universe is a diverse place.

I was regretting agreeing to tow that transport back. I didn't feel like dealing with Arakus and his band of uptight space assholes. I no doubt would annoy them with the Knights of Targoth uniform vest I wore. Anything that reminded them of my walking away would only serve to distance myself from them. That is what I wanted, though not the reason I wore the vest. I wore it because that is who I was. Who I still am. A Targothian knight.

I soon came upon the home offices of the Council of Bah'Tene. Landing the Hunter on one of the platforms, I turned off the engines, took one more gulp of my ale, and walked down the ramp of the shuttle, Sargotha at my side. To greet me there were all thirteen members of the Council of Bah'Tene. No, wait. Only twelve stood before me, and of those, I only recognized eleven of them. Who was missing?

Kop Va and Smoth were no longer in the group. Still, two members replaced by only one? This guy resembled a young Bah'Tene from back when I was fighting alongside Gostal. He looked like that Steve or Stave or whatever his name was, but I knew it wasn't Stave Steve because he was shredded by a durmivol. This man could pass as his twin.

I made immediate eye-contact with Arakus. He smile at me, I merely nodded. I was in no mood for pleasantries. The idiot addressed me by my birth name. "Oh, do forgive me, Sargas. I meant no disrespect." I nodded again, not showing my anger, though I'm sure they could feel it.

"What do you want of me, Arakus?"

He waved my question off. "First, let me introduce you to our newest council member, Artan Vi, son of Governor Dalteni of the Capitol City of Elginia." I didn't really care. "Kop Va died fighting several Fallen who attacked him on his way to visit a nearby space station." Wow, Kop Va went out in battle. That was almost unheard of from a council member. They were oddly silent on Smoth's absenteeism.

"Yeah, yeah, nice to meet you. Now, Arakus, what is it you want? Tell me what you want so I can say no."

Syltron, the tall blonde wench, stepped forward, her expression that of a woman who wanted to scream at her children for being talkative. "Look, barbarian half-breed. We will not let you show disrespect to..."

Arakus shot her a look and she shut up immediately. Turning back to me, he extended his hand. "Please, Sargas. This is better discussed indoors."

I nodded again, smirked at Syltron, and followed the one-member-shy group to their private chambers in their castle.

Hmm, one member short of a full thirteen. I had a strange feeling forming in the pit of my stomach. I was starting to think I knew the reason that they wanted me to come to Elginia. But, come on, I must be jumping the gun, I thought to myself.

Chapter 23

"Not no, but hell no," I said in a harsh monotone.

They had escorted me to their meeting chambers, the same place that I was brought to so many years ago when I was plucked from 1998 and brought to this time and place. The place that I had taken the Grand Test myself. This time, I was among them in the upper portion of the chamber. Where they sat and watched tene take the Grand Test, some of whom it was the last thing they did among the living, for not everyone came back. There were only thirteen seats up there, and one was empty, which had all but confirmed my suspicion.

I told them that it was just bad luck that I happened along to save a transport ship with Elginian troops on board. Arakus expressed that he didn't believe in luck and that the very universe itself wanted me to be at that place at that time. I did believe the universe had a mind of its own at times, perhaps that is what God was, he was the mind of the universe. I knew that demons were real. I also knew angels were real, especially since Michael empowered the first Bah'Tene and I had his essence running through my own blood.

They had heard that a ship with strange markings was assisting their troops. Ordering the transport com officer to send an image of the markings, the council immediately recognized it as the Seal of Targoth. Most of the council members had seen it as they were wiping out all records of

Targoth from the archives so that I wouldn't stumble across it.

They had offered the seat to me so that I could sit down and speak with them on more equal terms. I refused and stayed standing. Did they think letting me sit in a comfortable chair would make me leave Targoth and come back into their service?

After accepting that I would not sit, Arakus told me what they wanted.

Smoth, the brother of Syltron, had deserted his position and thrown his lot in with the Fallen. No wonder Syltron seemed even bitchier than I remembered. If her brother joined the enemy they must no doubt be looking at her differently. I remained silent as Arakus continued to tell me the situation.

"Sargas, my friend, we are in dire need of you. I know that we parted on not so great terms..." I did agree with him on that. "But please, see reason. You are Bah'Tene. You are powerful. And, you have a large fighting force, both Gostal's old army and your Targothian minions. We are prepared to offer you a seat on the council."

"Not no, but hell no." I said in a harsh monotone. Sorry, I guess I got ahead of myself earlier.

"They are my brothers, you dumb bastard. Not my minions. I will not put them in harm's way to fight your war. You have a large imperium, crossing the Three Galaxies. You don't need my people."

They then asked if I would be willing to just loan out Gostal's old army to them. Again, I repeated my words of negative response.

"But they are Elginian! They owe their allegiance to the Council and the Imperium!"

I stepped forward, noticing how they all slunk back ever so slightly in their seats. "They owe their allegiance to whatever their soul tells them, and they've chosen to follow me. I am not Gostal. I will not force them into servitude, be it for me or for you lazy cowards."

Sylton leapt from her seat and pulled her sword out. I smiled at her. I asked her if she was going to initiate the Challenge. Sneering at me for a few seconds more, she put her weapon away and sat back down, visibly shaken and angry, still giving me the evil eye.

Arakus then stood from his seat and held his hands up in a pleading manner. He never had any problem with being diplomatic. "Sargas, see reason. Every day, the Fallen create more incomplete Bah'Tene. Every day, nosferatus infect more tene into the undead ranks. Every day, we are losing citizens of the Imperium. Every day..."

I interrupted him. "Every day, tene die. Every day, wars are waged. And, one day, we all will die as well. Though, I think all of you will dust. I don't think most of you have it in you to actually get in the fight. I wager most of you are staying in these chambers while you send people out to fight and die on your behalf."

Seeing them cowed into silence, I continued with my rant. "I am shocked that Kop Va fought to the death. I bet he died putting up one hell of a fight. And Sylton, I think you have the stones to stand in battle, too. But the rest of you..." I just shook my head.

"Every day, people in this universe die," I continued. "My being here will not help nor hinder the natural order. By rights, I am not even supposed to be here, yet I am, thanks to you people messing with universal and physical law, and I will spend my time in this universe doing what I must. I will continue to lead and defend my people on Targoth, and do what I can to protect the Earth. I shall do what I will. I am Lord of Targoth, and I am a child of Earth. Which is where I'm supposed to be going..."

Arakus then interrupted me. "Earth? How long before Earth is in the crossfire of this war we've been fighting for thousands of years? I know nosferatus have been to Earth a time or two. Helsing, one of our greatest fighters, has fought them on Earth several times. But one day, he won't be enough."

I had heard of Helsing. He was a scientist and a doctor who had requested to take the Grand Test about three hundred years ago. He was older for a Bah'Tene, nearing fifty at the time. He wanted to have a longer life to develop better healing for the sick and to find a way to cure the nosferatus poison. Last I had heard of him, he had been on Earth, a few decades before I even came back to this time, tracking a vampire in the Sol System. Interesting. Perhaps that was how the vampire legend was born on Earth.

"I have never met Helsing," I said. "But from what I've heard, he is stronger than most. Don't even drag him into this discussion. I will not join the council, nor will I reenter service, and I will most certainly not loan out my brothers and sisters to fight and die for you."

The council had a group feeling of disappointment and anger. I half expected one of them to initiate the Challenge after all.

With a heavy sigh, Arakus slumped in his seat. "Then there is nothing more to discuss, Sargas. You know the way out."

For some reason, I felt a bit guilty. "I might be willing to be a consultant for you. Meaning that if you give me a call, I'll answer and see what I can do to help." I couldn't believe I was agreeing to help these guys in any form. But, people were dying out there. This would be my small part in helping. That seemed to satisfy them, more or less. Even Syltron seemed less hostile. I agreed to stay a few hours for a feast, but then, I had to leave.

It was a bit unexpected, but after I dismissed myself to go to the washroom, Syltron followed me in. We locked eyes for a mere second in time before she began to strip down. Figuring I might as well have a spot of fun, I followed suit and we ended up naked, sweaty, and rolling around for a while. After we finished, Syltron dressed again, gave me a look of contempt, and left me alone with my thoughts.

Did I really just have sex with Syltron of the Council? She was attractive enough and all that, but, by definition of who she was and what she represented, I despised her. Returning to the Hunter and starting the engines, I lifted off, bound for Earth finally.

Putting in a music disk of Goldmoon Dragon Revival, I punched in the coordinates for Earth and activated the LSD.

"She was pretty damn good," I remember muttering to myself as I flew away.

Chapter 24

This time, the trip was even more boring. No distress calls, no attacks by the Fallen. I saw a shooting star, which to me looked the way it would while standing on a planet. A star suddenly fell from view in the distance. It was probably several billion light years from me. More than likely it happened multiple millennia ago.

Soon I arrived at the edge of the Sol System. Maneuvering through the system, I took extra care in going through the asteroid belt between Mars and Jupiter. The asteroids were spread out a lot, but you never knew when one would come out of nowhere and smash into you. Finally, I arrived at Earth.

Seeing the moon come over the horizon, I decided to take a slight detour, and I steered toward it. I had seen it all my life on Earth. I never imagined I'd actually look at it up close like this. I didn't want to land on it. I just wanted to fly by. I thought about how in a few centuries, Neil Armstrong would plant the U.S. flag onto the surface of the natural satellite. I couldn't land on the moon and take that from Neil. I just sat there in the Hunter, looking at the moon up-close. About ten minutes later, I turned toward the Earth and entered the atmosphere.

Flying over the planet, I headed towards the North American continent. The current Earth year would have been in the middle days of 1518. Despite the obstacles and detours, I hadn't been far off schedule in my trip.

I had hoped for a quiet trip, though my Bah'Tene genes were glad to have the side adventures with the Nefarium and space vamps happen. Even my battle with the Fallen and his cronies was fun. We Bah'Tene like to travel and fight. I suppose I was truly conflicted in many ways. My Terran and Targothian blood. My Bah'Tene nature versus my tene upbringing. My wanderlust tempered by dedication to my people. But, even a planetary lord had to get away for a while. Being as I would most likely be alive for the next seven or eight hundred years, I'd no doubt have to have some "me" time once in a while.

Enough with the inner monolog, I thought to myself. I was back on Earth, even if only for a short time and a few centuries before I was even born. Time travel can be bewildering.

I scanned the planet and put in the coordinates that I was here for. Valley Center, Kansas, or at least where it would be eventually.

I located the area where one day the great state of Kansas would be born, and soon found the spot where the not-yet-made Valley Center would stand.

Valley Center. Named as such for its location in the valley of the Arkansas River. Valley of Progress, Center of Pride, or as the town signs would have you believe when you drove into city limits.

I had seen some strange things in that little town growing up, and I was really hoping to discover why. I'd have done this decades prior, but I was pretty busy at that time.

As soon as I entered the area of the unborn state of Kansas, I sensed something was off, and within seconds, my scanners revealed some bizarre readings. There was some sort of energy fluctuation right at the heart of the future Valley Center.

Landing the Hunter near a small hill, I headed out, Sargotha at my side, as I liked it to be. It was sometime in the late morning. The sun hadn't quite made it to the high point in the sky yet. All around me, fields of grass covered the flat plains. Shutting my eyes, I blocked out all outside distractions. The light wind blowing through my hair didn't distract me from my goal of reaching out and finding that strange reading I picked up earlier.

Several moments passed and a wave of vertigo came over me quickly, passing away just as fast. I knew then that I needed to head to the west. Walking for several long minutes, I soon found a hole in the side of a large hill. A hill in central Kansas? Weird.

It was big enough for a man to go through, so I held Sargotha out as I went through the entrance to the mysterious hole. It appeared to head in a spiral, so I followed it down.

It only went down about ten feet and then it became a straight tunnel. I went down the narrow passage, the light from the entrance getting dimmer and dimmer. I was in pitch black. Opening my right palm, I summoned a small fireball and threw it onto the ground before me. I saw that the tunnel went on much further into shadow. The fire soon went out, but not before I managed to grab a stick laying on the ground and then lit it on fire before the flames were gone. Using my makeshift torch, I continued into the tunnel.

I walked for about three or four minutes. The tunnel ever so slightly went downward. I estimated I was about fifty feet below the surface by this point. That feeling in my stomach came back as I descended down further. I literally saw a light at the end of the tunnel. The closer I got, the less I needed my torch. Soon, I came to the source of the light. A small cavern with a glowing sphere in the middle. I somehow knew that I was standing deep below ground in the exact center of the future town.

The glowing sphere was a beautiful shade of light blue. It seemed to have an unusual energy radiating from it. Looking closely, it appeared to be a piece of meteor that gave off a powerful glow which created that round appearance.

Throwing caution to the wind, I put my hand on the sphere. It passed right through, and I felt nothing. No cold, no heat. It was almost as if it wasn't there. It appeared as if the meteor in the middle was a hologram, but I felt in my gut that it was an actual piece of rock and metal. I had a sudden tingle in my hand, and just as I noticed it, it was gone. I had the impression of having blood drawn by a needle, but there was no puncture mark.

It gave off enough light to where the cave may as well have had track lighting on the ceiling. It had an ancient feel to it. This thing, whatever it was, must have been here a very long time. Possibly hundreds of thousands of years. For some reason, the words spatial anomaly came into my head. Was that what this was?

I thought back to all of the weird things I saw in Valley Center while I was a kid. The little monkey like men that I dreamed about, yet always wondered if it was a dream. The haunted basement on Park Street. The way the alleys behind the houses seemed to have ways of taking you across town suddenly as if you walked through a wormhole.

This was the thing that made it all happen, I was sure. This strange anomaly of space and time. Who put it here? Should I try and destroy it? I probably shouldn't, even if I could. Who knows what would happen? It might change not just the future I came from and wipe me out, but it may set off a chain reaction that could cause all sorts of future events from happening. It wasn't worth it. It had been around while I was a tene. Maybe it was a natural part of the planet. It wasn't for me to alter. It was one of those things that a Bah'Tene just knows that he shouldn't play around with.

Taking one final look at the glowing blue beautiful light, perhaps the very soul of the Earth itself, I left the cave. I made my way back up towards the surface. Once again being on the ground above, I took in the fresh air. It felt good to be back in the sunlight. The sun was now moving towards the horizon to begin another evening. How long was I in there staring at that blue orb? It seemed to make you forget about time itself. That could be dangerous.

Going back to the Hunter, I lifted up into the air and headed towards the cave. Letting out a heavy sigh, I aimed my forward guns and opened fire just above the entrance to the underground tunnels. One well-placed shot caused the rocks to crumble and fall, blocking the way. Another shot reduced the entire hill to rubble, causing it to collapse into the ground, filling up the entrance and sealing it. Looking at my handiwork, I knew now that the cave was sealed, though maybe not forever. I knew that one day someone would rediscover it. But, for now at least, the secret of what dwells below Valley Center, Kansas was safe. The strange happenings would still happen. I knew that much. That wouldn't change. But, no citizens of the planet would stumble across the anomaly. Valley Center would be built over it, and its residents would have to still deal with the strangeness that would follow.

It was pretty incredible to be in the location that the town that I grew up in would one day be built, standing in the distant past of the planet, alone in the knowledge of what made Valley Center different from other cities on the Earth.

I hovered over the ground in the Hunter. Sitting back in my seat, I shut my eyes for the briefest of moments. Without warning, my blood surged. My eyes shot open. My Targothian blood was calling out. My brethren were in trouble. Almost as soon as I felt the anxiety in my soul, my communicator sprung to life.

"Lord Sargas! This is Targothian planetary command. We're going to be under attack within moments!"

Chapter 25

The distress call was very frantic. Several ships bearing markings unknown had burst into the system and headed right towards Targoth, bypassing all other worlds in the system. I immediately fired up my engines and broke out of the atmosphere. As soon as I was far enough away from the gravity pull of the Earth, I activated my LSD and made a straight course towards home.

When I took over as Lord of Targoth, one of the many things I did was to put a call out to all of the Elginians that came with me. I sought out an information gathering expert, what on 21st Century Earth would be referred to as a hacker.

I found one not long after, a young man named Benaman who was barely out of his teens and looked almost like a grunge kid from the 90s with his unkempt hair and perpetual look of despair. He hailed from the capital of Elginia and had learned to break into most any defense system. I feared him one day doing something unsavory to our systems, so I decided to recruit him.

He was ecstatic. He actually smiled when I had asked him to break into the Elginian networks and find all information on all known worlds and peoples, things of that nature. I didn't plan on causing trouble, but I wanted to be ready for it.

He had found every known symbol throughout the Three Galaxies, and even dug up information on Targoth that the Council long since buried. Putting that info into our security database, we'd have an advantage in knowing who was visiting our fair planetary system.

So, needless to say, I was worried when the distress call said the markings on the attacking ships were of unknown origin. I believe my exact words in response were, "You've got to be shitting me." I had said it in English, and when the translation went through to Targothian Central Defense, they were a bit confused as to why I'd accuse them of defecating on me. Obviously they didn't understand 20th Century Terran slang.

I had my LSD going at maximum speed, the stars and planets I was passing were not even visible. I was moving so fast they weren't even streaks of white. It looked like I was traveling in pure darkness. The Hunter gave me a warning light telling me that the engines were fast approaching the overheating marker. I'd fly her apart if I must.

There was no need to worry for as soon as the warning light came on, I was almost to my destination. Pulling the lever back, I deactivated the LSD and came to a halt right outside of Targoth's atmosphere. Setting a course for my citadel, I went at maximum sub-light speed and within a matter of seconds I was approaching my home.

I saw all of my Knights of Targoth and the probies as well, fighting side-by-side against vampires. Vampires? There were hundreds, if not thousands of them. My knights were doing a grand job of fighting them. I hadn't seen a body of one of my brothers on the ground yet. It was a matter of time though before some of them were killed. I was angry at myself. I should have been here. Setting the ship to automatically fly away and land on the platform, I opened the ramp and jumped out of the moving Hunter.

It was only about seventy feet. I'd likely break my legs, but they'd heal instantly. As I fell, I held out my hand and summoned Sargotha to my side. In an instant, my right hand held my number one companion in this universe. The Sword of Targoth. The symbolic weapon of my ancestors.

Landing on the hard ground, I indeed felt the shock of the hit go up my spine, cracking several vertebrae, but no matter. After an ever so brief intense pain, I healed again, my spine once more intact. Several vampires saw me and charged towards me, fangs bared.

They were wearing Elginian civilian clothing from several different worlds. The fashions and styles of the Imperium was diverse, but alike enough to tell where it originated from.

Within seconds they were upon me. Four little vampires, and from the look and feel of them, they were newly turned. This was possible retaliation for my previous slaughtering of all those Nefarium and Nosferatus. It was rather brave of them to attack Targoth.

I held up Sargotha and with one swipe from my hand, all four of the vampires had their heads separated from their necks.

Looking up into the sky, I saw several ships from my battle fleet engaging with the assaulting crafts. Taking some heavy damage, my fleet finally destroyed three of the enemy ships while the remaining few turned and ran. My ships followed them out of the atmosphere and pursued them. I had every confidence they'd prevent the enemy craft from leaving the system.

The markings really were unfamiliar to me. They looked Elginian and military, however, so it was my guess that the ships hailed from one of the Imperium's deep space bases and they were overrun by vampires.

Pushing the pondering thoughts from my mind, I focused on the battle at hand. I saw three of my probies being cornered by over a dozen vampires. The three young men readied their blades, ready to go down fighting. I smiled at their bravery though their fear. True knights. A Knight of Targoth knew he may die, but they still did what must be done.

Holding out my left hand, I created a fireball and hurled it in the center of the attacking undead. One small explosion later, and there only stood nine, as the others were incinerated. I noticed that it took a lot less out of me to summon the flames than it usually did. With practice came ease of using that ability.

Turning towards me, the vampires growled in an almost lion sort of way. The advanced and my probies snapped to and jumped into the middle of the nine vampires, hacking them to pieces. Nodding at them for a job well done, I ran towards my Citadel.

As I ran, my sword swung to and fro, removing heads and arms as I went. The other vampires began to take notice of me. Many of them broke off from their fights and ran in my direction.

With my right hand, Sargotha swung about, destroying the vampires and sending them to whatever awaited them in the next life.

With my left hand, I continued to hurl fireballs, incinerating dozens of vampires at once. Each time, I felt my energy drain slightly.

The Knights of Targoth were now fully aware of my presence, and morale picked up. They fought harder and faster and more brutally.

I fought my way into the Citadel, where my Knights battled side-by-side with the Targothian army against the vampire invaders.

Tymber and Rasmussen were alone in the Throne room, back to back, hacking and slashing as the vampires surrounded them. I hurled Sargotha towards the progressing vampires, severing several heads in the process. Sargotha stuck into the wall on the far side. All of the vampires took notice, as did my two brothers.

"My lord," they said in unison as they bowed their heads and saluted in the Targothian fashion.

"Brothers," I saluted back.

"So," hissed one of the vampires in Elginian and who wore the uniform of an Elginian militia colonel. "This is the famous Sargas of Targoth. You do have the stench of a Bah'Tene."

"Yes, so I've heard from several of your kind in the past." I answered back in Elginian. "And who do you happen to be, skeezicks?" I used the Targothian word for 'young punk', something you'd refer to reckless teenagers as. It probably confused him more than insulted him.

"I am Colonel Devont, former leader of Elginian Defense forces on Moon Base 541. Now I lead my men for the glory of the Fallen and Nosferatus."

"What do the Fallen want with attacking my world?" I harshly growled back in response.

"Don't you know, fool?" Devont smiled. "You don't just slaughter a demon's base camp and not face the consequences." I was right. My little skirmish with the Nefarium and vampire base on my way to Earth. "We followed your trajectory and discovered that you came from this system. Your people fight well, but they die just as easily as all tene!" Devont leapt high into the air and landed several feet in front of me.

"I am going to tell you this once, Devont," I continued to speak in Elginian. "Order your forces to leave now and I won't kill or follow you."

Giving me a viper's grin, Devont asked me what if he refused. Wow, how cliché of him.

"Fuck it," I muttered in English and ignited a fireball from both hands and hit Devont point blank in the chest. With a primal scream, he fell to his knees and burned into dust and bones. Tymber and Rasmussen both let out a triumphant shout. The remaining vampires just stood there dumbfounded.

I held out my hand and Sargotha disappeared from the opposite wall and rematerialized in my grip. I pointed the sword at the confused cadre of Nosferatus. I spoke to them in Elginian. "Do you want to give it a go?"

One of them pulled out a communicator from his jacket and called for a retreat. Frantically, the vampires ran from the room. Rasmussen started to give chase but I told him to stand down. Another time for that, I told him.

Within a matter of moments, all of the vampires fled into their landing craft and headed out into space. I sent the order out to let them go. The siege was over.

However, I am not a very forgiving man. I called my fleet ships that had chased the Nosferatus attacking craft out of the system. They notified me that all ships were destroyed. I informed them that many landing craft were leaving Targoth, all of them full of Nosferatus. I gave the order to exterminate them all with extreme prejudice.

With that, I had my Knights go out and gather the bodies of our fallen people. Though only seven Knights died in the siege, fifty civilians lost their lives. In numbers, it wasn't bad, but in personal terms, one Targothian dead is too many.

We held a mass memorial for all of those that died, civilian and Knight. All were Targothian, even those that came with me from Elginia.

I then decided to get a hold of my Bah'Tene nature and stay put on Targoth for the time being. I stayed there, leading and watching over my people. I did the things I did before, too, like attending concerts and listening to the music of Targoth and traveling the system, meeting with the various planetary leaders.

And so, for the next several decades, I remained on Targoth.

Chapter 26

That time on Targoth was pretty uneventful. I did start an annual holiday to recognize those lost in the Siege of Targoth. Tymber had also considered retiring from the K.O.T. as he was getting older.

In Terran terms, he was in his mid-fifties now. But, as Targothians live on average of two hundred years, he still had some fight in him. He always talked of retiring and moving into a large cabin in the mountains with his family.

Rasmussen, too, was getting older. He always wanted to die in battle, but the problem was, he was just too good to die.

In my chambers, I kept a special calendar which held the dates of Earth. The Targothian calendar was a bit different from that of my planet of birth. A day was still approximately twenty-four hours, just like on Earth, and all months were exactly twenty-eight days. A week wasn't really used in the calendar until I came along. It was a new concept but soon the idea of four weeks in a month became popular instead of just twenty-eight days. A Targothian year was three hundred and seventy days. We didn't have leap year or daylight savings. The entire solar system was on the same clock.

I was still deciding on if I'd really move back to Earth when I caught up with my old life, or if I'd just stay here. Even if I stepped down as planetary lord, I could still stay here in my own cabin in the woods below in the Central Valley.

I could stay on as Lord Knight of the Knights of Targoth and just not be lord of the planet. Or, I could just retire and open up a bait shop for the local fishermen. Damn, I was really starting to sound like an old man.

Looking back on everything now, I sometimes wish I had gone into retirement. Targoth was a beautiful place to live, and I'd be happy there until I turned to dust at my one thousand year mark.

After several decades of uneventful peace on Targoth, I started to have uneasy dreams. I'd awaken without remembering what they were about. Strange for a Bah'Tene to not remember something, as our brains had many hidden parts unlocked upon resurrecting after the Grand Test.

The only thing I knew for sure, something was about to happen on Earth. Something dark.

Right now, on Earth, it was 1587. Something was beckoning me to come back. I think I was still tied to that spatial anomaly in Valley Center. Maybe that was the very thing summoning me.

The next morning, I called a meeting with the Knights. I informed them that I had to go to Earth. Something bad was going down. Tymber offered to come with me, but I turned him down. I didn't want my best warrior away from home in my absence. I reminded him I didn't want another Siege Memorial Day for fallen Targothians.

I had finally left and made the long trip to Earth. Well, long in relation to distance. With the Light Speed Drive on my ship, I made it there in a matter of hours. Our ships were protected by the LSD against time dilation, so in the outside universe, only about two hours had passed, just as it had on the ship.

I decided to land on a small island off the coast of what would eventually become North Carolina. Strange how this is where my feelings took me, though the Anomaly was in Valley Center. It was powerful and could no doubt detect darkness and oddness from around the planet.

It must have been around midnight, judging from the color of the night sky. There was something about this place and time I knew might be interesting. I wasn't sure what, but something from my childhood memories spoke to me. A mystery. Then it came to me. The lost colony of Roanoke.

In 1591 John White will return from England and find his colony abandoned. Food still on the tables. Clothing still in people's closets. No explanation except for the word Croatoan. There had been much debate on the meaning of that word carved into a post, but nothing ever was answered for certain.

It was only 1587. There would be about four years until White returned. How did the food stay unspoiled on those kitchen tables? I decided that I'd stay and see what I could discover. Picking a spot that was relatively secluded, I landed my ship and got out, ready to face whatever was out there.

As I drew closer to the colony, I sensed something dark and ominous nearby. A Nosferatus? No. This was different. A demon of some sort? Maybe. Demons were hard to get a read on. I had encountered a few before, but usually they were just doing their thing, not being concerned with the world of mortals. It might be a half-breed like the Nefarium.

I came across a great lake of ice and there were over a hundred people standing there, staring blankly, perfectly still on the frozen lake. Then, from the darkness around me, I heard strange chanting and then the ice turned into a glimmering portal and everyone fell into it, going to gods-know-where. I noticed a lone man standing there at the edge of the frozen lake.

I could sense gloom and hatred in him, comparable to that of what I got from Qal Dea. He was what I sensed earlier. He was cheering in satisfaction of what he had done. I felt in my gut the man standing down there was a witch. Not a minion of Satan by any means, but of some dark gods of magic. He was something that must be killed. I closed my eyes and focused on the dark energy I felt. I could almost taste it. I connected with it. I could feel that portal that those people fell into. They were beyond my reach. I didn't have what it took to save them.

My brain didn't get enhanced with any sort of psychokinesis. My clairvoyance was highly limited, good for only sensing others of my kind or some horrid evil close by. I had my fire, though. I knew long ago that some, actually most, Bah'Tene don't get any sort of special abilities. They are just strong and fast, seemingly superhuman in many ways compared to a tene.

I could see the witch several hundred feet from me. Aiming his finger at me, a black light shot out towards me.

I took the hit full on in the chest, but it didn't do any real damage. I felt like I took a blast of buckshot to the heart, hurting like hell. My anger bursting out, I held up my own hand and caused several dozen fireballs to hail down on the witch. He probably had no idea that I could do anything like that. I continued to rain down fire on him, and the witch waved his hand, bringing forth flames that came at me as fast as lightning. So, it was a firefight. Fine by me.

I jumped high into the air and flipped several times, landing on my feet in front of him, a mere foot or two away. My energy was drained from the excessive fire creation, but I was regaining my strength rapidly. His look of shock was priceless. Summoning Sargotha to my right hand, I ran my left hand along the blade, causing it to become aflame. It was a little something I had been experimenting with the last several decades on Targoth. I swung my sword at his skull, connecting flaming steel to bone.

It caused no harm, but it sent a shockwave up my arm, almost making me drop the sword. The witch began choking me with invisible fingers. I could feel them wrap around my esophagus. Lack of oxygen wouldn't kill me, but it would render me unconscious, and then he would kill me at his leisure. Thinking fast, I kicked his crotch and gave him a strong uppercut to the jaw, knocking him onto his backside.

He immediately chanted in some strange language and snakes began falling on me from out of nowhere. I have no fear of snakes, but that really disgusted me. Even at around a hundred years old, even after fighting two powerful fallen Bah'Tene, even after seeing some of the things I've seen, this was something that nightmares were truly made of.

Narrowing my gaze at the serpents, I slashed away at them, taking their little heads off. Bringing my eyes to the witch, I inadvertently caused his clothes to burst into flames as I simultaneously stabbed at his throat with my sword.

He jumped to the side, causing me to stick my sword into stone, shattering the rock into a thousand pieces. Those small rocks raised up in the air and flew at me like a volley of bullets. Several hit me but I managed to duck out of the way of most. They stung when they hit, but I healed up just as quickly as I bled. I wasn't sure how much longer I could handle this guy. Was this what was to finally take me out of the universe and send me on my journey to the other side?

No, I had come too far to go out like this. I summoned up all my strength and concentration and stood, bringing about a fireball the size of a man. I made it speed towards him with everything I had. It landed at his feet, exploding and sending him flying back, arms and legs flaying about. He landed hard on his butt and I stalked towards him, almost exhausted from the massive fireball I had created. Sargotha in hand, I was ready to cleave him in half. My strength was slow to return, but my anger and desire to kill this guy made up for it.

The witch stood quickly and ran and ducked for cover behind a large tree. I could hear him chanting again. The wind picked up once again with all the ferocity of a massive tornado. That familiar feel of crackling energy in the air meant that he was going to open another doorway and try to cast me in. I had already had that done to me once in my life. I didn't need to go back any further in time or to some other dimension altogether. Holding out my left hand, I sent another giant fireball at the tree, sending it into instant flames. I immediately fell to my knees, too weak to do anything else until my strength returned. That fight took a lot out of me.

That witch had no time to do anything about it. I could hear the chanting stop and he swore aloud. I didn't realize that word was used back then. Above that man of dark magic, another vortex opened in the sky, several feet above him. I must have disrupted his spell and caused him to foul it up and make it backfire. I was reminded of the thing that brought me to Elginia and the past. Was this a time hole as well?

Before I could think too much on it, the witch was pulled through and vanished. Had he gone to the same place he sent those colonists? I just assumed I would never know. It was sad, indeed, all those innocents taken like that. I could only hope that they were kicking the shit out of him wherever they were.

I sat down on the ground against a tree. I was tired from the fight. I hadn't used that much power in a long time. I knew I just needed to sit for a bit and rest. I'd be getting my strength back soon enough.

I ended up taking a nap.

Chapter 27

After an hour or so, I woke and decided to take a look around Roanoke colony. As I suspected, there were still kitchen tables prepared for a meal. There were boots half-shined like the person had gotten up suddenly to take a leak. All over the town, every home was in similar order. It was very surreal.

What sort of crime had they perpetrated on that he-witch to make him do this? Maybe they were just victims of a sociopath with magic. I figured it was lost to me so I decided not to think too much more on it. History would unfold naturally and perhaps one day, the truth would be discovered.

I suddenly felt another presence in the vicinity. This wasn't good or evil. Just powerful. I searched all around and found nothing. I turned a corner into the center of town and I saw someone standing there.

There was a man, or what at least looked like a man. He had a pasty skin and sharp features. He wore a black fedora on his head and was clad in a dark trench coat. It looked like he had a black suit on underneath. He was busy carving the word Croatoan into the post. I could hear him giggling lightly as he did so.

He must have sensed me, as he turned and suddenly smiled at me. "Come here, my friend," he spoke English in an accent that sounded bland and monotone. "Are you a Bah'Tene?" he asked. Responding in English myself, I asked him how he knew of my kind. "Oh, we're aware of pretty much everything in this dimension. It is the 3rd one, you know. That is why everything is in 3-D." He laughed as his own words. His demeanor was that of a dumb, bubbly blonde. "I'm from the 5th dimension. Everything there is live and in color. And five dimensions is a lot cooler." He grinned and danced a small jig.

"Ok, uh, sir?" I asked. "Yes, I am a Bah'Tene. What are you exactly?"

He stopped dancing and got serious. "I am a 5th dimensional being. We don't have planets like your dimension. It is rather one large, flat plane where everything is fifth dimensional. It is of the mind. We were once like you but have evolved. We left this dimension a long time ago. I was actually the last one born in this universe. You can call me Jack."

"I am Sargas."

He smiled. "Yes, of course. Well, I would love to stay, but that would keep me from leaving." I asked him what the Croatoan word meant. "Oh, sure. Like you don't know." Without warning, he pulled curved, rusty blade from his coat and attacked me. I instantly blocked his strike. I asked him what that was about. "Oh, sure. Like you don't know. You 3rd dimensional creatures, I swear!" He continued to attack me, and I continued to block every strike. He opened his mouth and breathed a small blue flame at me. This time, I grinned and formed a ball of fire in my hand and threw it in his face. "Ouch!" he yelped.

We continued to trade strikes for several more minutes. He shoved me back with a strength I didn't know he had. He put his knife back inside his coat. A great fighter he was, to block a sword like Sargotha with that pig sticker. "One thing I have that you dimension three people don't," he smirked. "I have spring heels!" With that he leapt into the air with a swiftness that I only saw in a Bah'Tene during a battle. He leapt high into the treetops and vanished from sight. I didn't sense his presence anymore.

"Springheel," I murmured to myself. "Springheel Jack!" I remembered reading about him in high school. During the Victorian period, and even earlier, in England were reports of a man assaulting people on the streets and leaping high into the sky to escape. Well, I thought, I will probably run into him again one day. Next time, I'd be ready to take his damn head off. But, that was the very last time I ever saw that guy. I'd heard stories in the time since, but that's another kettle of fish altogether.

The darkness I sense back on Targoth was now gone. I came all this way to kill a witch in Roanoke. So as not to make the trip entirely without extra benefit, I decided to make a quick stop in Germany before heading home to Targoth. I wanted to bring back some authentic German ale for my brothers in the Knights.

Heading back to the Hunter, I set in a course for Munich, Germany. I knew that Spaten Lager had been brewed there since 1397, or so the labels on the bottle would have you believe.

Soon, I was outside of Munich, hiding my ship behind some trees and trekking towards the town. After listening to some of the locals talk for about ten minutes, I picked up perfect German. It had many similarities with Targothian.

Asking around, I found the facility that brewed Spaten. I knew I didn't have any currency of the land, so instead, I managed to sneak into the storage units and I rolled out ten kegs of brew.

I didn't want to be a thief, so I headed back to the ship and found some Elginian gold coins. They were pure gold, and though not currency that the German brewers would understand, they could no doubt melt it down into whatever they wanted. Gold was valued on many worlds in the Three Galaxies.

One by one I carried the kegs back to my ship. I was amazed at the lack of security of the place, but I had to remember, this was Germany in the year 1587. They didn't exactly have security cameras or alarms back then. After the beer was loaded safely on the Hunter, I took off, hoping I didn't alert the locals who would be freaked out by a horseless wagon flying into the sky.

Before I left the atmosphere, I felt something else dark and vile. Another witch? I hoped not. No, it wasn't that exactly. Flying high in the sky, I found the source of the despair. I was soon landing outside of the German town of Trier. There was a witch trial going on.

I made my way into the small town. Five young women, all petite with dark hair and wearing filthy rags, were standing before a judge out in the middle of the town square. They were being accused of witchcraft and of mating with Lucifer. I had to try not to laugh at that. I could sense darkness and evil and these women had none in them.

But they had power. I could feel that they were like that witch I had just fought in Roanoke. They had the same sort of vibe, but without the vile murderous mentality.

I listened for a few minutes as the judge announced that in the morning at dawn, the witches would be punished, and if God forgave them, he'd accept them back into his arms, basically meaning they'd be killed. The primitive mentality of humanity.

I watched as they pulled the women away. They were all in their late teens at least. Far too young to die at the hands of self-righteous bastards like this. I had seen enough senseless death in my long life to put up with this mess.

I waited in a local tavern until nightfall came. Heading towards the town center, I forced my way through the main door and into the holding area where the five young girls were locked up. One of the girls was not alone in her cell.

A guard had her cornered with his britches down below his ankles. He was laughing at her tears. The other girls were begging him to stop. If they had power in them, it wasn't the kind that could cause harm. Witches of the Light. Perhaps they were too inexperienced to use their powers to protect themselves. They would have the chance to learn after this night.

Grabbing the handle to the cell's door, I yanked it open. The guard turned to face me, his erection deflating after he saw Sargotha materialize in my hand. I wanted to kill him, but refrained as I didn't know how it would affect the future.

Instead, I flung Sargotha at his head, hitting his temple with my sword's handle, knocking him into unconsciousness. He'd awake with a bad headache and possibly blue balls, but that was the extent of the damage. He deserved to have his head burned off of his shoulders.

"Ladies, nice to meet you," I said to them in flawless German. They were still scared, though now I think they were aware I had no intention to harm them.

I asked if they had family, and they told me their parents were killed by the villagers. All five girls were sisters and their parents died trying to keep them from being taken from their home. It made me want to burn the entire village to the ground with the Hunter's weapons.

Instead, I asked them if they wanted to come to a place where no one would hunt them for their abilities. I told them who I was, what I was, and where I was going. I invited them to come to Targoth where they could continue their studies in magic.

They told me they were learning from their mother but with her dead, no one could teach them. I told them to go home and get what they wanted and to meet me outside the town where my ship was. Fifteen minutes later, all five of the girls came, each with a bag of clothes and their books.

They asked me what they needed to do for payment for my generosity. They were beautiful. If I were a bastard, I would have wanted sexual favors from each of them. But, luckily, I was more or less a nice old man. Besides, I preferred women, not girls.

I told them the only payment was to study and become the best at their craft and to help benefit Targothian society. With that, they all seemed visibly relieved and they walked up the boarding ramp to the Hunter.

I showed them to the lounge and had them buckle in as I took off. Right before I lifted into the air, I could see several townsfolk coming, all screaming in German at me. Laughing, I flew off into the night's sky back towards home.

Chapter 28

Back on Targoth, I put the girls with a foster family in Talfurd. There they learned the farming trade while practicing their skills at white magic. Eventually, those girls built a school in the old Goldmoon Kingdom ruins where they taught magic to anyone who wanted to learn.

Magic was, after all, just one of many forces of nature in the universe that one could harness and control with the right mindset and training. What a Bah'Tene does can be considered magic of sorts. The ability to live longer, heal almost instantly, and sometimes even have the ability to create fire.

Those ladies did alright for themselves. They even found some lucky young men and formed families.

But, not everything was going great on Targoth at that time. In the short time I had been gone, a few skirmishes had occurred at the old border that used to separate North and South Abnu. Political tensions were forming. I came back just in time to see the Abnu government become divided and within weeks, the Southern factions left and set up shop at their former capitol in old Southern Abnu. The Northern factions did the same and moved back into their old castle.

I hated seeing Targothians acting like petty children like this. I suppose I was arrogant to think that I had been some sort of savior who united the planet. They were still tene, after all, and they had their tene mentality. I feared a civil war could break out.

I called for a summit between the leaders of both factions and asked for the Chancellor to attend as well. I brought in three dozen knights as security and had Tymber and Rasmussen with me at my side.

The meeting was at a neutral location. It took place at the small town of Tanara resting on the Ansaka/Katu border.

The talks took place over the course of weeks, which soon turned into months. I listened as both side argued their cases. The North was taking advantage of the work done by the South, and the South were refusing to work in order to punish the North.

In order to keep riots from breaking out, I had Knights and soldiers patrolling the lands of Abnu. Many citizens were arrested for trying to start fights and breaking into businesses. At one point one of my Knights arrested the son of the Governor of North Abnu. He demanded that we release his son, but I called a quick recess to the talks and personally went to the jailhouse to meet with the Governor and refuse his request. "Your son tried to assault an old man who refused to denounce his Southern Abnu heritage," I reminded the Governor. "He'll get a trial, just like any Targothian citizen."

The Governor was about to say something back when he abruptly turned and left. I returned to the meetings.

It was political nonsense. After a few more hours, I called a lunch break. I met with the Chancellor privately in a back office for lunch and asked what his opinion on the situation was. As we ate our steaks, he pretty much agreed with me.

Both sides of Abnu were being ridiculous. We were both concerned with the possibility of a war breaking out between the two small groups. The North might ask Kashm to help out like in the old days, and soon, war might break out across all of Targoth.

I felt foolish. What was I doing wrong? This never happened with Qal Dea. But, he was a tyrant, and he had an iron fist over the land, whereas I wanted people to be free to do their own thing. That was the problem. Freedom would occasionally breed stubbornness and violence. That was the price you pay for having a free land.

After all this time on Targoth, I was not about to let these children wreck the peace that had been achieved after the fall of Dea. I wouldn't allow it.

We finished our food. "Let's get back to it," I told the Chancellor. We met once again with both North and South Abnu leadership.

Soon, the bickering and arguing started anew, and I listened for almost an hour. Eventually, my anger grew too much and I slammed my fist on the table. A smoldering indention was left behind. I hadn't realized that my hand held a fireball when I slammed it down.

The entire group at the table stopped talking and looked at me, fear in their eyes, except for the Chancellor and my fellow Knights. They were amused that I scared the delegation so badly.

"I don't know why you all can't just get along like the brothers that all Targothians are," I scolded them.

"My lord, it isn't that..." the Minister of Defense of Abnu started.

"Do not interrupt me," I said in a low monotone. The Minister quickly shut his mouth.

"As I was saying, I don't know why you all are not getting along. And I don't care. I don't expect everyone to like everyone. You're all tene, and you all are Targothian. Emotion and passions run deep within us."

I stopped for a second to glare around the table. They all sat in silence, eyes wide in fear.

"Now, I am not Qal Dea. I won't rule with an iron fist and demand loyalty based off of fear. I want loyalty based off of respect and the fact that I am the rightful heir to the position of Lord of Targoth. But, I will not stand by while you people try to incite a war on my planet!"

The Governor of North Abnu stood, "You were not born here!"

I glared my eyes at him and his glass of water bubbled with boiling heat, shattering the glass into dozens of pieces.

"Do not speak that way of me!" I stood and put my hands on the table. "I am of the blood of Lorancano, and of all of his ancestors who ruled this world for generations before you were even born! Into the time of legends! I killed the madman Dea and claimed my birthright and freed you ungrateful bastards from the rule of a despot. I will not allow you to destroy all that we worked for!"

The Governor sat back in his seat, fear for his life clear in his eyes.

"As I said," I continued, "I am not Qal Dea, but I am your Lord. If you do not stop this inane bickering and disrespect towards me and our world, I will put garrisons in your countries to keep the peace."

Shouts of "You can't do that!" and "You haven't the right!" filled the room. My anger and impatience swelling, inadvertently I hurled a fireball into the wall behind the Governor.

The Chancellor now stood. "You will all find a peaceful solution to your problems, or else I will completely honor the wishes of Lord Sargas and have the army set up garrisons all over the lands of Abnu to watch your every step and ensure peace is kept."

"Well," I said, smiling at the Chancellor. "I see my esteemed colleague here has things well in hand politically. My Knights and I will take our leave. If anything other than peace is achieved here this day, I will make good on my promise of massive military presence in your countries." With that, I left the room, Rasmussen and Tymber following me. "Come gentlemen, to the Knight headquarters. We still have some of that German beer I brought back."

It had been too long since I just spent time with my brethren. The past few months so full of political tension and posturing. My brothers and I sat and drank beer and laughed and they told me of the goings on in their lives. Tymber told me his wife wanted to know if I had met a good woman yet and if not, she had a friend for me. I laughed saying that I hadn't time for romance. I had to make sure tene didn't do stupid crap.

Many hours passed and finally, the Chancellor contacted me. The Governors of both sides of Abnu agreed to resign and allow the people to elect new leadership in the nation in hopes of finding a binding peace for the land.

I knew that the old governors from both sides still hated me. That was good. Sometimes the best way to unite two groups is to have them hate the same boss.

Chapter 29

Targoth has a wonderful mythology to it. In the time of legend, people revered the gods. In those times, the tene of the world didn't call themselves Targothians. They called themselves human. Many worlds in the Three Galaxies had humanoid life, and many of them resembled the humans of Earth, and their DNA was similar enough to where they could produce offspring with each other.

Many theorized that humans came from a single world, long ago when the universe was young. Perhaps these beings became advanced and spread out throughout the stars. Perhaps over time, wars or other catastrophes happened and civilizations were destroyed and the survivors backslide as a society, forgetting their origins. They began anew, generations later they discovered old ruins and artifacts and pieced together their origin. Over the generations, over the eons, eventually everyone forgets where they came from.

But, that is only theory. I digress again. Forgive me. I do tend to ramble in my old age.

In the times of legend, the humans of Targoth walked the world with the elves, the dwarves, the gnomes, and dragons filled the sky. Magicians conjured spells and potions and clerics worked miracles on behalf of the gods of old.

Targoth has a singular mythology that everyone learns through story, unlike Earth, which has various myths: Roman, Greek, Norse, Egyptian, to name but a few. Targoth has only had one mythical creation and one set of deities. Many still worship them to this day, though there are atheists in the world who don't believe in any gods, but at least they are tolerant of their brother's faith in the old ways.

Eons ago, in the time before time, the universe was a black void, with no form save for the swirling pure chaos that flowed within. The nothingness was filled with a great silence that was deafening, and the chaos moved around the void, invisible. In this void one day appeared the Great Power. The Great Power was from another reality, another plane of existence that was full of spirit beings, both good and evil. The Great Power witnessed the chaotic energies and pure darkness that surrounded Him and He was greatly saddened, for He longed to create life in the nothingness. The Great Power held out His hand and spoke the sacred words of Creation.

From these sacred words, the chaos came to a halt. The energy that once swirled around without purpose and invisible was used to form a new world. The world was covered in water, and so the Great Power reached into the depths of the seas and pulled up land around the world. In the seas He formed life and plants to thrive in the watery environment. On the land, He formed animal life in honor of the spirit beings that were in His home universe. Some animals were bound to land while others could take flight. He created mighty trees and plants which bore fruits for the animals to feast on. Some of the animals fed on others instead of the fruits of the trees. Thus is the cycle of life.

But the Great Power's work wasn't done. Although the animals He created were great and full of beauty and grace, they were merely animals. The Great Power reached out into the vastness of the multiverse and summoned others of His kind.

The first to answer the call was Hanch, similar to the Great Power but significantly less in strength. Hanch created the first intelligent race of the world, the elegant elves, in his own image. They were slender of frame but powerful of body. Their ears were pointed and their hearing great like many of the animals of the forest. They were imbued with the energies of the universe and would be capable of wielding great magic of nature.

The second to answer the call was Lilith, a lesser being from another world long ago created by the Great Power elsewhere in the universe. She was once mortal, and soon fell from His grace and sided with a powerful god of evil in that world. That evil god had granted her power and she became a virtual deity. Now she was to make her home in this new world, and the Great Power allowed it so, for He knew that to have true good, you must have evil to balance it. She attempted to seduce Hanch, but he resisted her, for his will was strong. She retreated to the shadows of the world, nurturing her feelings of rejection into revenge against the world that Hanch and the Great Power were building.

Soon after, Forge came, and brought with him the dwarven race and the gnomes. The dwarves would be great builders, and the gnomes, inventors. The two races would work well together to build a better way of life for the other races that were to come.

Grubmesh followed Forge into the universe and brought forth his goblin races. Numerous they were, and as violent as the primordial volcanoes of the world. Lilith seduced

Grubmesh and soon bore his child, the young god Temash. Temash, as evilly seductive as his mother and as vile and brutal as his father, drew from the energies of life to create the state of undeath. He wished to ensure that all those who worshiped him would follow him and be bound to him even after their own death, unlike the other beings who after death move on to the spirit world of the gods. These undead children of Temash would be trapped in their own rotting flesh, forever in servitude.

Other gods followed, all from different times and places from throughout the countless universes in all of existence. Some brought creatures into the world, others brought wisdom, others forbidden things. The great Og brought forth his mighty ogres, tall and violent, they brought warfare to all those they encountered. The ruthless Blood Horn, fraternal twin of Og, took some of his brother's creations and corrupted them into the bovine Minotaur, thus making them resemble a race of diminutive beings from his home dimension that had the form of dwarves with cow's heads. These two races would soon become mortal enemies.

The Great Power gathered His fellow gods together and told them He'd be leaving for His spirit world haven. But first, He reached into the far depths of reality and brought forth a race called humans and placed them in the world. He then reached into the very fabric of time and space and brought forth the human Xavier, who hailed from a distant time in an impossible to fathom future. The Great Power elevated Xavier to a god and placed the care of the humans in his hands. The Great Power told the gods to name the world and then He'd leave it for them to rule. They called it Targoth, which means "The Vast Realm" in the ancient language of the gods that came before them that they themselves venerated. With that, the Great Power left the world of Targoth in the care of the gods and returned to His home.

Soon after He left, a great portal opened in the skies above, and the dragons arrived into the world. From a world far away they came, sent by their mother Iolat, and they quickly settled into the caves spread out all throughout the lands. Iolat had given them long life and power of fire breath.

As the times of legend advanced, the humans of Targoth spread out and traveled the world as nomadic tribes. The elven race spread out as well, forming several kingdoms across the face of Targoth. The gnomes and dwarves settled in the mountains and rivers. The wandering humans soon came across the goblin races, as they too were nomads. The two races took to an instant hatred of each other. Their first meeting was met with much bloodshed.

The humans would have surly died if not for the intervention of the elven people. The elves guarded the forests of the world fiercely, willing to kill to protect their domain. They saw a spark of good in the humans, and for the first time, they left the forest to help another race.

Together they fought back the goblins, scattering them and forcing them to flee for their very lives. The elves and humans forged a bond, forever allies.

As their societies became friends, soon the dwarves and gnomes reached out to them. The dwarves too were hunted, but by ogres, taller than two humans and stronger than anything they'd seen. These races all pledged to join together, and they all contributed.

The dwarves forged swords and armor with the metals from their mountains. The gnomes designed and built homes and cities for the humans so they could settle from their perpetual wandering and they built structures for the elves, helping them expand their kingdoms further. The elves taught the other races of magic and medicine. The humans developed farming, and soon taught the others so that they could grow crops and herd animals for food and work.

There is a great deal more of their mythology, but it is too much to go into here.

I bring it up because my interest in mythology led me to the great love of my life. A woman named Teak.

Chapter 30

It was in the Earth year of 1593 that I went to go into town to buy some books. It was during this trip to a bookshop where I met her. Teak.

She was short for a Targothian woman. Only about five foot six. Her long dark hair framed her beautiful face. Her brown eyes were soulful.

There was a new bookstore in Remet, a town near my citadel. I had gone to see what books it had to offer when I saw her. Teak's family had recently come into some money by selling their mining business and she was given enough money for her share to follow her dream of running her own shop.

Teak was a free spirit, more than I'd seen in longer than I could remember. She was young, at the age of twenty-five, which for Targothians and Terrans, that is about the same. You don't notice the slower aging for Targothians until the fourth or fifth decade of life.

It is funny, as at first she didn't recognize me. I came into the shop, in my K.O.T. vest as I usually wore. She just assumed I was a typical Knight of Targoth.

I asked her if she had any books on legend and mythology from the other worlds of the system. Without looking up from her book, she shook her head and apologized. "Sorry, only one Targothian mythology. I have some from the Elginian society if you like. They have over two hundred different pantheons."

I hadn't considered that. I was so into reading about Targothian legends that I never thought about our brethren that came with me from the Imperium so long ago. Though, now, they had all died of old age, but their children and grandchildren were still a strong part of our society.

I thanked her and went searching for the books on Elginian myth. I was serving their government for a decade and never even thought about researching their culture, though, to be fair, I was busy traveling with Gostal and fighting the hordes of evil demonic entities and their kin. Makes it hard to find time to crack open a good book with a cup of hot chocolate.

I found several books, each of them looked equally interesting, though 'The Guide to the Gods of the Three Galaxies' seemed like something that I'd want to get right away. The book was big, about two thousand pages at least. Well, the cultures of the Three Galaxies had been around for eons. They were bound to have some stories to tell. And this was just Volumn 1.

I went up to the front, ready to buy the books and then perhaps go out for a drink of ale. Placing the books on the counter, the pretty girl checked the prices on the covers and rang up the total cost. The machine looked much like a cash register from the 1950s.

After telling me the price, I took out a money card, very similar to debit and credit cards. It tied into the account for the Citadel's treasury. Taking the card, she got a confused look on her face and looked at me. "Are you sure you're authorized to use this for a personal purchase? I don't want to get my store in trouble." She sounded very concerned that any moment soldiers would burst in and arrest her.

"Don't worry," I assured her. "I am authorized to use this card." She nodded, stating that as a Knight of Targoth, I no doubt did, but she said she was thinking that the Lord Knight, also being the Lord of Targoth, would not want one of his Knights using government money for something personal.

I asked her what her name was. She told me Teakisis Kallag. She then asked me mine, with a flirtatious smile on her face.

It was at that moment that one of the probies of the Knighthood came in to make a purchase of his own. Seeing me there, he quickly knelt down, awaiting the command to rise. I hated it when they did that. I told them to not kneel. A salute is fine. That was when recognition dawned on Teak as well.

She curtseyed. "My lord, I am so sorry. Forgive me for not recognizing you. Of course your card is great for purchase here."

"Get up," I said a bit more harshly than I intended to the probie. "Go on, get to shopping." Standing quickly, he scurried off into the back of the shop, busily looking at books.

"Yes," I said as I looked at Teak. "I am Sargas. And your name is Teakisis, correct?" She nodded and stammered that people called her Teak. "Please, do not be nervous." I sometimes forget that the latest generation of Targothian only knows me from their parents and grandparents telling them the tale of how I arrived and killed the madman Dea.

"I'm not," she tried to reassure me with a smile as she ran the card and received the funding for the books. "I just never thought I'd meet you in person, my lord, especially in my small little shop."

"Well," I smiled back, "I prefer smaller shops to the big ones. I think you get a much better class of person in these places." She actually blushed. I was almost beginning to feel like I was twenty-three again.

Should I even be doing this? I thought to myself that I am technically married. To a junkie. Some four hundred years in the future. My wife's great grand parents weren't even born yet. I deserved to be happy. Maybe I could make things work when I caught up with my life, if I even decided to go back to Earth. But for now, I'm here on my ancestral planet. I had a good feeling about this woman.

"Teak," I leaned in to get closer to her. "I'd love to invite you out for dinner and a few drinks. Any place you want to go."

She was clearly hesitant. She was probably thinking that I was just trying to sleep with one of the commoners. If only she knew that wasn't how my brain worked.

It was then that the probie came up, waiting for me to finish my business. He was afraid to pay for his stuff while I was standing there. I turned to the probie and asked his name. "Dur'Ca, my lord," he responded.

"Son, go ahead and pay for your books. I'm just here talking." I nodded at him, and he seemed a bit relieved. Sad to think that younger Targothian Knights were this timid around the Lord Knight. His books were rang up, and by the time he scampered out, Teak had a new look in her eye.

A look of confidence. A look of assurance. "My lord, I'd be happy to accept your dinner invite."

I asked her where she wanted to go, and she said she enjoyed a café up the street. I told her not to worry about price, but she insisted. "If you want good quality, my lord, you have to go to the 'Mom & Dad' establishments." I liked the way she thought.

We went to the café and had soup and grilled fish. The fish were the freshest catch out of the Kyko Sea.

I had an incredibly wonderful time with her. I walked her back to her home, where she still lived with her parents. They were shocked to see the Lord of Targoth bringing their daughter home. They knelt down too. I told them to not ever do that again, but in a nice voice.

I saw her each night over the next three weeks. There was something about her. I had encountered a lot of incredible things in my long life. I knew there was something that awaited us after death, and that each being had an energy, a soul, that lived on. I didn't know what happened after this life, but I knew of the possibility of reincarnation.

I really think it was possible that Teak and I knew each other in a distant life, long ago, before we were born into these lives.

Time and space are truly relative things. It didn't matter that I was actually born almost four hundred years from now. Who knows how long a soul waited in between incarnations? Maybe it was a choice, and when you're in the realm of spirit, time doesn't mean anything, so waiting a decade, a century, or even a millennia was a drop in the bucket of time.

During the day while she worked, I left her alone, knowing that she was more or less busy, and I did have work myself to do. We were at a time of peace, and I didn't even go out into space to hunt vampires in that time. After that last siege, I didn't want to be away from the planet.

Every evening, I sent a car to her home to pick her up and bring her to the Citadel. I introduced her to Tymber, my best friend and brother-at-arms. He was now looking older, much older, but he was still as active as ever. His face was that of a man in late middle age, his once dark hair now salt and pepper, though still in the short cropped style he has always worn it in. A true soldier.

Those weeks of courting flew by fast. It was into the third week where we finally made love for the first time. I hadn't been with as many woman as you'd have thought with my longer life, as love was something I was too busy for. But when I was with Teak, it was as if the very fabric of time and space stood still. We were the only two beings in creation.

It was on the beginning of the fourth week that I asked her to marry me. I had gone into the archives under the Citadel and found many family heirlooms, from long ago, even into the time of Lorancano. I searched the rooms deep underground and I found a ring. It was the ring that Lorancano gave to his wife Enada, the mother of Sargas, my ancestor. It was a band of pure silver, several white gems on its surface, spaced out across the ring.

I decided it was a fitting gift to the future Lady of Targoth.

We were alone in my private library, drinking some cold ale and enjoying each other's company. I abruptly stood and knelt down before her. Without speaking, I pulled the ring from my vest pocket and took her left hand.

On Targoth, the wedding ring is worn on the left hand, just as it is in Terran culture. Perhaps something brought by Targothian refugees?

I asked her to be my wife and she instantly said yes. We embraced. We kissed. We made love right on the library floor.

The wedding was several days later. We didn't want to wait.

I asked the captain of my flagship to perform the wedding for us, and Tymber, my brother, stood up with me as my best man.

Twenty of my Knights flanked the walkway, swords held high in salute. Together, Teak and I walked out of the chapel, her in her beautiful dress of purple and silver. White dresses are not a Targothian thing.

We left for our honeymoon: a month cruise around the Grey Sea and the Kyko Sea with stops along the ruins of the Goldmoon Kingdom and the Isle of the Minotaur.

Sargas and Teakisis, husband and wife, Lord and Lady of Targoth.

Chapter 31

Being married to Teak was a wonder. It made me forget about the wreck of a woman I would be meeting in a few centuries.

I warned her before the wedding that we wouldn't be having children. Not that I didn't want to, but a Bah'Tene cannot reproduce. It was a side effect of the Grand Test. She didn't mind, she said. The people of the land would be our children. Her demeanor and attitude were regal. She was born to be Lady of Targoth.

As I went about the day-to-day business of leading my Knights and my world, Teak set about something far nobler.

After the siege, many children were left homeless. Teak set herself about at setting up schools all across the lands. They housed the children and taught them literature and art.

I had gone down there many times to watch her in action. She was like a natural mother. She taught the children to read and to enhance their vocational skills. She even set up lessons to learn other languages. Many of the children started to speak Elginian.

That wasn't necessary as all of the Elginian-born citizens had long since learned Targothian, and now Elginian was taught as a secondary language. I felt it was important to learn, so I myself even encouraged others to learn Elginian. I thought about teaching English, but as I was the only speaker, it didn't seem necessary. I decided instead to teach Teak. She picked it up fast. Her mind was a sponge of learning.

Along with her teaching reading and writing to the young, she took me up on an offer to learn the art of swordplay.

Several nights a week, I'd teach her the basics and soon she was able to spare. She managed to take me down in one or two occasions.

There were females in the K.O.T., but I didn't want my wife being a Knight, and she affirmed she had no desire to do so. Teaching kids kept her busy enough.

We were having a great life together. The two of us working to make Targoth better each day. Her with education and art, me with defense and leadership.

We had spent twenty-four great years together. In the Earth calendar, it was about to become 1617.

On Targoth, we were coming closer to another annual Festival of Legend. The turnout was expected to be huge. For several months the people were preparing. The Knights were devising security patrols and I was anxious to hear the great music and see the plays that the people put on. Teak had a group of children that were going to do a skit about the legends of the elven races.

The festival was underway and a new band, Kumbernestia Supreme, was slotted to perform on that first night. They were very similar in music style to Def Leppard, a Terran band from the late 1970s and on into the 80s and 90s. Very popular with the teenage population of Earth in those years.

The sun was close to setting as Teak and I lay on a blanket in the field. We weren't alone, surrounded by others on their own blankets and chairs. In order to better blend, I left the vest in my chambers. I wanted to enjoy it as a citizen of Targoth, not the Lord of the planet.

I could see Tymber and his family not too far from us. He had taken the night off as well. Good, he deserved to. He was there, surrounded by grandkids and laughing and eating cake with them.

The music played loud. I always liked it loud. I felt like a kid again, jamming to music, pretty girl at my side. As the band played their songs, almost everyone was on their feet, dancing and singing along.

I jumped to my feet and pulled Teak up, and together, we danced. I showed her how the old head bangers used to do it when I was a kid on Earth. I did some air-guitar and put my hand in the air, pinky finger and index finger pointing out, moving my head back and forth. I remember her giggling at me. She was so adorable.

Soon the band finished playing their set, and they bowed, and did an encore. It was a slower song, one that I didn't want to jam to, so instead Teak and I sat back down and ate some pie and drank some ale. We started to talk about the many things we enjoyed. The conversation went from books to mythology to a new bakery in Remet.

As we lay there talking, fireworks went off. That was a bit unusual as they usually saved that when the festival closed for the night, usually around the midnight hour. It took me a few seconds to process the situation, but those were no fireworks. That was laser fire.

Immediately, I took out my communicator and called Central Command. No answer. It was as if they weren't there, but I knew they were. Those lasers, they must have destroyed our communication satellites. The laser fire stopped and almost instantly, the ships appeared in the sky. Three ships, all capital sized warships, all Elginian. Were they attacking us? Did the Council finally decide that since I wouldn't join with them, I needed to be destroyed?

The ships moved closer, and they soon stopped, hovering several hundred feet in the sky. A single hanger door opened in the middle ship, and from it I saw a shuttlecraft descend. So the bastards wanted to parley with me. The people were clearly upset and disturbed, but they stayed put. Targothians are not usually prone to panic.

Within a matter of moments, many trucks pulled up, soldiers disembarking and getting into formation, their rifles at the ready. I saw Tymber hug his grandkids and draw his blade from under a blanket. He was soon at my side. "My lord," he nodded at me.

"Brother," I nodded at him. Holding out my hand, I summoned Sargotha, and instantly, my sword was in my grip, ready to strike.

I gave the order to all the civilians in the area to take cover. Some of them began leaving while others stayed behind, the look of fight on their faces. Targothians rarely want to back down.

The shuttle landed, close enough to where I could see the faces of those walking down the boarding ramp. Five men, humanoid, probably from somewhere in the Elginian Imperium. They wore simple black tunics and pants, boots were shiny and dark grey. Each one had a sword at their hip or a pikestaff on their backs. They had the bearing of

Bah'Tene, but I knew they weren't. They didn't give off the feeling. I realized what I was looking at. Pseudo-Fallen.

It was just these five. They had no guards with them. It was clear they wanted to talk. Not destroying our communications satellites would have made it easier to talk to us on the radio, but then again, these guys seemed like the type that liked to talk in person. And prevent us from having a warning.

"Ah, Sargas of Targoth. At last we meet," spoke the one that must have been the commander. He spoke in Targothian and his accent was almost undetectable. You'd think he was a native speaker. He was older than the others, looked to be in his late thirties. "Don't bother calling for your fleet. Your communications are out of commission. I didn't want anyone interrupting. Please tell your men to stand down." I turned and nodded at the soldiers. They lowered their rifles, but didn't put them away. Good men.

"You know me," I responded. "But, who are you that dares to attack my home?"

He put up his hand and waved away my question. "Sargas of Targoth, I am Kodan, commander of the 2nd Fleet and leader of the Neo Fallen." Neo Fallen? Is that what those idiots called themselves?

"We have come to make you an offer. We know you have no love for the Council. My masters invite you to join us in our effort to take the Council of Bah'Tene out of order and place a more suitable group of leaders in its place to give aide and advice to the latest Emperor. You have a vast army," he continued. "And together, you, the Lord of Targoth, and my masters, you can bring a new order to the Three Galaxies. A new prosperous regime to command..." with that, I launched a fireball into his chest, instantly burning his heart out. I felt no energy drain from it at all.

"I'm afraid I'll have to decline!" I shouted in Elginian. They didn't like my answer. I didn't want them to.

Chapter 32

I knew they'd attack. More or less, all of the civilians had taken cover as best they could. I still had a few hundred soldiers near me, as well as the sudden appearance of over a hundred Knights of Targoth. Rasmussen gave me a salute, his sword with a fresh shine.

"Sargas, be reasonable," one of the other visitors yelled rather loudly. "You and us, together we could conquer Elginia. Increase the influence of your culture and people throughout the Three Galaxies. Help lead us into a golden..."

His words were cut short when his boots burst into flames. I figured that would shut him up. He was lucky I didn't focus my energies on his skull, but this time I did feel a slight decrease of energy for a moment. "How dare you assault me while negotiating?"

Holding up Sargotha, I retorted, "How dare you attack my home unprovoked!" I was getting tired of yelling at this guy in Elginian. Returning to Targothian, I gave the command and the soldiers opened fire on the visitors, shredding two of them before the others leapt out of the way, blades in hand, and one with a pike staff, all ready for a fight.

As soon as the soldiers fired, the three ships hovering overhead released their forces on us, dozens of shuttles descended to the ground, all of them filled with more half-ass Bah'Tene. There were also a few platoons worth of Reptoids, those lizard foot soldiers of the Reticulans. My Knights rushed forward and I ran with them, yelling at a group of soldiers to take Teak to safety.

Together Tymber and I ran towards the fray, blades held high, our brother Knights running with us, soldiers firing at the enemy as soon as their feet hit the ground from the shuttles.

Within a matter of moments, our blades clashed with theirs, several of the attackers lost arms and heads right away.

More shuttles came forth from the ships, this time they held not pseudo-Bah'Tene, but real Fallen and tene ground soldiers. I wasn't about to complain, but I wondered why they didn't have air fighters. Fools probably thought I'd side with them against the Council of Bah'Tene.

Not more than ten feet from me, I saw a young probie Knight get ran through with a pike staff. The kid was no more than a teenager, probably eighteen or nineteen. He died almost instantly.

In a sudden fit of rage, I hurled Sargotha at the enemy that killed him, the pike staff still in his hands as he pulled it from a blood soaked chest. Sargotha found its mark and removed the bastard's skull cap. I quickly retrieved my sword and continued.

The soldiers were fighting well, too. As the battle went on, I saw them in formation, shooting their weapons and covering each other's backs. True brothers-in-arms.

My Knights fought with honor and skill. I saw a real Fallen and Rasmussen fighting one-on-one. As I fought my own fights, I saw Rasmussen claim his first Bah'Tene head.

Tymber had been surrounded by five of the enemy tene troops and two pseudo-Fallen. I went to go help him, but it wasn't necessary. Tymber went into an almost berserker-like rage and hacked and slashed them all until there was nothing but bloody appendages laying all about. He still fought well for an old man.

I found myself face to face with a Fallen. I could sense that he was older than I. He nodded at me and issued the Challenge. I hadn't heard that in years.

I agreed to fight sans power. I could see his eyes were almost glowing a bright red. I figured he was a fire master as I was, yet more experienced and powerful, not likely to weaken quickly from too much use of his gift. He was holding back trying to incinerate me.

We clashed our blades, his sword was more of a broad sword that was to be held with two hands. He held it with one.

A probie had come up behind him, ready to strike. I shouted at him to go, not to interfere or I'd have his head. He looked confused, as a Knight is to always have their brother's back. But, as all probies learn, do not question the Lord Knight.

As the probie turned back into the battle to go fight elsewhere, the Fallen and I continued our own skirmish. Our blades clashed again and again, several times coming too close for comfort to my throat.

Explosions went off all around us as the enemy tene fired rockets into the fight. They didn't seem to care if they hit their own people. One of the Targothian soldiers was hit dead center and I saw as he exploded into nothingness.

I decided it was time to end this fight, so I summoned all of my energy, all of my anger, and I swung my blade again and again at the Fallen, Sargotha almost a blur as I got ever closer to the Fallen's head.

At last, after almost fifty swings, my blade connected, slashing at the Fallen's throat, Sargotha moving through flesh and bone until his head toppled off of his shoulders.

The fighting around me went on. I noticed that the enemy soldiers were firing less. I saw that many of their corpses cluttered the area. My soldiers were superior.

Eventually, some of the enemy soldiers turned away and fled towards their shuttles. Most of them didn't make it as my troops continued to fire, slaughtering many of them as they tried to escape the battle they started.

Some of the shuttles managed to take off, though word had gotten to Central Command and over a hundred air fighters showed up, all of them bearing the Seal of Targoth.

In a brilliant flash, the fighters turned the fleeing shuttles into burning scrap metal.

The enemy soldiers finally surrendered. The pseudo-Fallen Bah'Tene followed suit. My soldiers and knights surrounded them.

"Rasmussen!" I called to my Sergeant-At-Arms. "See to it these prisoners are taken to the House of Kale." Rasmussen smile as he turned to carry out my orders.

I turned away and started looking for Teak. She was standing with a group of Targothian soldiers, safe and in one piece. She waved at me, a radiant smile on her lips. As she started towards me, she suddenly stopped, her face contorted with pain and a confused look. She fell to her knees and then forward, a knife handle from her back. It was almost in slow motion, or at least that was how my brain was recording it.

The group of soldiers didn't have time to respond. A man, he was a Fallen, was unexpectedly in the middle of them, and within seconds their heads were severed by a large axe.

My eyes were fixed on Teak as she lay there, too weak to move. I ordered my Knights and troops to hold their fire and go get doctors for my wife as I moved quickly towards the Fallen. He smiled and laughed and kept repeating "Challenge" over and over.

I was half a foot away from him and I accepted the Challenge, and then I grabbed him by the throat and all of my anger and hate focused into my hand and I burned through the flesh, his skull on fire, his screams muffled by flames protruding from his mouth. I know technically I broke the rules of Challenge, but at that point, I didn't care.

I tossed away his corpse and dropped down and held Teak close to me. Her breathing was growing shallow.

"Not enough time, my love," she said in a hoarse whisper. "We didn't get enough time together."

I told her to stay with me. I didn't want to face a long life without her. I needed her. She was the one good thing that the universe ever gave me.

She smiled weakly and touched my face. She said, "Until the next life, my love." With that, she died in my arms. I was numb. She was right. We didn't have enough time together.

For the first time in many decades and in the sight of God, the universe, and my people, I cried.

Chapter 33

The feeling of aloneness was indescribable. I picked up her body and carried her to a healer that was tending wounded. "Heal her."

"Lord Sargas, I am sorry, but I can't." The doctor turned pale as he said it, afraid that I'd punish him.

"Please, heal her."

Again, he told me he couldn't. She was too far gone. I had to accept that my wife, the love that I had found here in the past, was dead. Moved on to whatever awaits us after we pass from the universe. I laid her down on a cot and knelt by her side. I was there for a long time. I don't know how long.

As I knelt there, I felt someone approach. I turned and saw several of my Knights, one of them holding a body. It took me a second to register the face on the corpse.

It was Tymber.

During the course of the fight, Tymber, one of the greatest warriors I had seen in all my travels, was slain in battle. He had been stabbed through the heart and died instantly.

In the course of a few hours, I had lost my wife and my oldest friend. I wanted to scream, to burn the universe to cinder. That wouldn't honor their memory.

I had to keep in mind, I wasn't the only one who lost today. Many had lost sons and daughters, mothers and fathers, brothers and sisters, friends and neighbors.

In all, that day we lost twelve Knights of Targoth, ninety-nine soldiers, seventeen civilians, and one Lady of Targoth.

I only had two decades with her. Twenty-four years. As her last words said, not enough time.

It was three days later that a mass memorial service was held. I didn't want to make it just about losing Teak. It was about everyone that day.

The service was held at the Citadel. It was transmitted across the entire system. I named each name and said a small prayer to the gods of Targoth and to God Himself, or the Great Power, as is the name in Targothian religion and mythology.

Each nation's leader, the Chancellor, and several leading members of the priesthood all spoke after me, all honoring those lost.

Rasmussen spoke next on behalf of the Knights of Targoth. He spoke eloquently. His words soothed the families of the fallen Knights.

In the day prior to the service, I had instructed a group of military engineers to construct a wall in the courtyard of the Citadel. It would bear the names of those lost that day.

A wall with three sections, it listed the names of each Knight, each soldier, and each civilian. From here on in, any soldier or Knight who died in battle, and any civilian who lost their life in the name of Targoth would be listed here to be honored throughout time.

The evening after the memorial, I sat alone in my chambers. I still felt the guilt of the deaths of my people. I missed having Teak at my side. On any other night, I'd sit in my room and read or meditate and she'd be in there, writing in her journal or planning the classes for the schools. We'd often talk about anything.

Her lack of presence in the room was painful. I knew I'd never forget her and everyone told me that as long as you remember someone, they are never gone.

That just made it more painful. I didn't relish the next several centuries alone in the universe with a piece missing from my soul.

And, I had lost a brother. Tymber. My oldest friend on this planet. He helped me in defeating Qal Dea. He was a big part of forming the K.O.T. Of course I felt the loss of the others, but these two, my wife and my brother, I felt I'd never recover from that.

As I sat staring into nothingness on the wall, there was a knock at my door. It was Rasmussen.

"My lord," he saluted me. I only nodded, not even looking at him.

"Lord Sargas, I can't pretend to know how you're feeling," he told me. "But I know you feel guilt over the deaths that happened. You shouldn't. You showed true Targothian strength by not giving into the request from those bastards to join in their cause." I still didn't look at him, but I was listening. "Those that died, they did so in an unprovoked attack. They fought with honor and bravery. Please, honor their memories and don't give in to despair. That won't honor them at all." I looked at him, my face blank. "Live your life, lead your people, and guide your Knights. If not, then they will have died in vain." He turned to leave.

"Wait," I said to him.

Rasmussen stopped and turned to me. "My lord?"

I told him to sit. I told him how thankful I was to have brothers like him. And, he was right. I wasn't a private citizen who could just sulk and give in to my dark emotions. I had to be there for my people. He assured me no one blamed me for the attack. It wasn't the first time in history that people died in a battle, and wouldn't be the last.

I told him I would be honored if he took the post of First Knight and found a worthy warrior to be the new Sergeant-At-Arms. His bravery and natural leadership would be a benefit to the Knights as we moved on from this horrid event.

He declined, stating that he would be much better for everyone as the Sergeant-At-Arms. He suggested a younger Knight to be made First Knight. Someone who could learn and grow and lead for years and years to come.

Reluctantly, I agreed. I decided in the morning I would look over the files and see all of the possible candidates.

Out of all of the Knights, I found ten that seemed suited to be First Knight. I asked Rasmussen for his council on the matter.

Together we interviewed each one of them, one at a time. By the end of the week, we decided that we would go with the best choice. He was a young Knight named Robb V'Coine. He was a young man, in his early twenties, and hailed from a small farming community in Wheel. He had joined the Knights to see the system and for a sense of brotherhood that he had lacked in his life. Growing up an only child and farming, he had no real friends. The Knights of Targoth was the perfect place for him.

I watched Robb sparing in the training arena. He held his own against four Knights. He had a skill that I had not seen since I first witnessed Tymber in battle so long ago.

I called a halt to the sparing. All the Knights on the floor stopped and saluted me as I approached.

I told Rasmussen to assemble all of the Knights. He put the call out, and within fifteen minutes, every Knight in the area had arrived. I knew it would not be possible to have every single Knight active to come and bear witness, but it wouldn't be necessary.

I told Robb to kneel. He did so. I touched the tip of Sargotha to each of his shoulders and I so named him First Knight of the Knights of Targoth. I told him to rise, and he did, followed by every Knight, including myself, giving salute.

I knew he'd prove himself to be a worthy successor to Tymber. With that business done, I felt I could start to move on myself, and let the memories of my fallen comrades and Targothian citizens rest.

But, in actuality, letting go of Teak proved to be somewhat impossible.

Chapter 34

I set myself about the daily tasks of leading the Knights and attending to affairs of state. Along with the Chancellor, I tended to the needs of the people.

The days were long and difficult. Not the work itself, but the fact I was without my Teak.

I lost track of time as I went about my life as Lord of Targoth.

The Knights of Targoth continued to grow, and within a few decades, I had managed to strike agreements with the leadership of several other worlds outside of the system to allow garrisons of Knights to be stationed.

Many of these worlds were outside of the jurisdiction of the Imperium, and they wanted the K.O.T. to have a presence in hopes of discouraging the Elginians from trying to force them to join their Imperium.

It also helped to dissuade any of the Fallen from attacking. The Knights trained many citizens from those planets into the knighthood, and together with the planetary militaries, the worlds were well protected against outside aggression.

Of course, there were those that tried to attack. The Knights and the military fought back and repelled Fallen, pseudo-Bah'Tene, and even Nosferatus.

There were even a few Nefarium attacks, but with each assault, the Nefarium forces grew less and less. I soon heard reports that they were no longer a part of the alliance of Fallen/Nosferatus. The Nefarium were on their own in the universe. They would get no help from the Reticulans either. They were now considered weak and pitiful. Soon, it seemed, the Nefarium all but disappeared from the universe. Many speculated that they fled the Three Galaxies and sought dominion elsewhere. The more prevailing rumor was that some high-ranking lord of Hell sent them far away into a galaxy that was beyond our technology level to reach. Many of the forces of the Fallen seemed to accuse me personally of running the Nefarium out of the tri-galaxy area.

There was one incident about thirty years after the attack that killed Teak and Tymber. Five Reticulan ships had entered the system, but never made it to Targoth. The capitol ships of the Targothian fleet decimated them before they made it halfway through the solar system.

It was strange as the Reticulans never really had an issue with Targothians before. But, being as they were beings of demonic evil, they would no doubt be good partners to the Fallen.

Not long after the attempted invasion of Reticulan Grays, the chancellor grew ill and retired, prompting an election to replace him. Senator Ozman from Hanch, the fifth planet in the system. Ozman was a good leader, beloved by all of the colonists of Hanch, and would prove to be a good chancellor.

During this entire time, I had been harboring a depression that would come and go. I didn't want the people of Targoth to know of it.

I would still attend functions, and beautiful dignitaries from outside of Targoth would meet and greet me, some of them being blatant about wanting to marry for political unions. I would always politely decline. They probably understood but still didn't seem to care that I still missed my wife. And besides, the idea of political marriages bored me.

I know across many worlds, marriage is treated as a political tool. A way to unite kingdoms and create treaties between warring nations. I always thought that was bullshit.

There were better ways to settle differences than to force a princess to marry a duke, or a senator's son to marry a minister's niece.

I understood that in times past, even on Targoth, that was how things were done. I would not do things that way, however.

Doing the daily routine got me in a rut. Before I knew it, the 130th anniversary of the Festival Assault came upon us. One hundred thirty years since I lost the two most important people in my life. Those thirteen decades had gone by, and I started to notice I looked a bit older. I still looked like I was in my early twenties, but I saw that my face did seem to have aged, even if ever so slightly.

I stood in my chambers before going to the yearly memorial. I noticed on the Earth calendar, it was in the middle of the year 1747.

I went to the memorial, which was now preceding the annual festival. We didn't want to stop doing that. We all agreed that it would be an insult to our fallen and our ancestors to deny the celebration of the past.

I spoke to the crowds, leading all in a prayer to our ancestors to watch over our fallen comrades and to give us the strength to carry on.

Rasmussen, now much older, had declined in coming. He knew he was dying from his old age. Our science couldn't help him. He knew his time was limited and retired from the Knights, moving out into the wilderness of Katu. His last wish was that he was left alone to ponder his life until the end.

I had appointed a new Sergeant-At-Arms, a middle aged Knight named Tona Steward. Tona was a strong and brutal fighter, well known for his wielding of two swords instead of one. He kept his head shaved and his beard trimmed. I knew that together with an older and wiser Robb, the two of them would be more than capable of leading the latest generation of Knights.

The day following the memorial, I had gathered Robb and Tona, and the three of us went to the Chancellor's office. I informed them that I was taking a sabbatical and would be gone for several months.

I assured them it wasn't wanderlust. I had to get away and have some alone time. Away from the politics and daily tasks that I had to do. I told them of my utmost confidence in their ability to lead in my absence.

Of course, if I was needed badly, they had only to contact me and I'd be back straight away. They all told me they understood, and wished me well on my journey and would have everything well in hand until I got back.

I bid them farewell and went back to my chambers to prepare. I loaded the Hunter with some ale, some clothes, and of course, Sargotha. The ship had held up well over the centuries. It was used by Gostal when he was newly made into Bah'Tene, so I knew the ship had some miles on it.

The ship had one new addition. I had a portrait of Teak installed on the control console so I could look at her anytime I wanted.

I wasn't sure where I was headed. I was just going on a trip to nowhere in particular. A chance to go someplace where no one knew what I was, perhaps. A place to get right in the head after all these years. A century plus thirty years later and I still hadn't gotten over losing Teak.

Lifting off, I flew the Hunter into the skies and was soon out of the Targothian system.

I saw space and more space. It was as silent as it could possibly be. Normally I'd have music blasting, but I wanted peace and quiet.

I flew towards nothing and enjoyed the solitude, no one needing me for anything of importance. I felt really peaceful for the first time in one hundred thirty years.

But, I know the universe always has a way of interrupting things.

Chapter 35

Only six days after leaving Targoth and flying in interstellar space, I was fired upon

The blasts were weak. Merely warning shots, I surmised. I didn't show anything on my scanners, but I was still being shot at. I put up the shields and continued looking for the source of the attack.

The Hunter took a direct hit to the engines and the power went out, everything but life support. I knew I could fix it pretty fast if not for the mysterious visitor who wanted me out of commission.

My emergency alarm went off as a ship appeared right in front of me. It was vaguely Reticulan in design, but heavily modified.

Pirates?

Pirates were well known in salvaging derelict ships and using them to kill and loot the space lanes. None have ever attacked the Targothian system, and while I served the Imperium, none of them ever bothered us.

Most of them knew about the Bah'Tene and would not attempt to fight. These pirates must have thought I was just a lone ship out for a cruise. Easy target.

They activated a tractor beam and brought my ship closer to theirs. Soon I was mere inches from their craft, and a door opened in their ship. Five humanoids in dark gray space suits leapt out and began opening up my door. My sensors indicated that they had put a field around my ship so that the air wouldn't rush out when the door opened. They were probably planning on killing anyone they found. Good luck with that, I smiled. I could have them all decapitated in a matter of seconds if I so wished it. But, no. I'd let them take me prisoner and only kill them if I had to. What can I say? I had always wanted to meet a pirate.

Watching through the monitor, I could see them. The five humanoids took off their helmets after they entered my ship. They were all human looking. The scanner indicated they were Terran. Interesting. Earth people in space in 1747? Maybe they were time travelers that got their hands on some alien tech. I'd learn the situation soon enough. They walked along the ship until they reached the cockpit. They saw me and drew their weapons. "Aye! Who the hell are you, mate?" the leader of the group asked me.

"I'm Sargas," I responded. "Who the hell are you?"

Another one of the intruders broke to the front of the group. He was tall, a bit taller than me. He had darker skin than the rest. He looked like he was from the Middle East. "I'm Tylos. This is the crew of Captain Lawson. What is another human doing this far out in space? Are you Illuminati?" Illuminati? What did a secret society on Earth have to do with pirates in deep space? I shook my head.

"Well, in any case, you're coming with us," Tylos said. His face was expressionless. "We'll take you to the Captain. He'll decide your fate." They roughly pulled me from my seat and drug me to their ship. I tried to suppress a smile. This was getting a bit fun, now. So this Captain Lawson would decide my fate? If the bastard tried something, he'd have his own fate sealed. Sargotha was only a summon away, and I could also set his face on fire if I wanted to.

I was led through several corridors, no doubt towards the bridge to meet the captain of the ship. Several other crew members were at their post and they eyed me warily as I was escorted. Some of them weren't human. He had recruited some aliens it seemed. One was an Ephant Min, a race of humanoids with an elephant-like head, complete with trunk and small tusks. His flesh was orange, one of three colors of Ephant Mins. The others were blue and brown, though I had never met a blue before. Another alien crew member was an Alturian male covered in dark gray hair. He looked to be fixing an electrical problem. I saw a few other crew members, all of them human, most likely Terran.

I finally made it into the bridge where I saw a man standing there facing the window. Instead of a helmsman flying the ship, it seemed the Captain did it. It had a wheel like you'd see on an Earth seagoing vessel of that century. He seemed to be dressed like a stereotypical pirate. His long black hair was in a ponytail. I couldn't see his face.

"Sir," Tylos spoke. "We found one person on that small craft. He appears to be human." I smirked slightly. "He is unarmed." I grinned.

Without turning around, the Captain spoke. "Strip him naked, beat him bloody, remove his balls, then send him out of the airlock." The men grabbed me and began dragging me away.

"Wait," I said. "Don't kill me. I know where to find some buried treasure!" They stopped pulling me and the Captain turned around to face me. They all laughed.

The Captain spit on the floor, his face full of a week's worth of stubble. An eye patch covered his left eye. "Fool!

We don't fall for so-called buried treasure tales. Do you take us for storybook pirates?" I considered the irony of that. "It's your ship we want for salvage. As for you, I don't like your face, so I'll have my men cut it off of you before sending you out to die in the cold vacuum." This guy really had a dark side. If I didn't know better, I'd think he was a Fallen.

"Well," I retorted. "You're a fool if you just kill someone you don't know. You don't kill people that you don't know. What if I'm a cop? What if I'm a prince? If you kill someone you don't know, you never know who will come hunting for you."

Captain Lawson considered my words. "Very well, friend. I am Captain Lewis Lawson of the Death's Head. This is my first mate Mr. Tylos. These are my crew. And so, who are you?"

I smoothed back my hair. "Sargas. Lord of Targoth and former member of the Elginian Imperium. Now, you can kill me as you know who I am."

The captain and his first mate exchanged glances. "Sargas? Of Targoth? Elginia? You're a Bah'Tene?" All of his men drew their guns. They looked to be Pax Draxian weapons. Leave it to the Pax Draxians to sell weapons to pirates.

I bowed. "At your service. And now, I have only one word to say to you. Sargotha!"

Chapter 36

I held my hand up and my sword materialized in my grasp. In one smooth motion, I swept my blade across and severed three heads. Mr. Tylos lunged at me and I held out a hand and sent a ball of fire into his chest, blasting its way through and incinerating his heart in an instant. Lawson hit a button on his steering wheel and yelled, "All hands to the bridge! Hostile intruder!"

He pulled his own pistol and blasted at me, but I still had some flame coming from my hand and I melted the bullet in mid-air. Interesting how he still used an old fashioned pistol but his men had laser weaponry. As soon as that thought went through my head he pulled out a laser pistol and opened fire. I dropped to the floor as the bolts flew past me.

Lawson headed out of the door and seconds later, his crew had burst in, firing at me. I had already gotten up and I threw Sargotha at the pirate in the lead, the Ephant Min. My blade severed his skullcap and then embedded itself into the chest of a human behind him. I leapt forward and pulled the sword from his carcass and swung it, severing the Alturian in half down the middle, his two twin-halves falling to either side.

As laser blasts flew past me, I was a whirlwind of movement, Sargotha flying and taking more life and limb with it. I was hit a few times, but I healed almost as quickly as I took damage. The Pax Draxians didn't sell them very high quality weapons. Granted, a Bah'Tene is harder to kill than a regular humanoid, but it could have done worse damage to me. Or maybe at my age, I was just a fast healer. Either way, it didn't matter.

The fight itself only lasted a minute or two. The end result was me standing there, Sargotha in hand and the bodies of twenty-two pirates strewn all around me. Some of them had smoldering corpses. Others were merely without heads. It wasn't over yet. I still had Captain Lawson to contend with.

I could sense that it was only the two of us on the ship now. I bent down and picked up the weapon Tylos had used. It was a rare find. A Pax Draxian made Sienna model pistol. This hasn't been in production for at least half a century. Putting the gun in my belt, I figured I'd put it up in my bedroom back on Targoth. I had a few other weapons I collected over the years mounted on the wall. This would make a fine addition, indeed.

The pirate captain was nearby. Heading into the hall, I searched room by room until I found him near some escape pods. Before he could enter the pod, I threw a fireball at the door, blocking his entry. He turned and drew his gun, but I flung Sargotha at him and severed the pistol in two.

"Captain Lawson, your entire crew is dead now. Give up. I can take you to the House of Kale. You'd probably end up running the place before the day was out. We don't have to end this with your head on the floor."

The captain sat on the floor, propping himself up against the wall. "No, I won't go to any prison. You're going to have to kill me."

"I suppose, if I must," I responded. "But first, I don't suppose you'd mind telling me your tale. You can't let your legacy end without telling it to the man who will kill you."

He stared at me for a minute. Then, shrugging his shoulders, he proceeded to talk. He told me his name was Lewis Lawson, and that he was a pirate in the Mediterranean Sea until he met the Orions and the Illuminati who were in a secret war with one another. He was offered this ship by the Reticulans, allies of the Orions and for almost the last decade, he had been robbing cruise liners and supply ships, killing all on board. No survivors meant no descriptions of the attackers.

He had taken a lover, the wife of an Illuminati man he killed. She had come to the stars with him, but was soon taken by some Pax Draxian traders. They offered him either weapons or his woman. Had told them to keep her and he took the weapons. They had sold her to a group of cannibals on Earth and he felt no remorse. Women were plentiful, especially now that he was flying in the space lanes of the Three Galaxies.

He and his crew had only been in the sector for about a week before they came across my ship and decided to take everything useful on board and scrap the rest into a black hole. He had never met a Bah'Tene before, only heard about them in legends. True, we were pretty damn legendary. He didn't believe anyone could actually conjure fire or energy. Strange as he dealt with Orions who were said to be the creation of Satan's legions beyond the stars and Orions supposedly kept company with demonic entities. Maybe this

Lawson never ran into them. He stopped talking and took a sip of his bottle of rum. I asked him about his eye patch.

He told me he was born without that eye. Strange birth defect. He had a patch of skin there. When he was a small boy, his drunken father had taken a knife and cut the flesh open, thinking he'd reveal a hidden eye. It was just bone underneath. Lawson lifted his patch and I saw a nasty scar and no sign of an eye. Pretty freaky, indeed, but I had seen much stranger stuff in the last few centuries.

I considered his words. He was a violent sociopathic pirate who was prepared to have me beaten naked and tossed into space while still alive. He and his crew were no doubt responsible for a lot of innocent deaths in their pursuit of money. I of course wasn't going to let him go free. I did the only thing that made sense. I lunged toward him and kicked him in the face. While he was holding his bloody nose, I launched the escape pod. Now, the pod bay was empty. I opened the door and threw him inside. I hit the launch button again, but with no pod, when the door opened, it tossed him into the depths of space. The look of fear in his eyes before I hit the button was priceless, well worth the effort. I smiled as his body flew further from the ship. He should have stayed on Earth for his piracy. Space is a completely different kettle of fish.

I went through the ship and explored a bit. I found the cargo bay and it was full of stuff. Currency from fifty different planets. Gems and jewelry. Weapons, both legal and not. Artwork. These guys had tons of loot. I decided to set the distress beacon and hope that whatever passed for law enforcement would come by and collect the loot and give it back to whom it belonged. I didn't want to mess with it personally. Let the locals do it. I felt a lot better about life and I decided it was time to go back to Targoth. This little adventure had given me a good time and reminded me of who I was. But, I took all the alcohol. That stuff was high quality dark rum. My favorite hard liquor.

I made my way back to my ship and set the course for home. I'd keep it on autopilot and get some rest. I accelerated the ship forward and engaged the Light Speed Drive. As soon as I did that, the ship's lights began to flicker on and off and strange beeping came from the LS unit. Around me, the stars faded away and for a second, it seemed as if the universe itself had vanished.

But then, after a moment, everything came back into view and all seemed normal with one exception. The pirate ship was gone. My position was the same but the vessel had vanished. I didn't know what to make of it. I had the sudden urge to get the hell out of there as soon as possible, so I double checked the course, and set my way back to Targoth.

I got closer to the Targoth system and something was off. The usual ships that patrolled the area were gone. The House of Kale was gone, as well. What happened to it? I accelerated to top speed. I needed to get back to the Citadel and find out what happened.

As I landed on the platform next to the Citadel, I noticed something quite disturbing.

The flags bearing the Targothian seal were gone, and in their place was a symbol that looked very similar to the Elginian Imperium.

Chapter 37

Things were certainly starting to go south, and in space, that is quite a feat, as there are no directions in the true sense of the term.

My light speed drive, the good old LSD, had malfunctioned in the oddest possible way, and now, I knew not how, Targoth was a very different world.

I landed the Hunter onto my personal platform where I was greeted by guards. That was common enough. I was always greeted by either Knights or by soldiers, but these guys, they seemed like they didn't belong.

Instead of the leather uniform vest of a Knight of Targoth or the all black fatigues of the members of the military, these troops wore a uniform that was awfully similar to the one I once wore myself while I served under Gostal and the Elginian Imperium.

My instinct was to take Sargotha and start removing heads from shoulders. Somehow, the Imperium had come and conscripted the Targothian forces. No, that couldn't be. I knew that the K.O.T. would have contacted me, or I'd have been otherwise warned.

Yet, the sight before me was plain as day. Elginian troops in my citadel. I picked up my pace and walked towards the six guards that stood at the end of the walkway. Calling Sargotha to my hand, I readied myself for the strike.

All six Elginian troops knelt down before me.

I stayed my hand. They weren't hostile? Since when?

"Rise!" I commanded them in Elginian, and they stood up with a speed that showed more fear than respect. They were right to fear me. I could incinerate them into nothingness.

"My Master, apologies, but we didn't expect you back so soon."

Back so soon? Why would Elginian troops be expecting me back at all? Why were they on my planet?

"What is the meaning of this?" I demanded. They nervously shot side glances at each other. "Well!"

"Forgive us, we're not sure what you mean?" The guard was young, no more than fifteen or sixteen. He held his bearing well for such a young man.

Another guard approached, this one with slightly different markings on his shoulders, and I knew what that meant. I had seen these before in my days fighting for the Imperium. He was a commander.

He bowed. "Master Sargas, it is good to see you again. Is there a problem with these men? Shall I punish one?" He called out for his men to wash the Hunter, except he referred to it as the Soul Hunter. That just sounded weird. He looked strangely for a moment and went to take a closer look at the Seal of Targoth on the ship. "Forgive me, master, but did you lift the ban?" Ban, what ban? I only narrowed my eyes and let them flash red, the flames just hinting at exploding out. He quickly turned and rejoined his men.

"I'll be in my chambers," was all I said as I stalked off.

The Citadel itself was the same on the outside, but instead of the Seal, everywhere were banners with the damn Elginian Imperium's flag. A red upside down star in a black circle. But that star was upside down. It should have been right side up. Did they change it or did some idiot hang the Elginian flag wrong?

At least it wasn't Gostal's skull or the face of Qal Dea with that insane glint in his eye.

I walked slowly down the corridor leading to the throne room, noticing people averted their eyes from me. What the hell happened while I was away?

My curiosity turned to confusion as I came to the throne room and saw a giant portrait of myself hanging above the throne, except in it, I had hair to my shoulders and a goatee.

I believe the words I uttered then were in my native Terran tongue.

"What the fuck?"

Chapter 38

My words did elicit some strange looks from the people around me. They never really heard me swear in my old language. I needed to get someplace private to think. Still carrying Sargotha in my hand, I headed for my bedroom.

My room hadn't changed too much, at least. I had only one bookshelf, though, for some reason.

Deciding to check it out, I saw a lot of history books of both Targoth and of the Elginian Imperium, though with that new symbol instead of the one I had known in my earlier decades. And what was even more peculiar was that none of these books were in Targothian. Everything was in Elginian.

I tossed Sargotha on the bed and sat down in the big comfy chair next to the bookshelf. These history books were just plain wrong.

I started reading 'History of the Royal Targothian House' and it had some new information I don't recall knowing before.

First off, there was no mention at all about Lorancano dying at the hand of Dea. It started with Henra Haron as the Lord of Targoth a full five centuries before Lorancano's time. He was an ancestor of mine from further back. I remember learning about that when I studied my family history.

How could the writer of this history book gloss over the sacrifice of Lorancano? His death allowed his son Sargas, from who I took my name, to escape to Earth with tens of thousands of Targothian refugees.

I had been on Targoth for centuries, and I had led them fair and just. How could they just up and turn their backs on their own history?

I wanted to go out and start throwing fireballs at everyone, telling them to snap out of their dream state. It had to be some sort of mind control. Drugs. Evil alien clones of the entire population of Targoth. Maybe I was hit in the head and imagining all of this.

No, I knew those ideas were ridiculous. The Targothian people wouldn't just toss away all that has transpired since I first arrived.

There were many on this planet like my old friend Tymber. The old man had died a warrior's death in a cowardly attack at our favorite festival. God, it seemed like only yesterday, even after all this time.

Thoughts of Teak came flooding to me, too. Her portrait was supposed to be all over the place in this citadel, and a wedding picture was supposed to be hanging in this very room.

I didn't know why it wasn't hanging in its rightful place.

Even my collection of weapons was missing from the wall.

Maybe there was something in one of these insipid books. The so-called history of Targoth.

I scoured the books for the next three or four hours. No mention of the wife of Sargas in any of them.

Sargas. It hit me. I needed to see what these books said about me. I felt like an answer would lay there.

I found 'Lineage of Targoth'. That book read like a laundry list of names. It went back to the times of legend when a group of the world's leaders got together and decided to appoint the wisest as the Lord of Targoth to lead the people in a united peace. My ancestor Bradalay, king of Ansaka, was chosen, and since that time, it was passed down from father to son, all the way down to Henra Haron, and from there to Lorancano and his son, Sargas.

The book really offered no help.

I found another book that looked interesting. An astronomy book of the Targothian system. It looked like one that you gave to schoolchildren. Teak loved to teach children.

All the planets were listed, but none of the colonies were listed alongside them. Shouldn't they be teaching that there are dozens and dozens of colonies throughout the system?

Looking further, I read something disturbing. Each of the other planets in the system were uninhabitable and would never be again. All were lifeless rocks in space.

No, that wasn't right, not at all. I couldn't believe what I was reading.

On a hunch, I grabbed another history book. It told of the revolt that Lorancano led that ended with his execution.

To further punish the Targothian people for their insolence, powerful nuclear devices were deployed, rendering every other planet uninhabitable. All of the indigenous life they held, blinked out of existence forever. They might not have been sentient, but it was still tragic.

I threw that book into the wall, too. These books, such nonsense. I wanted to find the idiots that penned those lies. It was almost as if history was just changed overnight. Who would do that? Who would dare print that falsehood?

At times, even with my Bah'Tene enhanced mental capabilities, my brain can be slow on the uptake. Every once in a while, I can put two and two together and come up with four.

The malfunction with my light speed drive. The Elginian uniforms on my guards. No Seal of Targoth flying high and proud. These peculiar books in my chambers.

My LS drive had managed to propel me into an alternate reality.

Chapter 39

The thought of being in a parallel universe, an alternate reality, seemed impossible, even to me. I'd fought with undead, monsters, and even my own pseudo-immortal kind, but the concept an alternate reality was unheard of. I knew other dimensions existed, but they were the realms of beings unlike anything in the physical plane.

But, apparently, I had somehow found my way into one. I couldn't even begin to understand how it was possible, but I knew that my LS drive was the cause.

By some fluke of science, that thing had flung me into this universe. A universe where my beloved planet was under Elginian control.

My namesake ancestor had never even left Targoth with any refugees. He died here with his father Lorancano.

I started to think about the way the guards reacted to me when I landed. They were afraid of me. I expected that behavior in my enemies, but not my own people. Not from a Targothian, or even from a Targoth-born Elginian. What manner of man was I in this place?

There was little help from those insipid books in the way of my own history in this world. Two hundred fifty years as a Bah'Tene and I once again felt the way I did two and a half centuries ago when I was first brought into the past.

Oh, how long ago that seemed now. My time fighting alongside Gostal felt like it was in another life altogether. The memories even seemed like I watched them through someone else's eyes. But, that happens when you get older.

Memories, no matter how vivid, can seem like they're somehow not real.

With no help from my personal library, I decided to venture out into the citadel and see what I could learn from the people. I'd like to call them my people, but I knew that wasn't the case. Their loyalties were with another version of me, one that was completely not like me at all. What was up with the goatee and the hippie hair?

The citadel itself hadn't changed in structure. Every room I went to, it served pretty much the same function as it did in my home. Armory, guard's quarters, kitchens, dining hall. Where my private meeting area for K.O.T. business should have been instead was a supply closet. Now, that just seemed out of place. That room was huge, almost fifty feet by fifty feet. On its walls should have been portraits of the great leaders of the past.

Instead it held brooms and cleaning supplies. This version of me was an idiot with apparently no concept of Targothian culture. He was a true Elginian, no doubt.

Maybe in this reality Gostal managed to convert him into a Fallen. Now, that was terrifying. Sargas, Lord of Targoth and Lord Knight of the K.O.T. a Fallen Bah'Tene? My own temper was horrendous at times, and I was one of the good guys. A truly villain version of myself, that made my blood run cold.

I had to find out more. What had this version of Sargas done to my planet? He must have been tyrannical in order to illicit fear from the populace. Some people were tense around me, sure, but they knew I'd never turn into a dictator and wipe out families and the like.

But, even heavier on my mind was how was I going to get out of here to my own world?

I figured I'd have to just experiment with the LS drive and hopefully find a way to get back home.

But, for the time being, nothing I could do about it but explore the citadel and observe the people.

Again people would avert their eyes. The guards would drop down and kneel before me. It was unsettling to see Elginian armor on my guards. Even more wrong was the lack of the Seal of Targoth anywhere. That had been the unifying symbol of the planet since the old days.

Bad enough that Dea had taken it from the people but I managed to bring it back. Here, it seems like it was still cast away in favor of another group of oppressors. Well, even in my own world, the Bah'Tene had just let Dea do his thing and never stepped in to help Targoth. I guess this place shouldn't be any different.

A thought had just occurred to me as I wandered through the citadel. No one spoke Targothian. Everything was in Elginian, just like the books in my room.

A commotion from down the hallway caught my attention and I hurried to see what it was, calling Sargotha to my side. Civilians were running away from the source, only to see me and become even more scared.

I came upon a group of guards in a circle. One that I recognized as a lead guard was severely beating one of his men.

"What's the meaning of this?" I demanded. The lead guard immediately stopped and knelt down, as did all who were standing around watching.

I wasn't having it. I stalked up to the lead guard and told him to get on his feet. "Again, what is the meaning of this? What do you think you're doing?"

The lead guard was out of breath. "My master, this man has broken the regulations code of the Royal Guardians."

I asked him to which code he was referring to.

"His uniform is out of regulation. He has failed to properly install his rank insignia onto his shoulder. He must be punished."

I had heard some messed up stuff in over two hundred years of life. I thought maybe he broke some ethics code at least. Perhaps tried to force a girl into doing something or stealing money from the treasury. But this? A uniform regulation violation. That was, well, I had no words for it.

"Help that man up, now." Without hesitation, the other guards scrambled to help up their fellow guard. "Get him to the doctors immediately."

The lead guard began to protest. "My master, I was to understand you gave me complete authority to..." his words were cut short when I hit him across the jaw with Sargotha. It wasn't meant to cut him, though it did draw blood from his jaw and a tooth came out.

I called several other guards over and ordered them to arrest this one and put him into the holding area. They seemed confused at first, but only for a few seconds. They hurriedly cuffed the lead guard and dragged him off.

Of all the crap I've heard in my time as a Bah'Tene, this was some of the most ludicrously vile I ever came across.

And to think that in this universe I actually promote behavior like that among the ranks. This place needed the Knights more than anyplace I'd been before.

Before I left this parallel world, I'd be making some changes to it. After all, what if I didn't get to go? I'd be stuck here, and I wasn't about to let Targothians treat one another like this, even if they weren't "my" Targothians.

Chapter 40

I called in the leadership of the planet. I had to act the part of a tyrant, so I did. I told them I was testing their loyalty and knowledge of history.

From asking the generals and the political leaders questions about the Elginian and the Targothian citizens, I came across something that brought out a lot of anger in me.

Not only did the K.O.T. not exist here, but the military itself was comprised almost entirely of Elginians and tene from other member planets. Almost no Targothians were serving.

It appeared that the Elginians like to keep a tight hold on this planet. Hundreds of garrisons were scattered throughout the planet, and they'd regularly detain citizens for questioning. It helped instill the fear and maintain control over the populace.

I dismissed the leaders and told them to get back to their jobs. Everyone seemed confused by my actions, but they were too afraid of me to question it. That could play to my advantage, unless someone notified the folks back on Elginia.

If I wanted to keep them in the dark, I'd have to act more like the asshole they thought I was.

But, how was I supposed to do that. While, true, I could make the rulers of Northern and Southern Abnu sweat bullets, I only did that because I wanted them to see things my way.

But, to treat the citizens as such. What monster was their Sargas?

A horrid thought went through my mind at that moment. What if I had that tyranny inside of me now? Something happened in this universe to their Sargas to turn him into what he was.

If something similar had happened to me, then I could have been far worse than Dea and Gostal combined.

Dea and Gostal. I wondered if those two were still alive here. Out there in space somewhere, secretly recruiting Bah'Tene and tene alike to join the Fallen. Dea, likely not. If he didn't have that meteor to enhance his lifespan, he'd have dusted by now. Gostal. That was a possibility. Gostal may have been out recruiting Fallen all throughout the Three Galaxies.

Had their Sargas helped them with that?

I went outside and stared at the spot where there should have been the Wall. Tymber should have been listed first on that wall.

I wondered what happened to my old friend in this place. I shuddered to think that their Sargas killed him or that he was a minion of the Fallen, out there in the Three Galaxies, fighting alongside someone like Gostal.

I preferred to think that he somehow managed to avoid any harm and had his family. I hoped he had grown old and died in his sleep, peacefully and loved by his children.

Teak. Was she here in this world? She may have married another and had a family, too. I hated to think that she had also been corrupted by the Fallen here. Maybe the other

Sargas took a liking to her, and murdered her when she rejected him.

I felt like I lost them both again, and I hadn't even met their alternate versions yet, if they even existed, that is.

Times like that, I wanted to go into the Council Chambers of the Bah'Tene and incinerate every single one of them for bringing me into the past. I wanted Sargotha to take off their heads and violently send them into whatever awaited them in the afterlife.

But, those feelings of hatred and anger wouldn't do any good without control and focus. Those feelings combined with the discipline of two hundred years of battle served me well.

Ok, to be honest, I didn't fight for two hundred years. A lot of my time on Targoth was day to day boring business as usual.

After bloody battles and run-ins with the undead forces of evil, I enjoyed getting reports of labor disputes and requests to be present at a debate.

Sometimes, boring was divine.

That would all have to wait until I fixed this place up and got home.

Yes, I would get home again. By hook or by crook, hell or high water, by any means fair and unfair, I would find my way back to my own universe.

But, I felt I owed it to the people of this Targoth to help them. Even though I wasn't the same Sargas as they were used to, I felt responsible in an obscure way and wanted to set them on a better path.

This place needed three things. It needed the Knights of Targoth in place to protect the citizens. It needed zero influence by the Elginians. And, most importantly, it needed its own rat bastard version of Sargas to go on a one-way trip into oblivion.

Chapter 41

I'd have to go out and start meeting some of the people. Slowly work on them trusting me. They perceive Sargas as a cruel master who must be obeyed at all costs. I needed them to know I wasn't that person. I could help them make Targoth a better place, but to do that, I had to earn their respect and loyalty.

I decided to take a trip to the closest garrison. There was one in Ansaka, not more than a mile from the citadel.

I was about to go to the Hunter when several maintenance personnel began to work on the ship. They apologized for interrupting my flight, clearly fearful that I would kill them. I assured them I didn't need the ship that badly and asked if there was any other transport.

Confused looks came from their eyes, but one of them did speak up. He told me I had several other vehicles in the bay ready to go. I thanked them and left. I could hear as I walked away that they were shocked that I didn't kill them for their failure to have the ship ready at a moment's notice.

Again, what sort of bastard was I in this reality?

I went over to a large building that had to be the bay they spoke of. I saw several other craft in there, all of them bearing that idiotic symbol that infested my citadel. I longingly looked over at the Hunter. If they removed the Seal of Targoth I might just have to sever some heads.

I had to decide which craft to take. All of these ships seemed, I don't know, bland. They were mostly shuttle craft, though several different designs.

I then saw what I needed. Something that almost made this venture into an alternate universe worthwhile.

It was a motorcycle, not unlike the one I rode many decades ago when I liberated Targoth from Qal Dea. A gift from Tymber.

This might even be the same bike, I wasn't sure. Might not have lasted all those years, but I did have incredible mechanics working for me. They kept the Hunter working like a new ship, and that thing was old when I inherited it from Gostal.

I took a few moments to ogle the bike. It was worth the time. It looked so much like a Harley. Handle bars were ape hangers, though. If this was my original bike, then it got modified. All black. Even in this reality, I preferred my vehicles in darker shades.

I suddenly remembered I was wearing the K.O.T. vest still. Good. It would do the people of Targoth a great benefit to see me bearing the original seal. Hopefully it would help to get them on my side and we could eventually push out the Elginians.

Scary proposition, though. I doubted this Targoth would be strong enough to hold off the entire Elginian fleet and the Bah'Tene as well.

Things to worry about later. I figured I'd burn that bridge when I came to it. I started up the bike and savored the rumble of the engine.

The trip to the garrison of Ansaka was actually enjoyable. The day was sunny, yet cool. I loved Ansaka. Always a cooler temperature than the rest of the planet. And the Central

Valley, that was my favorite. Always like an autumn evening down there.

I got to the garrison, and soldiers and civilian alike were scattering to greet me. It was nice knowing that the Elginian troops were as afraid of me as my own people.

The garrison commander came and knelt before me. I told him to get on his feet and stop embarrassing himself.

I called the garrison together and spoke to them of change. I told them that a new time was coming to Targoth, and everyone must choose between Targoth and the Imperium of Elginia.

They were clearly disturbed by my words. They probably thought it was a loyalty test.

"I can assure you, this is no test," I spoke as soothingly as I could.

"My master," the commander spoke up. "But, the glory of the Imperium is all."

I laughed at that. "Seriously? The Elginians are pompous, arrogant scum. Present company excluded, of course." I nodded towards the Elginian troops. "I mean merely the Bah'Tene power elite and the Emperor."

They were all gawking at me now, afraid to speak up for fear I may strike them down for failing to show proper loyalty to the Imperium. "I can assure you that I am not the same man you've known all these years. And I..."

My words were interrupted by a loud explosion.

We all ran outside of the meeting hall and saw the smoke coming from the Central Valley.

"Master, it was the rebels. They blew up the fuel depot down there. Not to worry, my master. Soldiers are looking for them now." Rebels? That was who I needed to get in contact with.

"Answer me this, Commander. Why hasn't the Council of Bah'Tene sent more help?"

"My master," the Commander answered me with fear in his eyes. "You know that we have only the limited resources that they granted us. No more troops are to be sent to Targoth. The High Command refused last time you requested help in hunting the rebels."

So, they really are as lazy and unwilling to intervene as they were back home. Well, that is for the best. They didn't help me when I liberated Targoth, but I was glad they didn't help this world's me when I requested help in further strangling the people of the land.

High Command. I supposed in this universe, they are called the High Command instead of the Council. Subtle change, but didn't make them any better people.

"Everyone listen up!" At my words, they all stopped and listened. "We need to get down there with a medical team. Look for any injured. Don't worry about hunting down the rebels at this time." That caused seriously perplexed looks. They must have expected me to order the Central Valley burned down.

A loud popping sound in the distance hit my ears as I felt an explosion of pain in my chest.

I just got shot by a faraway sniper.

Chapter 42

Luckily, the bullet only hurt. Extremely, but pain passes. The wound healed almost as quickly as it had formed. Surely they knew a bullet wouldn't kill a Bah'Tene. Rebels being ever defiant. Now those are the Targothians of this universe that I needed to find.

Many of the soldiers came to my aide. "Master, are you injured?" Of course I wasn't, not really.

"I'm fine. Do you know who shot me?" I was desperate to find out who. If anyone had been that brave to open fire on me, then that was the person I needed to talk to about contacting the rebels.

"Yes, master. One of the rebels. We're searching them out now."

It took several hours, but the soldiers finally found the shooter. A young man with thick, unkempt black hair. Maybe he was in his late teens. He was dressed as a peasant, which I had gotten rid of in my own Targoth. All of the peasants were integrated into the work force of the system and the shelters for the poor were always keeping them fed and clothed. I hadn't seen anyone like that so destitute in ages.

The most interesting aspect of this young man was that he had a black armband on his left bicep. It had the Seal of Targoth on it. Yes, these were the kind of people I needed to find.

I ordered them to bring him before me. One of the soldiers, a lieutenant by the look of the Elginian insignia, brought him over and rammed the butt of his rifle into the kid's back, forcing him to his knees.

I reached out and grabbed the lieutenant by the collar and threw him rather harshly to the ground. I warned him against further abuse of the prisoner. Very shakily he acknowledged my order.

I asked the kid what his name was. He didn't answer. I liked him even more. I wanted to ask where his rebel compatriots were, but even if he did answer, I didn't want the Elginians to find them.

"Very well," I continued. "Why did you shoot me? Surely you know who I am."

The kid looked me right in the eye after that. "You're the piece of Elginian loving scum that has ruined the lives of my people!" Ah, his words were Targothian. I was beginning to think I'd never hear anyone speak that here.

I answered in Targothian. "Why do you think I'm a lover of the Elginians? Maybe you should take me alone to your friends and we can talk. I can guarantee safe passage. The Elginians wouldn't be coming with us." The soldiers were confused, as I suspected none of them spoke Targothian at all. I got the feeling they didn't teach a secondary language here like back home when I took Spanish for three years.

For this young man to know the language of the land, there must be some true Targothians in the underground waiting for the right time to topple their Sargas from power. Now that I was here, I was going to help them get liberated, but I'd have to be discrete.

He didn't believe my words, I could tell. Just like the Elginian troops, he probably thought I was testing him for a response.

"Very well," I said in the most calming tone I could muster before I switched back to Elginian. "Take this prisoner to the stockade. And he is to remain unharmed, is that understood?"

The troops nodded and left with the young sniper. I'd have to go down there and talk to him later on tonight. I didn't want to risk anyone overhearing me talking to him in Targothian.

If these guys were beginning to suspect something about me, I didn't want to give them a reason to strike. After all, a Bah'Tene isn't invulnerable. Likely one of them knew how to take me out.

"Wait!" I called out. Before they took him down there, I had to know one more thing, so I'd ask in Elginian just to make sure that the guards would understand the question and hopefully the answer. "Why did you shoot me with a normal bullet? You didn't think that would kill me."

The kid smiled and looked me dead in the eye again and I was happy that he answered in Elginian. "Because, Sargas. We wanted you to know that we're not afraid to strike at the Master of Targoth. We wanted you to not get hurt, only know that we're able to get to you anywhere. Everywhere." His eyes opened wide and he let out a primal scream and shouted in Targothian. "We are the true Targothian people and we will not bow to Elginian scum like you anymore!"

It was official. This kid was my favorite person in this alternate reality. Smiling, I ordered him taken immediately to his cell, again emphasizing he wasn't to be harmed.

I was also happy that he didn't refer to his friends as the Targothian Liberation Front or the Free People of Targoth, or something like that. He put it as simply and properly as one could.

We are the true Targothian people.

Chapter 43

Later that night I waited until about an hour until the midnight shift change. I figured that the guards would be tired and less likely to question my going down to the holding area, though, truth be told, they were already very afraid of me and wouldn't question much anyway.

I soon found myself standing in the corridor that lead to the young prisoner's cell. Several guards were standing at their posts. I knew it wouldn't be a problem to deal with.

They knelt down immediately upon my arrival. I told them in a rather harsh voice to rise and get out of there. I wanted to speak to the prisoner alone. I knew this was the Sargas they were used to dealing with.

The senior guard, or I assumed he was because I recognized his Elginian military rank on his collar, actually asked me if I needed a guard for my own protection. Normally, I'd have probably smiled and declined. My own Knights and soldiers would have offered, of course, but out of loyalty. This guy was afraid.

I decided the only way to convince him was to act like the tyrant they believed me to be, so I pulled Sargotha from my side and held it to his throat, slicing deep enough to draw blood but not actually hurt him. "Go!" I growled the word at him and for a moment, I was even afraid of myself.

"As you wish, my master," he said, very professionally, too, as he quickly walked away, followed by his comrades.

I stood before the young man in the cell. He was propped up on the floor, against the wall, dozing off, but he quickly awakened.

He was so young. Only a teenager, but his look of defiance and pride was equal to that of a man twice his age. One who had loss and pain. He was very much like the Targothians I met when I first came to the planet so long ago.

I imagined he was how Tymber was as a kid, before he was recruited into Dea's imperial guard. "Master Sargas," he said, with a lot of sarcasm and distain on the word 'master'. I liked this kid a lot.

"Please, tell me your name," I responded. "I can't just call you young man, now can I?"

He shook his head, almost smiling. "Very well. I'm Artoro. That is all the information about my name I'm giving you." I nodded. At least I knew what to call the little skeezicks. "But, I can't help but ask, Sargas. Why are you speaking to me in Targothian? What about the ban on the language?" Again with a ban. In this world I guess I had banned anything relating to Targothian heritage. Well now that I'm different than the man they're used to, things would be changing. I just wasn't sure how to go about it quite yet. If only I had the resources that I was used to back on my own Targoth.

"No, no ban," I told him. "No ban anymore. Things will be different." He asked what I meant, and I told him that the Targoth of old would once again reign on this planet. He was dubious, and I couldn't blame him. "Let's just say that there's a new Sargas in town. One that believes in the

Targothian people and isn't a big lover of the Elginian Imperium."

"Well, somehow, I believe you, but I can't explain why," he said thoughtfully. "You have a different vibe about you. But I still can't trust you. Even if you're serious, I know your soldiers won't let you do anything against the Imperium."

That was true, but if I could rally the people, then we could do it. I told him that I was in fact a different Sargas, and that I was from a reality where Targoth was a free and flourishing society.

I could tell he wanted to believe, but it was a fantastic story, very farfetched. The concept of a parallel universe has been theorized all over the Three Galaxies, and back on Earth in my time many books were written on the subject, both fiction and scientific theory. But, no one has ever discovered them.

I told him about how I liberated my Targoth from Qal Dea and set up the Knights of Targoth. How I have hunted the undead and other forces of evil. He told me that he had heard legends of the nosferatus, but they've never been to Targoth. People didn't believe they existed. Most likely, the Bah'Tene of this universe kept them away.

That suited me fine. That was one less headache to deal with here. It must have been something in my voice or my eyes, but he came to accept that I was telling the truth.

I asked him to explain his life and people to me. I wanted to learn about the resistance. He was hesitant, but eventually gave in and told me about his people, the True Targothians.

For the next several hours, he explained to me that there has been pocket resistance groups for decades. Only recently had they joined forces. They had a strong desire to make Targoth like it was in the days of old, when Bradalay was the ruler of the planet. At least that was something both versions of Targoth had in common.

The True Targothians preferred to only speak the native language of the world. They only spoke Elginian when out in public. They were united, but still spread out.

They caused disruptions in military operations and acts of vandalism and sabotage. They acted out as often as possible, knowing that the Elginians would receive no reinforcements from their own Imperium. Their Master Sargas didn't want to appear weak to his own masters.

Maybe it was the Universe itself that caused that malfunction in my LS Drive and brought me here. Here as their new Sargas I could help them.

I had to hand it to the True Targothians. They were brave, defiant, and extremely willful. They faced grave danger from the occupying Elginians.

But, as the Targothians on my own world say, it is better to die fighting than live in servitude. Unfortunately, as on my own version of Targoth, these people have been under tyranny so long, they accepted it as a fact of life.

I wasn't about to let these people suffer further. I would do what I had to and make contact with the True Targothians. They were the only thing standing in the way of a free world and continued slavery under a dictator.

I explained to him that I was going to break him out of jail. He had a light in his eyes at my words. He believed what I said, despite his brain telling him that it was a preposterous story. He could tell that I was a true-blooded Targothian as he was.

I held Sargotha in my hands and shut my eyes. Focusing all of my strength and emotion into my arms, I swung the sword across the lock on the cell door, shattering it into thousands of metallic shards.

Sliding the door open, Artoro leapt forth and stood at my side. I asked him one final question before we made our way out. I asked him if the True Targothians were worried about the Elginians wiping out every citizen of the planet.

"If Targoth is wiped out by genocide, we'll have died fighting like our ancestors did. Our souls will dine with the gods of old. We will have died as Targothians and not as slaves."

And with that, I saluted him as my knights saluted one another. He recognized the gesture and saluted back. And then we were off.

The guards were true to the order I gave them and were nowhere in sight. Even the guards that were further up the corridor were gone. Did I scare that many away?

With Artoro behind me, we quietly crept through the halls of the stockade. I was amazed at how many cells were empty. I supposed as much as they arbitrarily executed people, the jail was unused.

I figured we were in the clear. If anyone questioned why I had the prisoner out, I'd simply say that I was taking him for torture. That was something that they were used to hearing.

At the door of the stockade, I knew we were home free. Soon we'd be in the Hunter and getting to the True Targothians in the area.

I opened the door and for a split second thought that there was a mirror in front of me. But my clothing was different. Why was I wearing an Elginian uniform and not the K.O.T. vest I was certain I was just wearing when I came down here? And why was my hair longer?

"So it's true," my reflection said to me. "You are wearing forbidden symbols."

This was no reflection. I was looking at a doppelganger in front of me.

Chapter 44

I suppose it was my own misunderstanding of parallel universes that led to this. I could have been more careful.

I was assuming this whole time that when I came to this alternate reality, that I took the place of the Sargas of this world. By jumping into this world, I became their Sargas. I never suspected that the Sargas of this universe was still here.

But, it was better than him being in my own world instead. I could only imagine what my Knights would have thought of this guy.

"And, just where do you think you're going with my prisoner?" He sounded just like me, but with an Elginian accent when he spoke Elginian. It was as if he was raised there. Maybe in this reality I, or rather, he, was.

"I take it you know who I am," I said sarcastically.

"Yes, a dead man," he growled at me. I wondered if this was considered talking to myself. He called out for his guards, and they came pouring into the room. Dozens of them.

"When I arrived from my council meeting on Elginia, I was told that they didn't know I left. After beheading the guard who spoke that way to me, another begged for his life, stating that I had already arrived back early a day ago. I killed him, but several other guards made the same comments. One of them showed me the shuttle I arrived in with that disgusting Targothian symbol on it. I figured that it was a test by my Elginian masters. Apparently it was something else.

I called Sargotha to my hand and held it out, pointing the blade at the other Sargas. He did the same, but his sword was no Sargotha. It was an Elginian issued sword that most of the Bah'Tene carry. Very similar to the one I used back in my days serving with Gostal.

"Where did you get that?" He glared at me. "I had that damn thing launched into a star to be forever destroyed."

"I took it from the insane Bah'Tene that stole it from Lorancano. Why would you want to destroy a great symbol of Targothian leadership?"

He called out for his guards to attack. "These people don't need any hope from the ridiculous relics of the past. They must learn that Elginian rule is absolute."

The guards closed in. Artoro was without a weapon, but he held his fists up as if ready to brawl. I handed him my sword. He wouldn't be able to do the things with Sargotha that I could, but he could use it to defend himself. I had a different weapon at my disposal.

"But then you are weaponless," he said as I put Sargotha into his hand. I told him to let me worry about that. The guards closed in.

I held up my hand and the temperature went up slightly. I'm sure they noticed it but still they advanced, not seeming to understand.

They were mere feet from Artoro and myself now. They were caught off guard as balls of fire engulfed them as they advanced. Their screams filled the halls as they fell to the ground, trying in vain to roll around and put out the fires that were inside of their armor.

"Damn fire master!" The other Sargas was very upset. I figured he never gained this ability when he took the Test. Good. He'd be dangerous enough as is.

Artoro tossed Sargotha back to me as he picked up a sword from a fallen guard. More guards piled in and he fought them brilliantly. He was trained by a good teacher.

I focused my attention on the other me. I rushed at him and our swords clashed. We traded strikes back and forth. I managed to throw a fireball at him, hitting him in the chest and knocking him back into the wall.

I took that opportunity to aid Artoro. I flung Sargotha at a guard who was about to take the kid's head off with an axe. My sword pierced the guard's temple and pinned him to the wall. Artoro looked at me wide-eyed for a second before returning to the fight. There were only five of them left out of the original twelve. The kid was good.

The other me had regained his footing and was about to run me through. I managed to summon Sargotha to my hand and block the strike, pushing my attacker's blade up and inadvertently stabbing another Elginian guard in the back of the neck. You might think that was skill, but it was just dumb luck.

Ten more guards came in to join their comrades in the fight. I launched a barrage of fireballs at them, hitting several and causing the others to dive for cover. They've never dealt with someone with this ability, I could tell. The fear they emitted was powerful enough that a durmivol could probably smell it from three systems over. My energy drained a bit but regenerated almost immediately after I stopped tossing the flames at them.

I took a quick look over at Artoro and he had managed to get his hands on a second sword and was duel wielding them. I turned to my own adversary just as Artoro had scissored off the head of another guard. That kid was one brutal fighter. If I ever made it back to my own world, I'd have loved to take him with me to make into a Knight of Targoth.

The other me hit a button on his sword handle, and the tip of the sword fired outward, hitting me in the throat. It healed quickly and just as fast, from within the sword another tip popped out. That sword was no mere Elginian Bah'Tene weapon. I was actually impressed.

More men came into the mix, but these weren't guards of the stockade. They were Elginian soldiers armed with rifles. They opened fire as I jumped out of the way, though I was hit by several bullets in my leg and lower back.

It did hurt immensely, but I healed up fast and my anger and impatience with the fight began to boil.

I rained some fire down on the soldiers and many of them cried out as their uniforms burst into flame. I almost felt bad as one poor young soldier's hair was on fire and he ran screaming into the line of fire from his fellow warriors. A little friendly fire put him out of his misery.

Soon I was surrounded as was Artoro. It was harder and harder to fight everyone off, and moments later, I am not sure how long, I blacked out as I was probably hit from behind by the butt of a rifle or some sort of other blunt object. Even a Bah'Tene can be knocked out, but it is hard to achieve. I must have been out of energy from the fight.

I couldn't have been out for long, as like other injuries, I'd recover fast from a knockout. But it was long enough to toss me into a cell down in the stockade.

I looked and I saw the other me and many of his soldiers standing outside my cell, the other Sargas laughing at me. One of the guards was holding my sword and admiring it. I summoned Sargotha to my hand, and I saw the look of shock on his face as the sword vanished and was somehow in the cell with me. I swung out and struck at the bars, only to receive an electric shock.

"Go ahead and try to break out. The bars have been energized. It tends to strengthen them. And as for your little fireballs, I can order this room flooded with explosive fuel. You'll only burn yourself to death, and we both know that a Bah'Tene can only handle so much damage in a short amount of time. You'd never survive a massive fire in that confined space."

I leaned up against the wall and propped Sargotha next to me. "So, what's the plan? Leave me in here as a prisoner until the Bah'Tene can come get me?"

The other me shook his head. "No, I'm not even going to mention you to them. I don't need them down here interfering with my world. You can just stay down here and rot. Maybe you'll luck out and starve to death before you dust. Never heard of a Bah'Tene dying of starvation. Could be interesting." Laughing, he took a sword and stuck it into the ground a few feet from my cell. "I do have a companion to keep you company."

One of the soldiers brought in a bag from the other room. Reaching in, he pulled out the severed head of Artoro and shoved it hard into the sword handle, now acting as a pike to hold up the kid's head.

Chapter 45

I became angrier than I had felt in a long time. Not since I lost my beloved Teak and my brother-at-arms Tymber. I quickly hurled a fireball at the soldier who planted Artoro's head, incinerating him into a husk in mere seconds.

Laughing, the other Sargas nodded. "Well, I owe you that one, I suppose." He ordered his men out of the room. "I want to ask you some things, and I don't want the men to overhear." He switched to Targothian. "Just where did you come from?"

I don't know why I felt obliged to answer. I didn't feel threatened or coerced. I was full of rage over the senseless murder of the young Artoro. But, I somehow knew that this other version of me wouldn't lie to me and I felt like I shouldn't lie to him.

I sat on the floor against the wall and let out a deep breath. "Well, where to begin?"

I didn't tell him everything, just a few of the basics. About being brought from 1998 to 1498 and taken to Elginia. How I went through the Test. Fighting alongside Gostal for a decade before realizing he was a Fallen and issuing the Challenge. About how I was told Targoth was gone but eventually found out that I was deceived and when I got there, I had to liberate it from Qal Dea. He'd heard the name Dea before, but not Gostal. Perhaps Gostal never became a Bah'Tene in this universe or maybe he was never born. I didn't tell him about Teak. If she existed in this world, I didn't want him knowing about her.

When I was done, he nodded thoughtfully and left for a moment and came back with a chair. Sitting down, he proceeded to tell me about his own personal history.

He was born in 1975 on Earth as I was, of course, but as an infant, he was stolen and brought back to 1498, such as I was. Instead of the grown man, they had the baby, and they raised him to be the perfect Elginian in his ideology.

He was trained as a powerful warrior. Adept at anything with a blade, he had led campaigns on behalf of the Emperor, who was really just a puppet leader, serving the Bah'Tene. That seemed about right.

The Bah'Tene in this universe had a much different history. They were created by Lucifer to battle Michael's own warriors called Peace Keepers. They were closely matched in power and abilities, though the Peace Keepers still aged like normal tene.

The Peace Keepers were wiped out about a century ago in an epic battle. This Sargas served as a general of the tene army, and he personally killed the commanding Peace Keeper in battle. This Sargas was thirty years old when he fought in that bloody battle.

To reward him for his service, the Council had taken him for the Test. They revealed that they brought him from Earth as a baby to raise, knowing he was the descendent of a powerful Targothian warrior. That part was at least similar to my own story.

He took the Test and was soon raised as a Bah'Tene to serve alongside his brothers and sisters for the Archangel Lucifer.

Michael was imprisoned in one of Hell's dungeons and this Sargas was asked to prove his loyalties now that he was given his new life as a warrior of the darkness.

He traveled to Earth in the year of 1527 and brought a large battle fleet with him. He laid waste to the entire planet, blasting it until it had become a second asteroid field in the Sol system.

I don't understand why that didn't wipe him out of the timeline, but as I've said before, time travel is a tricky business.

He then went on to conquer planet after planet for the Imperium. He earned the nickname of conqueror of a hundred worlds in a hundred years. Sargas, War Lord of the Imperium.

He then had been given permission to travel to Targoth and rule it for the Imperium.

With several battle ships and tens of thousands of Elginian soldiers, he came and told the current planetary ruler, Garron who was a great, great grandson of Lorancano by a second wife, that he was taking over. Garron refused, and in response, that Sargas broke his neck in one swift move. Taking Sargotha from Garron's dead hands, he proclaimed himself rightful ruler.

The Targothians knew there was no way to stop a man like that, so they did what they thought would save more lives and offered their obedience and swore they'd not fight back.

The last time there a revolt, in the time of Lorancano, he and his son, Sargas, from whom we both apparently took our new name from, were killed and the wife of ancestor Sargas fled to Earth with many refugees, though not as many as in my timeline.

This Sargas was as brutal and vicious as any Fallen Bah'Tene I had ever come across. He was a cold blooded murderer and I was questioning if he had a soul. I hated him as much as I hated anyone else, perhaps more.

I know now why I hated him so greatly, but at that time, I didn't really get it. True, how can you not hate such a bastard? But, deep down, I was afraid that I had that same brutality in me. If I had been trained differently or listened to Gostal more, I might have become a Fallen myself, and I'd probably be just like this alternate reality Sargas.

I might have destroyed Earth or enslaved it.

It was hard to wrap my mind around the fact that Lucifer had created my kind in this universe, and he even managed to lock Michael away in the depths of the pit.

"Answer me this," he spoke to me after explaining his horrid life. "Where did you get that weapon? I had it destroyed." I growled the question of why he did it. Why would he destroy Sargotha? "I had to destroy all elements of hope and tradition on Targoth. Garron had been keeping tradition alive, and that is why Targoth needed it taken away, to prove that sentiment is a weakness and tradition only serves to take away focus from the goal of serving the Imperium."

This guy was apparently a true believer in the Imperium and the Bah'Tene. I smiled at him and asked him why he wasn't able to be a fire master. He glared his eyes and was about to say something, but stopped himself short.

I felt like changing the subject. I asked about the House of Kale. His demeanor changed and he seemed almost friendly again. It happened so fast that it was disturbing. He was mentally unhinged. A true Fallen.

"House of Kale? I didn't need that trash in my solar system, so I had a fleet decimate it much as I did to Earth. Though, I did send down some pods with some of the local villagers in them. Figured I'd get rid of some tene scum while I was at it. That insipid orphanage in Ansaka occupied may of the pods." The glee in his voice and twinkle in his eye as he spoke of murdering children was unbearable.

In a rage, I charged the bars and swung Sargotha at them.

I suddenly found myself knocked back into the wall, spread eagle and falling forward onto my face, Sargotha still in my hand. My doppelganger laughed. "You moron! Bars have a powerful charge in them, remember?"

Chapter 46

I slowly got back up, eyes locked on his. He could tell I wanted to rip him apart and feed him to the hounds of hell. If I could have gone to hell and dragged him with me at that moment, I would have.

"Why so angry, my friend?" He was taunting me. "Well, I am growing bored with this little conversation we're having. I'll be off now, but I'll check in from time to time. I'd like to see if one of our kind can starve to death, or if you'll survive long enough to dust."

I yelled out a string of Targothian curses and swears that would have embarrassed most in polite company, but his man was a definite exception. He turned to respond when an explosion elsewhere in the stockade caused him to turn around and call out to his guards. No one came.

"Idiot tene," he mumbled under his breath as he stormed out down the corridor, ready to personally behead his men for failing to come when he called.

I sat back down, unable to do anything else. I felt very useless and alone in the universe.

A firefight from down the corridor broke me from my thoughts. The body of one of the Elginian troops came flying through, his head halfway hanging from his neck. Dozens of men came piling through the door. They were dressed in simple clothes of villagers and fishermen. One of them, an elderly gentleman who had the calloused hands of a blacksmith and not a single hair on his head, approached the cell and proceeded to unlock it with a set of keys. I asked him what he was doing.

"My lord, we're here on behalf of the True Targothians to free you and get you to our safe zone."

Here I was, upset that I never made it out to meet with these people, and now they're rescuing me. Not often does a Bah'Tene need help from tene villagers.

As he worked the keys, trying to figure out which key would unlock the door, he told me that a village elder with the second sight had seen that an opposing Sargas would arrive from beyond the stars to help them defeat the Elginian influence on their world.

I asked them if they knew who I really was and they said the visions of their elder showed me coming from another Targoth, far off in another dimension. A free Targoth, and that the god of the gods had brought me here to help them.

I explained that it was actually a LS drive malfunction. Another one of the villagers, a young woman with short dark hair and almost as tall as I was, laughed lightly. "Often, you'll find that most malfunctions and accidents lead to great destinies. God of the gods touched your ship and brought you here."

I wasn't one to argue with people who helped me. I knew there was a god, especially since I had battled evils that came straight from Satan himself. I wondered if maybe each universe had its own god that created it, and they all answer to a higher god. We Bah'Tene didn't know everything about the nature of the universe. We barely knew anything when you thought about it.

We fought evil and often times, each other. The Bah'Tene were a more powerful version of most tene cultures. On Earth, humanity has spent countless millennia trying to kill each other. Same on other worlds. The Bah'Tene, supposedly so advanced and wise, did the same thing.

The sad truth was that conflict was in the nature of the universe, and, it seems, in other universes, as well.

Maybe throughout the whole of the multiverse there was war and murder and aggression. Perhaps no species or spirit ever outgrows or evolves out of it.

Finally, the old man got the lock open. "I'm Sal, by the way. This is my squad. We're going to get you out of here and get you to our people in Ansaka. From there, we'll be off to the ruins of the Kumbernestia Empire of the long gone race of elves. There you'll be able to help us."

Kumbernestia. I read about them a lot back on my own Targoth. Too bad in this reality that the other races of Targoth didn't stay. Can't blame them for leaving though.

The multiverse was a big place. They could be on any world, any dimension, any plane. Some of them may have passed through a portal in Valley Center, my home town from Earth.

I suddenly remembered that there was no Valley Center in this universe. Earth was destroyed by my other self here. Just to prove his love and loyalty to the Council. The thought made me feel physically ill. I wanted all of their heads in my hands so I could throw them into a black hole.

As the firefight continued outside, Sal looked at me and apologized. "I cannot make you come with us, I know. If you wanted to leave and try to get back to your own home, we'd understand. But, we must implore you, will you fight beside us and help us cast down Sargas the Demon?"

I didn't answer with words. I just looked at Sal. He saw it in my eyes. He saw my anger and rage and disgust at what their Sargas, a Targothian by bloodright, had done to his own world. Both worlds. The destroyer of Earth and the tyrant of Targoth.

The look in my eye was their answer, and they knew I'd join them. I wasn't about to let this Targoth remain under that bastard's rule.

Sal nodded and everyone pulled out large guns. Larger than a pistol but smaller than a rifle, I had seen these before. Personal defense weapons of the officers of the Elginian Imperium. I knew that they had taken these weapons from the dead hands of their oppressors. I couldn't help but smile.

"Are you ready, Sargas?" The dark haired woman of the group asked me the question with no trace of fear in her voice. She was a tough one, I could tell.

My answer was to bring a fireball to life in my hand and I cast it into the corridor at an Elginian soldier that had just entered. His head imploded from the impact.

Chapter 47

The fight was on. Many more soldiers and guards began to filter through the doorway. I felt a rush of pleasure knowing that I was about to have a nice and proper fight.

My companions opened fire, taking out many of the oncoming troops. I wanted to show these Elginians that no matter what reality you're in, Targothians will always triumph.

I almost felt like I didn't even need to assist my new found friends. They fired their guns, bodies continuing to hit the floor. But, I didn't want to just sit back and watch. I launched another fireball into the chest of a captain of the guard. It flew with such force that he never caught fire because the flames went through his chest. A charred and smoking hole was left. It was a clean shot. He fell dead almost instantly.

With a primal scream I jumped into an oncoming trio of Elginians. With a spin and a kick I took off all three men's heads with Sargotha and knocked them into the middle of another mob. Several troops tripped over the severed heads and fell on their faces. It was almost comical.

I didn't sense my other self anywhere near. He must have fled the scene. I was hoping that he would have been as ready to fight as me, but I suppose we really weren't all that much similar. He probably learned to throw soldiers at a problem and if they fail, punish them. I came up differently.

Gostal and Dea may have been murderous madmen, but they never backed down from a fight.

It dawned on me what I needed to do. The next time I ran into that bastard, I'd have to initiate the Challenge to him. I hoped that it held the same power over a Bah'Tene's honor as it did back home.

But, for the time being, I had my hands full.

It looked like we'd soon be overrun. I prepared to rain down fireballs on the crowd, hoping that I wouldn't hit my comrades. I never had to do that, though.

The wall behind me exploded, debris flying out everywhere, a few pieces impaled a young Elginian private through his temple.

When the smoke cleared, I saw the outline of something familiar. Then it came into full view. A hovercraft.

This was an older Elginian militia model, used mainly in law enforcement. Basically just a large grey oval shaped craft with six gun turrets on both sides and a tail gunner in the back. It would seat twenty men. I noticed that the Elginian flag was burned off and a crude but still impressive Seal of Targoth painted over it.

The pilot of the craft, an older man with half of his face scarred beyond recognition, waved over at us. "Get your butts on the boat!" He spoke Targothian, which was likely to be expected. With one final fireball thrown at the crowds of troops, all of my companions and I rushed onto the craft and it took off rather abruptly into the night sky.

These ships weren't designed to fly like that, only hover about three feet from the surface. They did some heavy modifications in order to get that hunk of crap off of the ground.

Above, several other hovercraft concentrated fire at the Citadel, taking out defense craft as they tried to launch. A powerful explosion in the Southwest tower of the Citadel caused the tower itself to topple over, crushing a large tank on impact.

The pilot looked over at me. "Well, he certainly looks like the old skeech." Ah, skeech. A Targothian word that was roughly the equivalent of the word 'asshole'. Sal spoke to him, assuring him that I wasn't their Sargas. I was indeed from another timeline.

With the ground below going by in a blur, we were heading east and very quickly, we were out of Ansaka and in Talfurd. It was almost an hour later that we were seeing the Grey Sea below us. I asked where we were going.

Sal came over and stood by me. "Have a seat, please. It will be another hour or so before we reach Kumbernestia."

Of course. The ruins of Kumbernestia. Abandoned for centuries, if not longer, they were once the home of the Kumbernestia Empire of the Elf races. Elves held several kingdoms in times of ancient Targoth. Goldmoon. Silverstone. They even held a couple of seats of power in the Republic of Free Wills. But, they were gone, lost to the mists of time. Most believed they were merely legend and never existed.

I believed they did. My own ancestors before Lorancano, back to when my bloodline first was made Lords of Targoth. My ancestors ruled alongside elves and dwarves and other beings.

I sat down and enjoyed the view. I noticed that the sky was starting to turn light. The sun was coming up and a new day would be upon us.

It was full daylight when we finally arrived in Kumbernestia. It sat on a large island next to the main continent. It was very large, about the size of Kashm's territory. The ruins took up almost the entirety of the southern half of the land. To the north was the Republic of Free Wills, at least back home it was. I doubted that it was allowed to survive in this backwards version of Targoth.

The ruins went on for miles. Half erect palaces and thousands of stone houses. Where beautiful gardens once sat, now dusty ground and rotted trees.

We soon arrived at the secret base, located in a large structure that I was told used to be a library and school for elf children.

Deep in the building, I was taken to their command central. Over a hundred men and women were busy with whatever tasks they were performing when they saw me.

They stopped dead, fear in their eyes. They thought I was the other guy. Sal explained to them that I was the one that their elders spoke of. I was from another universe, sent by the God of Gods to help.

One who I knew had to be the leader approached me. I knew he was the man in charge. He had that look about him. Something familiar in his eyes.

He introduced himself as Val, proud first born son of Robb. Robb as in my elderly current First Knight back home. Small world.

Unfortunately, here Robb died, though not in battle. He was a simple baker, loved by everyone in the small Central Valley village of Nilbog. Master Sargas, their horrible planetary ruler, came in one day when Val was only a boy. Sargas, for no other reason than he was bored, ordered his men to murder Robb. Val was left there alone but soon several villagers came in and took Val to one of their homes. He was raised there and he harbored his hatred of Master Sargas.

Letting me know to ask any questions, he sat patiently as I inquired about a few others that I was interested in the history of.

Teak. No one knew of her. Likely she was somewhere in the world, older and wiser and with a family of her own. I didn't want to find her. It was too painful to even consider.

Tymber. Val knew that name well. Tymber was a blacksmith. The Elginians didn't like to let the locals join their ranks in the military and law enforcement. Only in rare cases did they recruit. Very rare cases.

Their version of Tymber joined the resistance against Master Sargas when he was in his late teens while maintaining his day job blacksmithing. For the last century there have been pocket groups of rebels, and Tymber was in one such group. Mainly using guerrilla tactics, their group was successful in procuring food and medical supplies for villagers across Targoth's mainland. Fifty years ago, he was killed alongside fifteen other rebels as they raided a food storage building.

At least my brother died in this world fighting, just like in mine. That didn't make it any easier to hear the news, though.

Chapter 48

After meeting with the leaders that night, I stayed with them for the next several weeks.

I spoke many times with Val about starting a Knights of Targoth here after Master Sargas was finally cast down. He liked that idea a lot.

I told him about how our rank structure was set up and how they'd travel the system helping people and fighting criminals and others who'd hurt the innocent. Even in my great world of Targoth, there were still assholes.

He told me some more about the history of this Targoth. A lot of that information was disturbing.

In the northwest part of the continent where Steel sits, the large nation of hard working builders was nothing but rubble and bomb damage after forty years. Master Sargas grew angry at the citizens of Steel. He accused them of building bombs and weapons to conquer the Throne, so he preemptively destroyed them with concentrated strikes from one of his Elginian warships.

The Isle of the Minotaur, a place I knew well. The entire island was a prison camp and a reeducation center. Dissident citizens were taken there to be made ready and fit to reenter Targothian society.

In several cities in Kashm, young girls were taken from their families and trained to be love slaves and sold off world to senators, businessmen, and other rich and elite people in the Imperium.

The thought of doing that to any other living being was horrid. No matter the world, I never understood how people could perceive their fellow sentient beings in such a cheap fashion.

This Sargas, this alternate me. He had nothing of me in him. Whatever he was, he was no Targothian. He wasn't even Elginian. He was a piece of excrement that needed to be flushed.

More and more I didn't just want to take the Throne of Targoth from him. I wanted to pull him apart with my bare hands and feed the pieces to a durmivol.

I decided to lighten the mood a bit. Everyone gathered around as I started talking about my Targoth.

I told them how I took Sargotha from Qal Dea, a Bah'Tene who had lived unnaturally beyond his one thousand year life. I told them of how I started the K.O.T., and not just on Targoth, but on a few other worlds.

I spoke of how the Elginians don't even come around, and how they've even asked for my help a few times over the years. I told them of the House of Kale and how I and several Knights liberated innocents from that prison.

I told them of our music, which they knew of already, but it was outlawed. That didn't stop them from singing their songs and playing on their makeshift instruments.

I told them of the Robb and Tymber of my world. How bravely they served the people and family.

I told them of the terrors of the nosferatus. They were almost unheard of here. At least the Bah'Tene were keeping the vampires under control.

Someone asked how I was able to create fire from inside. I explained to them that sometimes my kind can do that, but it is uncommon. They remarked how strange it was that their Sargas couldn't do that.

"Don't complain. We have enough to worry about with that bastard," I told them. They all agreed. The last thing we needed was to have a fire master on the opposing side.

We continued speaking for hours. They asked a lot about my home, both worlds I called my place of origin. I told them about the Earth of my time and how strange it was for me to see my birth world in the distant past.

With that, someone brought in some containers of a very familiar liquid. Beer. Not quite as good as some of the beer I've drank, as this was brewed in less than desirable circumstances, but it still tasted great. A bit of moonshine feel to it.

Val silenced us for a moment and whispered something to a young man of about fifteen. These rebels recruited young. The boy blushed a bit at first, but then he started to sing an old Targothian song of prayer before battle.

"God of the gods, hear my words, and guide my heart today. I go now into battle, let me not falter and stray. I'll fight and I'll die if I must, but if I do then please. Take my soul to the heavens above and for eternity I will feast."

He began singing the same words again, and this time everyone joined in, including myself. I hadn't heard this battle prayer in years.

It was during the middle of the third time that the walls and ceiling shook lightly. Not very noticeable, but enough that a few of us stopped singing. After a few seconds, the vibrations grew harder and louder. In the distance I could almost hear popping sounds.

That was when the bloody alarm went off.

Chapter 49

The last thing I would have expected to see in this reality was an army of Nefarium. They were unmistakable. Bald heads and small horns coming from their temples. Back home, they were all pretty much gone, believed to have been teleported to a galaxy far beyond our Three. Rumor was a demon lord opened a wormhole and had them flee, afraid that the Targothian Son of Michael would wipe them out. Probably the demon that fathered their ancestors. The way things were here, I speculated that they were probably allies of the Lucifer worshiping Bah'Tene.

I hadn't tangled with them in many a decade. I knew this would be fun.

All of the Targothians scrambled to get their weapons ready and they fired into the oncoming horde. Nefarium hit the floor one after the other, but more came. Summoning Sargotha to my hand, I ran into the fray, hacking and slashing, making many a head fall from its home on the shoulders.

The shock that I felt from the Nefarium was thick and heavy. I knew that they had dealt with my kind, but they didn't seem like they understood why I'd be fighting back. The Bah'Tene of this universe were true scum if they allied with these guys.

That was the most truly disturbing part of this universe. There really were no true Fallen. The entire population of Bah'Tene were tainted. If there were any good guys here, they'd be outnumbered and most likely hunted all the days of their lives. Against their Lucifer empowered brethren and the Nefarium, and I suspected all of the other alien races that were often friendly with the forces of the Fallen back home.

With all of this to contend with, who needs the undead thrown in?

The fight was relatively short, but just as brutal as any I'd seen in a long time.

As the demonic minions piled in, they were dispatched, but some did make it through. I saw several of my Targothian friends die horribly, but they fought all the way down. Not one of them died without taking several of the Nefarium with them. They all would have made great Knights of Targoth.

I burned several Nefarium into ash, but not as many as I decapitated. My energy didn't seem to be draining as fast from the fire I was dispensing. Sargotha moved at almost a blur. The demons fired their weapons and hacked away with axes, but we still stood our ground and took them out of this life.

Finally, their numbers thinned out. We managed to overpower them. My comrades went around and killed any stragglers they found. I managed to subdue four of them and had them bound.

As my people finished off the wounded enemies, I held a ball of fire in my hand, moving it in close to the faces of each of my prisoners. I demanded to know why they were here. Who sent them? I somehow already knew the answer. It was pretty obvious, but I needed to hear this asshole say it.

One of the Nefarium laughed. "So, it is true. You only look like him but lack the drive and ambition we all know and love from him." That was the one I needed to talk to. I took Sargotha and beheaded the other three demons in one swipe. Putting the sword to the one who spoke, I asked the questions again.

"You did, or at least the real Sargas. You're some imposter. What are you? A clone?"

I backhanded him and asked where they came from. He spit on the ground so I stabbed him through the knee.

"Why are you torturing me? I'm just the hired help. A traitor gave the location."

So, we had a spy in the mix. I knew Targothians were just as flawed as any sentient being, but it still pained me when one was capable of turning on his brethren. "Who?" I demanded as I stabbed him in his other knee. I was very happy these guys felt pain the same as any other being.

"You'll just have to kill..." his words were cut short as I sliced off his head. He was right. He wouldn't talk, especially knowing I'd likely kill him anyway. Not like I'm going to let a Nefarium walk away.

We had a spy in the group. Maybe he was already dead, one of the Targothians killed in the fight, and we'd never know which one. But, that didn't make sense. Why would the spy stay around and fight and possibly die?

"Where's Val?" I heard someone ask. No, I didn't want to believe it. Val, kin to Robb, even in this universe, couldn't be capable of being a spy.

"I'm right here," came Val's voice. We all turned to look and saw that he was standing next to another survivor. A young man, no more than twenty. I had seen him in the crowd earlier before the battle. The fear in his eyes was evident. "I found this one trying to escape the fight." So, at least now we knew, Val was no traitor. He caught the culprit.

My anger was barely controlled as I moved over to speak to the vile bastard who'd betray his fellow fighters. "Who are you, treasonous skeech?" I asked the question as I raised my sword up to his throat.

"I'm a true believer in the rule of Sargas! You came here to take him from us!" This kid's fear quickly dissipated as he ranted. "I am here to strike back at you so called True Targothians. If you were true, you'd follow Sargas as our master. As his family before him, he is our lord and ruler!"

I actually felt bad for the kid. In his eyes, my counterpart was the rightful Targothian ruler and we were insurgents.

Back home on Earth, my own nation's forefathers were insurgents against a tyrannical king. Had they failed their revolution, history would have branded them as traitors and they'd have been executed by the king. I could understand his hatred of us.

In his own way, he was a patriot, much like I was for Targoth and for my own country back in my future time.

I knew that my fellow Targothians present wouldn't necessarily feel that way about him. He was an evil young man who needed to be punished. As much as I wanted him tortured to death, I couldn't let it happen.

With a swing of Sargotha, I granted the kid a quick and painless death. It may have seemed like I was punishing him to everyone else, but it really was an act of mercy.

Val was the first to speak, breaking the awkward silence. "We need to evacuate."

He was right, of course. The other Sargas would be sending more people soon, and not Nefarium mercenaries. He'd probably be sending Elginian troops. Maybe even force Targothians to come and try to kill us. Anything seemed possible in this crazy parallel world.

I asked what the best place to go would be and they all agreed that Talfurd was our destination. There was a small outpost in the mountains there. Many underground tunnels to hide in.

In a matter of minutes, we were all on the move. We had all the weapons we could carry. I even grabbed a rifle myself.

The trip to Talfurd took longer than expected. It was back across the sea on the mainland, of course, but we traveled north along the western edge of the small continent that held Kumbernestia. We went halfway up in the Republic of Free Wills before turning west again and hit the main continent.

We arrived in the lands that once held the Silverstone Kingdom of Elves. Landing in the Silverstone Forest in the south, we went on foot into Talfurd.

Once there, the mountains were close by, and before we knew it, we were in the caverns that held the secret outpost.

I only hoped that this place held no loyalties to their Master Sargas.

Chapter 50

We were greeted by more people than I'd have thought. Val explained that they sent coded messages to the other outposts a few days ago. The plan was to eventually meet in these mountains. It was just bumped up much earlier because of the little spy.

Every outpost and rebel leader was here to meet me. They could hardly believe that I was not their Sargas.

But, at least, they believed it.

I found myself surrounded by thousands of my fellow Targothians. The look they gave me was confusing to say the least. A mixture of distrust and hope. How do those two mix? Water and oil come to mind.

I told them I was honored to be among them and I explained to all what happened, though the word had spread about my origins, I knew they'd need to hear it from me.

Once that was out of the way, they began to ask questions about my Targoth. What is life like there? Are the people happy? Do the Elginians have a presence? Of course they did, though not in a bad way. I told them about how when I killed my mentor-turned-enemy and inherited his forces, they all defected from the Imperium to my side and helped me take Targoth from Qal Dea.

I truly felt bad for the situation they were in in this universe. It wasn't like an alternate timeline, not really. It was an entirely parallel universe with Lucifer created Bah'Tene running around.

Once the questions and answers were finished up, I announced that I wished to attack the Citadel that very night. They said they wished to wait a few days, to train and mentally prepare themselves. I wanted to take command of them and make them march with me, but I knew that wasn't the way to do it.

These Targothians had been living with an evil asshole version of me. They were willing to fight, but it was their way to prepare and pray and ask the gods of old for guidance. They had been secretly worshiping for the last several centuries. Bad Sargas regarded them as nothing more than a powerless cult. Simply praying to the old gods was punishable by public beheading.

I couldn't just take their faith from them. I told them I'd agree to wait a few days.

It would prove to be very slow. Time dragged. As long as I've been alive, I learned to be patient, but there were times that I was as impatient as I used to be in my youth as a tene on Earth.

My mother used to tell me to stop worrying. I was too young to be in such a hurry. If only she could see me now.

She would, eventually, if I managed to survive to the point when I was taken back in time.

Then it occurred to me that my mother would never exist in this particular universe. Earth wiped out centuries before her birth. That son-of-a-bastard Sargas of the Imperium should have been erased as well, but he was protected from any future timeline changes. As I've said before, time travel is a strange thing.

There were two people, more than anyone, that I wished to have at my side at that moment. Neither of them I'd ever see again.

Tymber, my brother and comrade in arms. He was the first person on Targoth to really show me any trust. I never met the Tymber of this universe, but I knew he'd be as honorable as the man I knew back home.

And of course, my love Teak. It is embarrassing to admit, but after all this time, I still wake up expecting to have her presence next to me in bed. Even as I write this, when all of this stuff happened so long ago, I still wish I could turn to the side and see her sitting next to me.

Even if I were to meet the Teak of this universe, I wasn't sure if I'd be able to love her like I did my Teak. The thing about parallel universes I don't understand is that if you can exist in both, are your souls separate entities or do you share a common soul, a source of life and energy? Did I share a soul with the demon Sargas or were we two separate spirits who just happened to have identical DNA in two different realities?

I've had a chance to think about all of that and more over the years, and I still can't sort it out. One of those things you no doubt learn in the afterlife after you die. Lot of good that does, to learn about life after you're out of it. One of the biggest jokes that the Creator of the Multiverse came up with. Who says God doesn't have a sense of humor?

For a day and a half I waited. I dined with the people. I listened to their life stories. I learned of the loss they've endured. I grew more angry and hateful of my other self. Could I have gone that bad if I'd have stayed with Gostal?

I came from a universe where Michael was our founder. We can still turn bad and become Fallen and serve the cause of Lucifer.

And that brings me to another question about multiple universes. Are there more than one Michael and Lucifer? Hopefully not. They are beings of pure light and spirit. They primarily exist in the spirit realm, so time and space are different. They probably exist in all realities simultaneously. Something that a mortal mind cannot truly comprehend.

And while my mind wasn't completely mortal anymore because of my Bah'Tene nature, I was still a finite being who would die one day, albeit a longer time out than if I'd have stayed tene. I was still mortal, true, just a more empowered one. And that is why I could never figure out the nature of the universe.

Any of them.

But, here I go again, digressing off topic. Forgive me. I'm an old man.

I was having a drink with several of the local fishermen when I was summoned to the meeting hall. They were ready to march on the Citadel.

There were a few voices of opposition. They were afraid that Master Sargas would call upon Elginia for help. I knew he wouldn't and if he did, they'd say no.

I knew now that the Elginians weren't interested in Targoth anymore. Just like in my own universe. If their Sargas fell, they'd just let it be. They didn't think the Targothians capable of being self-sufficient.

That idea made me smile, because I knew once we defeated our enemy, the Elginians would leave them alone, and one day down the road, these Targothians would be a force to be reckoned with. They'd be able to spread out and grow.

And Elginia would have to watch out.

But, that day was a long time coming, and I wouldn't be there for it, at least I hoped I wouldn't be. I still needed to get back to my universe, but not before I set these people on their path.

Looking around at my comrades, I knew it was time. I held Sargotha into the air. "Brothers and sisters! We ride!"

Chapter 51

It was a sight that looked familiar to me. I was in the lead of thousands of Targothians, marching to the Citadel. Instead of an insane Bah'Tene Fire Master, I was going up against myself, more or less.

This time I didn't have a motorcycle. I was in a regular transport truck. Every one of the vehicles had the Seal of Targoth on a flag, high up so that all could see it coming. Every one of the men and women had the Seal on their backs or on their chest, some even had it tattooed on their arms.

It was a further distance than the last time I did this. Master Sargas would knew we were coming. And, if he was anything like me, he'd be arrogant enough to let us come.

I was hoping that we'd kill minimal Elginians. I had a gut feeling they'd be giving up if too many of their troops were killed and they'd retreat off world. The Elginians would write off this world and eventually forget it.

At least, that was what I had hoped for.

The destiny of this world would have to be determined without me in it. But, I knew Targothians, and even in this backwards universe, they'd be better off without the Imperium's reign holding them back. They'd be able to work on colonizing other worlds in and around their system.

But, I didn't have time to be concerned with that. I had to lead them into a rebellion against that Elginian-loving version of myself.

On the trek to the Citadel, we did meet some Elginian troops out on the open road. They offered no resistance.

They, instead, asked to join our convoy. I left it up to the Targothian rebel leaders, and they agreed to let them come, provided when the time came, they'd fight alongside of them against Master Sargas. They readily agreed. I assured the leaders that if these Elginian troops got out of line, I'd incinerate them, and I made sure to say it loud enough for everyone to hear.

We moved fast and nonstop, only ceasing when we needed to fuel the vehicles. It wasn't really that long before we ended up in Ansaka, and then to the Citadel of Master Sargas.

As I expected, several legions of Elginian troops awaited us. Master Sargas stood in the front of his soldiers, a vile smirk on his lips.

It was still unsettling to see my own face looking back at me like that. It reminded me a lot of my own Test, fighting a doppelganger of myself and then getting impaled. That was a psychological trial, though. This was real world, and I knew I'd be able to kill him.

Just looking into his face, I felt a pure hatred. If he was anything like me, he shouldn't have gone this path. It only proved that if I didn't remain vigilant, I may too become Fallen.

I knew I could kill him, but if I did, how could I rely on his men not slaughtering every last Targothian here? Fine warriors they were indeed, but even superior numbers could end them. It might have even ended me.

"My simpleton twin!" Master Sargas greeted us when we finally had the caravan come to a halt. Both of us in the lead of our people, we were mere meters from each other.

"I see you have your imperial stooges with you, Fallen," I shot back. He gave a light laugh. "Something I said?"

Nodding, he stopped laughing abruptly. "Not what you said, but how you said it. You say it with such confidence, not realizing that you are vastly outnumbered." I responded by telling him that one Targothian commoner is worth a dozen of his Elginian troops. "Oh is that so? Will your powerful fighters really last against the Emperor's finest? Or me?"

I hated to admit it, but he had a good point. Just as I earlier feared, what if I just got these people killed. Genocide on Targoth. But, there was one thing I knew about a Bah'Tene, and I was sure that it would carry into this world. Pride.

"Challenge!" I yelled. He was taken aback. I asked him if I had stuttered. He and I approached each other, both ordering our people to stand down for the time being. We hashed out the details. We'd fight right there, right now. And, I added in that he'd order his men to withdraw from Targoth in the event he lost. No retaliation. He was quick to agree. He thought he'd have an advantage over me, he said. He had grown up fighting and without me able to use my fire abilities, he'd surly claim my life.

I only smiled at him. I asked if he was ready to do this. He agreed. We both told our people that if I fell, Targoth would have to remain under his rule. If he fell, his Elginian troops would have to swear a soldier's oath to return to Elginia. That was no problem. I suspected that without Master Sargas to order them around, they'd have no problem really leaving, but I still had to ensure they wouldn't attack afterwards.

We raised our weapons. He in his flowing gray cloak, sneered and narrowed his eyes at me. I noted that they seemed a bit older than mine, but that made sense. He became a Bah'Tene later in life than I did. I still looked more or less twenty-two, though I had begun to notice some slight aging.

The fight was on. We both fought hard. He swung his blade fast and furious. He fought like a berserker, and at times I was hard-pressed to block the blows.

Our men were cheering us on. The cheers for 'Sargas' were the loudest, and I knew they were meant for me. All of his cheers referred to him as 'Master' but they weren't as sincere.

Where he had some years of training on me, he had grown over confident in his fighting skills. He likely didn't fight as much as I had of late.

Master Sargas had grown too sure of himself, and it was just a few moments later on that I had the upper hand. My strikes were coming faster than his. I let my hatred of him guide me. I thought about his potential to do good in this universe and how he merrily murdered his fellow Targothians and especially how he destroyed his own planet of birth.

I struck him across the shoulder, causing him to drop his sword. I raised up Sargotha to claim his head. The blade was inches from his neck when he called out "Forfeit!"

I immediately stayed my blade. It was rare, but it had happened before during the Challenge. One of the Bah'Tene could surrender the fight.

He was on his knees, the look of fear in his eyes was enough to make me almost feel sorry for him. That sorrow quickly turned to disgust. I hated him even more. We were both named for a brave and honorable ancestor. He was disgracing the name of Sargas, son of Lorancano.

I called out that I had won, and that the Elginians were honorbound to not fight back. I told several of my fellow rebels to take him to the dungeons of the Citadel. Several Elginian troops approached. They requested that honor. Master Sargas was an appalling leader and they wanted to escort him themselves. I left it up to the rebel leaders, who agreed.

As the coward Master Sargas was led away by his own men, many Targothians were laughing and pointing at him. Words were shouted at him, such as "coward" and "skeech" as well as a few words that were so offensive, that I don't even wish to put them here.

Chapter 52

Many called for his head, but the rebel leaders concocted a much worse fate for Master Sargas. Banishment.

It probably would have been a mercy for me to take his head but at this point, I was out of mercy for his kind of evil.

But, this wasn't my world. This was their Targoth and they had to start to make their own way. And so, Master Sargas was sent away, back towards the Imperium.

It gave me a dark joy to know that he'd likely be tortured and killed very slowly. The thought of him sickened me and caused my blood to boil. I know it was because I saw myself in him, and I knew there was the potential that deep down, I was capable of the atrocities he committed. I was fortunate that in my universe, Michael started the Bah'Tene. Lucifer didn't have a great history of creating beings that did the world any good. But, I know, that wasn't his purpose in things.

As Master Sargas was imprisoned in the shuttlecraft, he looked back and swore that we hadn't seen the end of him. Such a cliché threat to make. I knew we'd never have to look into that insane set of eyes again.

After the ship had taken off, programmed to fly straight to Elginia, the rebel commanders all convened with the current national leaders. I was asked to sit in as a third party, one that wasn't prejudiced towards the rebels or the national leaders.

I stayed with these Targothians for the next month. I wondered if my own people had been missing my presence at this point. Likely not. They were used to me being gone for long periods of time. The Lord of Targoth was allowed certain freedoms when it came to coming and going. And why not? I was Lord of the planet. I sometimes felt guilty for taking these little trips, but I had also stayed on Targoth for long lengths of time as well.

A lot of those times were uneventful. That was a comfort, however. I had dealt with a lot of action and drama out in the Three Galaxies and going to a boring desk job was nice. OK, I know it wasn't a desk job. I sat on the throne of leadership for an entire planet. For an entire solar system.

As they all met and planned and negotiated a new world government, all of the Elginian troops were rounded up and given a choice of staying here and integrating into Targothian culture or going away. They didn't have to go back to Elginia but otherwise they couldn't stay here.

They all opted to stay. Targoth now had over fifty thousand Elginian refugees, all of them pledging loyalty to whatever government Targoth chose to create.

They were terrified of going back to their own world. None of them had families, as their military wouldn't allow them to have any other attachments. That could dissuade absolute loyalty to the Emperor.

I knew in my soul that these men weren't evil. They were the product of their own culture and were doing this out of a sense of duty. They had known their duty wasn't always honorable, but they were loyal in their own way.

But, they needed a change, and they chose to become Targothian, in spirit if not in actual blood.

I offered to help start a Knights of Targoth here, an Order of dedicated men and women to protect and serve the system.

Everyone saw that as a grand idea, so I was asked to start it up. I approached Val and asked him to become the Lord Knight of the Order. He accepted but asked why I didn't take that on, and I told him I'd have to leave soon and find a way home. I had an idea of how to do it, but wanted to make sure all was well here before I did.

Val had appointed his own 1st Knight and Sgt-At-Arms. Two good men. I remembered seeing them before. They were sparring with practice swords. They were both young and would grow into incredible Knights of Targoth.

Meanwhile, all of the governments of the world along with the rebel leaders established a congress to govern Targoth. No central leader was wanted since I wasn't staying.

Elections were set up for the future, but I'd be gone by the time they came around. Leadership had been taken temporarily by each current national head. They were open to elections. I had explained to them how they worked in my home country of America. I left out the part about political parties, however. I didn't want them to fall into a two-party system and become nothing more than "liberal vs. conservative" in their nature. Elect the person, not the party. Finally, I was ready to leave Targoth behind to find its own destiny.

I was met at the Hunter by thousands of Targothians. They all were shouting out thanks to me. I felt honored to have helped my people in another reality. They may not have been the Targothians of my world, but they were still Targothians.

I bid them farewell and Godspeed and started my engines. As I took off, I looked towards the Citadel. The Seal of Targoth was back where it belonged. All remnants of Imperial signage were cast away and burned.

The statue of Master Sargas was still there, but they had made some changes to it. Now he stood there, holding a sword that looked a lot like Sargotha high in the air. Instead of a cloak and armor, he wore the vest of a Targothian Knight. I began to tear up. They made it look like me. Though they hadn't shortened the hair yet.

One last look back at the assembled crowd. I put my fist over my heart in a Targothian salute and accelerated out of the atmosphere.

I set a course for the spot where I popped into this alternate universe. I did have an idea of how to get back, and if it didn't work, then I didn't know what I'd do.

As I flew I thought a lot about those I had left behind and about those who I was hopefully to see again.

I worried that there was a chance that this Targoth would be attacked by the Elginians, but that worry soon evaporated. Somehow, I knew in my heart and soul that they'd leave Targoth alone.

The bigger worry was if Targoth would one day seek retribution for their treatment by a Bah'Tene. I couldn't even call him a Fallen, as they were all that way here.

I had half a mind to go to Elginia and burn down the Council, but that would have been a bit much. I'd likely not make it out of the system if I did that. Elginia always had high security and this version would be no different.

Besides, if I did that, I'd deny my doppelganger his hellish fate.

Chapter 53

My alarm went off, announcing that I was nearing my destination. I turned off the LS Drive and saw the section of space that I had entered into this universe months ago.

Had it been that long? Time passed pretty quickly it seemed. This area of space was so far off of the beaten path that no one else likely came through here. I wondered if that pirate existed in the parallel reality. Likely since he hailed from Earth, he'd never have been born here. Damn that other Sargas for destroying Earth in the past. It was unfair that my parents, well, his parents, were never born either because he destroys the planet centuries before they were even born, but because of the nature of time travel, he manages to survive their erasure from existence.

I'd have to amuse myself with thoughts of his being burned alive and beaten into a pulp so mushy that even his Bah'Tene healing wouldn't work to save him.

Never before had I felt such a hatred towards anyone. More so than Dea, Gostal, or anyone else I've done battle with. He was me, in a way. Bastard.

I had to focus on the task at hand. I had been thinking about this for weeks, and now was my chance.

I flew the Hunter around slowly, opening my mind to my surroundings, searching for the right place to do this.

It took a few moments, but I found the right spot. The exact spot in which I arrived.

The feeling was familiar, but where did I feel it before? Valley Center. Yes, long ago when I discovered the anomaly that causes the area where Valley Center was built to have portals and other strange occurrences, I felt this. An energy that seemed almost alive and sentient, as if I were standing in the presence of a powerful entity. I never did discover where that thing under my home town had come from, but whatever and wherever, it was related to the forces and energies that brought me into another universe.

Nevertheless, now was the time. I held my breath and slowly moved my ship into position. I wasn't really sure if I needed to be precise, but the closer the better. After inching my ship forward, I was finally satisfied that I was in the right position.

I set my coordinates for Targoth, as I had originally. I muttered a small prayer, something that rarely escaped my lips. Activating the LS drive, a strange glow came over the cockpit consol. My stomach lurched forward, feeling as though I just leapt off of a cliff into an unknown darkness.

My clock began to fluctuate the time. I sincerely hoped that I didn't go further into the past, especially if it was still in this universe, or worse, another one altogether. I knew there had to be many parallel universes, but I had no current interest in visiting them.

The Hunter began to vibrate in the same manner that it did when flying through a magnetic field. Was I travelling through the fabric that separated realities?

Almost as quickly as it started, it stopped, and the engine cut off. I quickly checked the power and controls. It wasn't dead, just turned off. Starting up the engine again, my ship returned to life.

Checking the clock and coordinates again, I saw that I hadn't moved, neither in space nor in time. Had it not worked?

Looking around through the cockpit window, I saw a welcome sight. The pirate vessel that I had encountered before being thrust into another universe.

A disturbing thought of being in yet another reality where there happened to be a pirate ship in this place swept through my brain, but I quickly dismissed it. It was a feeling in my gut, but I was sure it worked.

Only one way to be sure. I put in the coordinates for Earth. Even before Targoth, I had to make sure my planet of birth was still there. It was a bit out of the way, but I just had to know.

I arrived as quickly as I could. My mind fell instantly at ease. Earth was still spinning around Sol as it had always done. The moon was nearby like a constant companion walking alongside Earth.

It was still only 1747, though many days since my departure. I knew that in that other place, Earth was long gone. I sat there, looking at the planet for about an hour. I took in its beauty. I really never thought much about my home world, but I didn't want to stop looking at it.

But, I had to go see Targoth again. I wouldn't truly be at ease unless I saw that everything was as it was supposed to be there, too.

I quickly made my way through space and back into the Andromeda galaxy. I eventually made it back to the Targothian system.

The House of Kale. Still there. Several blockade ships guarded it against unwanted drop offs.

I remember letting out a breath I wasn't aware I was holding. Delving further into the system, I passed each planet.

I saw the colonies where they should be. I saw supply ships coming and going. I saw patrol ships making their rounds.

I was soon upon Targoth itself. Heading into the atmosphere, I flew directly towards the Citadel. The Memorial was where it belonged. I saw Knights walking to and fro throughout the area.

I was home.

Chapter 54

I quickly fell back into the routine of daily life. I had gathered my trusted council of leaders together and told them of what I had gone through. They were all amazed that a Targoth could exist in another reality. Most of them never gave much thought to other universes and timelines. I told them that the universe was a big place, but it was still small in the grand scheme of things.

I went back to being Lord of Targoth. I knighted new knights and traveled the system making my presence known and greeted my fellow Targothians.

Things were pretty slow, really. It was another several years later, around the Earth year of 1756. I was sitting in my chambers reading some poetry and thoughts of Earth sprang into my head.

Not the Earth that I grew up on, but the one that was long gone back in that other place. Yes, the universe was a big place, and there were a thousand and one threats out there. I couldn't always be there to protect and defend.

I put the word out to all of the K.O.T. I wanted to establish a division on Earth. One that would stay behind the scenes and protect the world. Recruiting worthy Terrans would be essential, but I'd need some Targothians there to do it.

I asked for volunteers to relocate to Earth indefinitely. I had hundreds of volunteers step forward. I only needed thirty or so, so I ended up selecting thirty-three of them, each one a single man or woman that had no family or children tying them to Targoth.

I told them about how the Earth was primitive compared to Targoth. They had never dealt with the machines and spacecraft that Targothians took for granted. Seeing a bicycle was the highest tech they had. Electricity itself had only recently been harnessed by Ben Franklin, though he didn't actually discover it. It had been around. He simply studied it and did great things with it.

I told them about my home country of the United States. It wouldn't be around yet. But, in several years, it would come into being. I asked them to help the Colonials in fighting the British, and they swore they would.

We didn't take the Hunter for the trip. I had one of my battleships fly us out to Earth. I had assigned several ships to patrol the outer edges of the system and I had instructed our ship to join in the patrol, relieving one of the other spacecraft that had been here on a several month rotation.

But before that would happen, I had us go into an orbit around the Earth. Flying down in several shuttles, I showed the Knights to their new home.

They all understood that they'd likely be here for life, but that is why they volunteered. They'd be intermarrying with Terrans. I had instructed them to keep secret their alien heritage. I knew that there were already some mix-blooded Targothians, and even some pure blooded, and they'd be likely keeping the same secrets.

I did stay for a few weeks to help them assimilate. Not that I knew much about this time period, but at least they wouldn't be on their own. They had quickly picked up

English, which gave them unusual accents. It was a strange mixture of German and Irish. But, they could be easily understood, and that was key.

We had ended up on the edge of the Colonies. Under the cover that we came from small communities in England, we were here to start a new life. The locals told us that the Crown still held a tight grip on the lands. I smiled inside.

The Redcoats would soon learn what it means to mess with America. And, to make it even better, Targothian Knights were among them.

We did meet a young man, the local blacksmith, who had Targothian blood in him. I could sense it. He was well over six foot and he had the dark hair that was very common on Targoth. The eyes, looking as if he saw a reality that very few would ever understand.

I spoke to him in a few words of Targothian, and he answered me back. Excited to meet someone from the homeland, we went back to his home and I met his lovely wife, Annabel. They were descendants of the original refugees of Targoth. I knew it must have been difficult to keep together with only Targothians. I told them that Dea had been defeated and Targoth was free.

The man, his name was Joseph, he showed me a holographic portrait that had been passed down from father to son over the years. The face looked a lot like mine. I told him I was a descendant of Sargas. I didn't go into detail about being from the future. That would have sounded like a bit much I imagine.

Upon telling him, more or less, my story, about how I was from Earth, though I didn't go into detail about where exactly, and how Targoth was liberated, he asked to come back to Targoth with me. He and his wife wanted to return to the homeland.

Who was I to say no? I told him about the K.O.T. and he said he'd be honored to join and even return to Earth to serve here, but they wanted to actually touch the ground of home. To see the Citadel, home of the Lords of Targoth since ages past.

I agreed to bring him home, and I knew it was possible they'd wish to stay on Targoth, which was fine. Was I altering history? Maybe it already happened this way before. Time travel is a big pain in the ass.

He introduced me to his brother-in-law, Michael. The dark blonde man was mostly Targothian, too, having a Terran mother, the first Terran blood in his particular family line. Michael knelt before me, obviously well educated in dealing with the Lord of Targoth.

I told him to rise and asked if he wanted to join his Targothian brethren in the K.O.T. of Earth. Explaining all of the details and introducing him to the rest of the men that came with me, he swore his loyalty to the order of Targothian knighthood.

I felt comfortable with the people I was leaving behind on Earth. They had an exciting destiny awaiting them. They'd be there when the United States started. They'd fight the English and serve the people from behind the scenes. They'd fight any undead that happened to come to Earth. And I knew it would happen. Vampires are no stranger to the Sol System.

Bringing Joseph and his wife, I bid my men farewell and promised to check in on them from time to time.

On the trip back, Joseph and Annabel told me of how their Targothian ancestors settled in the areas of Europe that formed Germany and the regions of the Slavs. They eventually found their way across the globe. Some stayed in Germany.

Many came to England and Ireland. A lot of them eventually migrated to the Americas. A couple of them had gone missing in Roanoke Colony. That gave me chills. That dark magician I battled with so long ago had sent them to I know not where.

Annabel spoke a lot about her cousins who took the last name Scott and moved to Scotland. They were incredible singers and musicians, she said.

When we arrived on Targoth, I set my two new citizens to their new life. Joseph became a probie for the Knighthood and Annabel began to study history with the hopes of being a historian for Targothian culture.

Eventually, Joseph became a Knight of Targoth and I was honored to knight him that day finally. I had an interesting job for him. He was to be the official liaison between the K.O.T. of Earth and the central command on Targoth. He jumped at the chance.

Soon, the Festival of Legend was near. That always got me thinking extra about Teak and Tymber and everyone else we lost on that horrible day so long ago.

Now with the Festival always came a memorial service to honor the men and women that died that day.

I went as I was expected to. I said words of comfort and love and respect. I spoke the names of each and every person who died that day, saving Tymber and Teak for last.

As the music began, I withdrew from the festival and went back home to the Citadel.

Like a typical tene, alone in my chambers, I wept.

Chapter 55

For the next five decades or so, things went back to normal. They always do, but of course, it doesn't last.

In that time, we lost Robb to natural causes. He died in his sleep. I appointed a new First Knight, a young warrior named Fynn, who was an Elginian by blood, but a Targothian at heart. He was welcomed as the new leader. We also had a new Sergeant-At-Arms, as that position was vacant due to the current Knight, Darnan, retiring. I felt bad as I wasn't there for him being appointed to that position. It happened while I was away in the parallel universe.

We even had a new Chancellor elected. Milton of Ansaka, a former colonel in the army who retired from service to lead in the political arena.

New generals and admirals had been promoted to command the fleet and the soldiers of the army. Even though a Targothian lives over twice the span of a Terran or Elginian, their lives are quick and fleeting to an aging Bah'Tene.

I was in that other world for a short time, but its effect lasted well beyond. For years, I had shut myself off from my Targoth. It reminded me of the things their counterparts went through. Targoth itself had suffered tyranny in the past and I helped them with that. I helped the other Targoth, but I saved them from an evil version of me.

Again with that, that was in my head for a long time. Did I have that in me? It got repetitive and annoying, and over time, when I started to become more involved with my

Knights and didn't just come out for a Knighting or other such function, I began to heal inside. I could finally let the other Targoth go. They'd be fine.

As I said, five decades went by in relative normalcy and peace. It was nearing the turn of the century on Earth, and I went back for a visit.

I'd been getting reports from Joseph. He aged quicker than a full blooded Targothian and was starting to get old. He requested to retire back on Earth with his wife. I granted him my blessing and I flew him back to Earth myself.

The K.O.T. had grown quite a bit since I left before. I learned that they attempted to recruit General George Washington during the American Revolution, but he declined, stating that he already owed his allegiance to another order called the Masons, thought they did band together to combat a mysterious group called the Illuminati.

King George of England had fallen victim of a vampire and so had to be put down. A Bah'Tene had come to do the deed. A man called Helsing. I knew him by reputation.

I visited with the Knights and they held a banquet for me. I was honored to be there with them and I told them of the events of Targoth in the time since I left.

After a night of drinking and revelry, I flew back to Targoth. I needed to come to Earth more often. After all, someday I'd be relocating back here. Or would I?

Once I got back home, things fell into the usual daily drudgery I had dealt with over the last fifty years. On the Earth calendar it was now just turning 1803.

I was having a staff meeting with my generals, admirals, and Chancellor Milton. While an admiral's aide was discussing a budget request, the meeting was interrupted with an urgent message from Central Command.

"Yes," I immediately answered. Something to break up the boredom.

"My lord, you have an urgent message from the Elginian Council of Bah'Tene."

All eyes turned to me, each one with a look of dismay. Why would the Council be bothering me after all these years? Couldn't they just leave me the hell alone?

But, I did think that it couldn't be any worse than sitting through another budget meeting or proposal for building another garrison on another world.

Yeah right. Couldn't be any worse....

ABOUT THE AUTHOR

Larry Yoakum III was born in Wichita, KS, raised in Valley Center, KS, and joined the Air Force almost 2 years after graduating high school.

Larry currently lives in Dallas, Tx with his wife, Allison, where he continues to write stories to amuse and abuse the public.

Larry maintains a website, The Yoakumverse, at larryyoakum3.webs.com

Here you will find links to all his social media, links to buy books, and other fun stuff.